PRODIGAL SON

ALSO BY THOMAS B. CAVANAGH

Head Games
Murderland

PRODIGAL SON

THOMAS B. CAVANAGH

THOMAS DUNNE BOOKS

ST. MARTIN'S MINOTAUR NEW YORK

This is a work of fiction. All of the characters, organizations, and events portrayed in this novel are either products of the author's imagination or are used fictitiously.

THOMAS DUNNE BOOKS.
An imprint of St. Martin's Press.

www.thomasdunnebooks.com
www.minotaurbooks.com

Library of Congress Cataloging-in-Publication Data
Cavanagh, Thomas B.
    Prodigal son / Thomas B. Cavanagh.—1st ed.
        p. cm
    ISBN-13: 978-0-312-37707-6
    ISBN-10: 0-312-37707-X
    1. Private investigators—Florida—Fiction. 2. Cancer—Patients—Fiction.
3. Missing persons—Fiction. 4. Murder—Fiction. 5. Florida—Fiction. I.
Title.
PS3603.A8995P76   2008
813.'h—dc22   2008013404

First Edition: July 2008

10 9 8 7 6 5 4 3 2 1

9/08

For Pam, for always

ACKNOWLEDGMENTS

Thanks to all those who assisted me in writing this novel. Whether you read drafts or offered comments, you know who you are and you have my gratitude. I'd like especially to thank my wife and son, who always understood why I was so often sitting alone, typing late into the evening. I would be remiss if I didn't recognize my agent, Daniel Lazar, who believed when few others did. Thanks, Dan. And a special thank you to my editor at Thomas Dunne Books, Peter Joseph, who was unwavering in his encouragement, advice, and relentless pursuit to help me become the best writer I can be. Finally, I would like to thank all the people touched by cancer who contacted me after the publication of my previous novel, *Head Games*. I was humbled by your comments and awed by your courage.

. . . bring the fattened calf, kill it, and let us eat and celebrate; for this son of mine was dead and has come to life again; he was lost and has been found.
—Luke 15 (23–24)

PRODIGAL SON

CHAPTER 1

There is no death like a child's death.

This piece of wisdom occurred to me as I sat in a pew at St. Joseph's Catholic Church, listening to the presiding priest describe the dead seventeen-year-old stretched out in the gleaming white casket before him. My daughter, Jennifer, sniffled quietly beside me.

Any death is a tragedy, of course. The person was, after all, someone's grandfather or aunt or husband or mother or whatever. But one thing we all have in common is that somewhere, sometime, we were all someone's child. The younger the deceased at the time of death, the more acute the pain of the loss.

The reason that it's so painful, I suppose, is the wasted potential. The younger the person is, the more likely that he would have gone on to do great things in his life. Cure cancer. Fly in space. Be a good citizen and parent. But those who are snatched from us prematurely never get the chance. Whenever we hear of a death or read an obituary, the first thing we look for is the deceased's age. If someone dies at age ninety-four, we tend to smile ruefully and think that he had a good run. But the younger someone is the more likely that we'll shake our heads and mutter about what a shame it is. He was so young. She left three kids in school. He hadn't even graduated high school yet.

The potential unfulfilled in this case belonged to seventeen-year-old Victor Madrigas, a classmate and friend of my daughter. What made this death even more painful were the circumstances: a suicide by overdose. Add in the mortal sin of self-murder to the devout family's shock and loss, just in case the situation wasn't tragic enough.

My ex-wife Becky—my first ex-wife—had asked me to chaperone Jennifer and two of her friends to the funeral on that sunny Thursday morning. Becky and her new husband each had weekday commitments and couldn't chauffeur the girls, who were taking a day off from school. None of the girls had her license yet, despite all having reached or being on the cusp of reaching that all-important milestone of the sixteenth birthday. Good thing I was available. Of course, being unemployed, my only real daily commitment was *SportsCenter*.

I hadn't known young Victor, but the funeral truly depressed me. I thought that my former career as a detective had hardened me against death. You see death as often as I have, even the deaths of young people, you build up emotional calluses. I saw a lot of young kids lying on sidewalks or in crack-house closets, a pool of dark blood drying black beneath them. I delivered the bad news to a lot of parents. I thought I had become immune to any emotional connection with the victims or their families.

But there I was, blinking my eyes and swallowing a hard lump in my throat. Maybe it was my distance from the job. Maybe it was seeing my daughter so upset. Maybe it was a "there but for the grace of God" type of empathy. But, more likely, it was the close, personal relationship I now had with the grim reaper. Over the past nine months, Death and I had become good buddies.

The service ended and I loaded Jennifer and her friends into Becky's Lexus, loaned to me for the occasion with strict instructions "not to scratch anything." My battered pickup was left at home, its cab too small to comfortably accommodate us all. I flipped on the Lexus's headlights and pulled out into the long, slow procession that led to the cemetery. If we were going to have to inch along like this, at least we were inching in style.

If anything, the graveside service was even more depressing.

The sight of the coffin being slowly lowered into the dirt eliminated any abstraction. This was a real death. Victor was being buried. For many of Victor's friends, this was their first funeral and it hit them pretty hard. When it was over, I stood off to the side under an old live oak while Jennifer consoled her friend Gwen, who was sobbing uncontrollably.

A man approached me. His black suit was neatly buttoned and his eyes were red. As he stepped up next to me I realized who he was: the deceased's father.

"Excuse me," he said. "Are you Mr. Garrity?"

"Yeah," I said and shook his hand. "I'm really sorry."

He thanked me and introduced himself as Ben Madrigas. "Can I ask you something?" he said, running a hand over his close-cropped graying hair.

"Of course."

"My daughter Carrie, Jennifer's friend, tells me that you're a private investigator."

"Sort of. I don't have my official license yet."

"But you used to be a cop, right? A detective?"

"That's right," I said.

Madrigas paused, took a fortifying breath. "I want to hire you." My eyebrows went up. He continued. "Victor didn't kill himself. I don't care what the police say. He wouldn't. He didn't. I want you to find out what happened."

I waited for a moment before responding. "I understand how you feel," I said, forcing myself to go slowly. "It's perfectly normal to feel that way. But the police are professionals. They know what they're doing. You don't want to waste your money hiring a guy like me."

But he was already shaking his head. "No. No. They're wrong about Victor. I know my son." He produced a business card from his coat pocket and pushed it into my hand. "Come by my office. Monday morning. Okay?"

"Look, Mr. Madrigas—"

"Monday morning. My secretary will set it up. Okay?" He fixed me with his sad, bloodshot eyes, and I knew that there was no way I could argue with the guy just a few minutes after he had buried his son.

"Okay," I said, pocketing the card.

He nodded. "Good. Thank you. I'll see you Monday." Then he turned and rejoined his family at the graveside. I sighed and looked up into the cloudless Florida sky. I'd go see him Monday and politely decline. Nobody wants to believe that his child committed suicide. That kind of thing happens only to other people.

I dropped off my daughter's friends and returned Jennifer to the house she shared with my ex and her husband Wayne, the orthopedic surgeon. I reluctantly switched the Lexus for my dented F-150 and headed out. Looking in the rearview at the Lexus, it occurred to me that not only did Becky drive a Lexus, my other ex-wife, Cam, drove a Porsche. The fact that both of my ex-wives drove luxury cars while I rumbled around town in a battered pickup probably had some sort of poetic significance. I could possibly have figured out exactly what it signified if I had cared enough to dwell on it. But I am far too shallow for that type of introspection, which might partly explain why I have two ex-wives in the first place. Besides, I was hungry, and I don't think well on an empty stomach. Instead, I found a Bob Seger tune on the radio and cranked it up. The music covered the pinging of my truck's engine.

I pulled out onto Orlando's main artery, I-4, and shoved my way into the unrelenting traffic, forcing a spot between two cars that tried their best to refuse me entry. A nice benefit of driving a crappy truck is a complete disregard for dings and scratches. I checked my watch. No time to go home and change out of my one and only suit, but I had a few minutes to grab a sandwich before I needed to be at the meeting.

I couldn't go in there with an empty stomach. Some of those people were in a very delicate state. The last thing they wanted to hear while they bared their souls was my stomach growling like a garbage disposal. So I pulled into a nearby deli, ordered a pastrami on rye, and tried not to drip mustard all over my tie.

For the second time in a day, I found myself sitting in a church contemplating death. Although I was now technically in a Sunday-school classroom and had moved from the Catholic St. Joseph's to the Lutheran St. Luke's, the general environment and subject were the same.

Both Victor Madrigas's funeral and the cancer support group I now sat in were about God and Death, not necessarily in that order. For young Victor it was about the tragic death that had just occurred. For me and the other survivors sitting in the church classroom, it was our mortality on the agenda. Death was the invisible guest in the center of the room. While none of us ever acknowledged him, we all knew that he was there, one leg crossed comfortably over the other, patiently waiting for each of us, a knowing smile on his colorless lips.

"It's just so hard, y'know?" a fortyish woman named Francine said. A dozen of us sat in a general circle in the church's folding chairs. Francine wiped a tear from her cheek. She had dyed blond hair and about fifteen extra pounds. "I mean, I have to be strong for my kids and my husband and pretend that I'm fine, that I'm keeping it all together. If I don't, they don't know how to handle it. They kind of fall apart, y'know? But inside I'm scared to death. . . . I'm *not* keeping it all together. Sometimes I just need someone to pretend for *me*." Another woman, a black woman about the same age—Barbara, I think—leaned over and embraced Francine while she tried unsuccessfully not to cry.

The group facilitator, Jerry, leaned forward, his elbows on his knees. "I think we can all relate to what Francine is talking about. The need to be strong for everyone around you while, at the same time, needing those around you to be strong for you. It's tough. It really is." I liked Jerry. How could you not? He was professionally trained to be empathic and likable. He was youngish, early thirties, with almost shoulder-length hair and a Fu Manchu mustache. He looked like a narco cop I used to work with. I always liked that guy, which was probably also part of why I now liked Jerry. "You may have noticed that we're one short tonight," Jerry said and then paused. The whole room froze, the air suddenly heavy and still. Nobody fidgeted in his seat. Francine and Barbara disengaged and sat back in their chairs. No one breathed. We had heard these types of announcements before. "Andrew won't be coming back to the group. He's entered hospice care. If you want to send a note or some flowers, just let me know afterwards and I'll give you the address."

Andrew was in his late sixties, a retired army colonel with some service in the military police. He was a quiet, soft-spoken, tough old bugger with a shiny head. Rather than fret about his hair loss, he'd gone on the offensive and shaved it all off himself. Said he felt like he was back in the army. He liked me because, like him, I used to be a cop, before we both got our new gigs as Cancer Patients. I was sorry to hear that he was now in hospice care. That meant his time was short.

On the other side of the circle, a woman named Debbie caught my eye and offered the slightest of sympathetic smiles. This was only her third meeting and she didn't know Andrew as well as I did. I offered an equally slight nod of appreciation.

Jerry looked around the group. "Why don't we take five or ten minutes and then regroup to wrap things up, okay?"

We all stood awkwardly. Some headed for the restrooms, others for the supermarket cookies and Diet Cokes. I chose a cookie.

"Hi, Mike." I turned and saw Debbie. She took in my suit. "You look nice. How are you?"

I nodded while chewing the bite of cookie in my mouth. Debbie was about my age—early forties—and pretty. Dark brown eyes. Smooth, pale complexion. Small wrinkles at the corners of her eyes and mouth that gave her face character. She wore a red kerchief around her head, a fairly common sight in the room. The chemotherapy drugs were a lot better now but some people still suffered hair loss. It bothered the women more than the men. They talked about it a lot in the group sessions. In their eyes, the loss of their hair seemed somehow to diminish them and their femininity. It obviously wasn't as bad as a mastectomy, but it was a surprisingly close second. Chemo-induced hair loss wasn't something I thought about very much. Here was a sad twist for the ladies in my support group who, like Debbie, had lost their hair: Despite the chemo, my hair never did fall out (except for my preexisting alopecia, which continued to surrender territory to my forehead with French-like consistency).

However, Debbie hadn't complained. She appeared to take her hair loss in stride and had even selected a bold red scarf. Her eyebrows were drawn in brown, so I presumed that was what her hair color was. I tried to picture it and decided that it would look nice. Maybe shoulder length. This was only her second session, but we had chatted amiably during the previous week's meeting and spent an enjoyable hour or so over coffee afterward. She had leukemia and had not yet shared her prognosis.

I finally swallowed the bite of cookie and smiled at her. "Good. I'm good, all things considered. How about you?"

"Just a little tired. But I feel okay." Her eyes dropped from my eyes to my mouth and she grinned.

"What?" I said.

"You have . . ." She gestured with her hand and then reached up and rubbed my chin, brushing away a large cookie crumb. Her hand lingered on my face for a second too long, an extended moment that sent an involuntary jolt of excitement through my brain. I didn't know her well and her touch was innocent enough, but, for that one instant, it felt surprisingly intimate. She removed her hand.

"Thanks," I said.

She smiled. "Can I interest you in coffee again this week? My treat."

"Sure. That would be nice." We chatted for a couple of minutes before Jerry called the group back. We wrapped up the session, gave each other the usual encouragements, and headed out into the night.

I got Andrew's hospice information and followed Debbie into the parking lot, refusing to acknowledge the invisible grinning Death who tried to block my way.

CHAPTER 2

Her last name was Watson. Debbie Watson. So far, I had learned that she liked cream but no sugar in her coffee, was partial to pecan pie, and was fighting against cancer for her life. We appeared to have a lot in common.

We sat in a Denny's not far from the church, sipping coffee and poking our forks at pie. She asked me to tell her about myself and I gave her the short, sordid history of Mike Garrity. Somehow we hadn't gotten around to the personal histories the week before, spending most of the conversation on our treatments and on the dynamics of the support group. We also chatted about the growing hurricane named Lorraine currently churning its way across the Atlantic on a general course for Florida. After the last few years of hurricane onslaughts in the Sunshine State, the slightest little drizzle west of the Canary Islands got the whole peninsula's attention.

So I filled her in on what we'd never had the chance to share the previous week. Garrity 101: two ex-wives; one teenaged daughter, who lived with ex-wife #1; former career as an Orlando police detective; tumor recently removed from inside my skull; embarrassing golf handicap.

"So what do you do now?" she asked.

"What do you mean, for work?"

"Yes. Do you have a job?"

"I am currently between opportunities," I deadpanned. I took a sip of my decaf. "By coincidence, though, I do happen to have a job interview tomorrow. My first in almost eighteen years."

Her penciled eyebrows went up. "For what?"

"Private investigation."

She considered. "That makes sense. With your background as a detective, I mean. You should take it."

Now my eyebrows went up. "I don't even know anything about it yet. I might hate it. Or they might hate me. It wouldn't be the first time." I took another sip. "It's strange to think about a new job. Not that long ago, the future wasn't exactly my biggest worry."

"That's why you should take it. Believe in your future, Mike. You have to believe in it. Make a commitment to it."

"Maybe I should just get a puppy instead."

She laughed. "You should do that, too." I liked her laugh. It was sincere and borderline goofy.

An overworked waitress refilled our coffee mugs. "So, Debbie Watson, your turn to tell me about yourself."

She gave me the abridged version of her life: divorced after eight years of marriage; worked as an administrative assistant for a lawyer who had a private practice; no kids; cancer in her bone marrow; enjoyed scrapbooking.

"Scrapbooking is my commitment to my future," she said. "If I keep memorializing my past, it implies that I'll actually have a future when I can look back on it." She chewed the inside of her cheek, thinking. "Does that make sense?"

"Yeah. It makes perfect sense."

She gave me an awkward, almost grateful smile and downed her last bite of pie.

I had been pretty skeptical about attending the cancer support group, but, talking to Debbie, I now appreciated its value. Here she was, alone, scared, walking that razor line between life and death every single day. Just talking to someone who understood was a comfort. She wasn't really alone. I wasn't alone.

I'm about as social as a hillside hermit, so I initially resisted joining the group. But my doctor had insisted and Cam had kept on me until I finally agreed to go, mostly just to shut her up. And, though I usually kept my mouth closed during the sessions, just being there, knowing that other people were feeling the same things I was feeling, actually helped my state of mind.

By then I had met Debbie, which was another reason to be glad that I had joined the group. I wasn't quite sure what was happening there—friendship, a date, commiseration—but I enjoyed her company. While I wasn't particularly interested in sharing my thoughts with the entire group, I found it easy to talk to her one-on-one. Just chatting with each other seemed to help both of us. Given the way that cancer beats you down physically, emotionally, and mentally, finding something—anything—that helps should be appreciated and cherished.

We finished our coffee and pie and I walked her out to the parking lot. When we reached her green Toyota Camry, she stopped and turned to me.

"Thank you for the coffee," she said. "And pie."

"Thank *you*. You paid."

"My pleasure. Good luck on your interview tomorrow. I hope you get the job."

"Thanks." I shrugged. "We'll see."

She lingered for a beat, reluctant to get into her car. "I . . . uh . . ." she said and fell silent. Then she lifted her arms and embraced me. "Thanks for talking," she said into my shoulder. "I get so scared sometimes, you know?"

I returned the embrace and held her. "I know." We didn't say any more for a full minute, holding each other in the lamplight of the Denny's parking lot. When we let go, she wiped her cheek in an attempt to hide a single tear.

"See you next week?" she said.

"I'll be there."

We exchanged phone numbers before she offered another awkward smile, got into her car, and drove off.

I loitered in the parking lot for another minute or two, hands in my pockets, looking up into the night sky. I thought about my future. Debbie was right. I needed to make a commitment to it, to let my future know I would be there for it so that it could be there for me. I had no idea what it held or how long it would last, but I was going to do my best to find out. It was as dark and mysterious as the sky I now peered into. Between the lamplight and the clouds, I couldn't see any stars. But I knew they were out there all the same.

I headed downtown—specifically, to the big SunTrust building, my destination being on the twelfth floor. I loosened my tie, knowing that I would have to tighten it back to my throat again when I arrived.

For the second day in a row, I was wearing my one and only suit. It emerged from the closet only on rare occasions—funerals, weddings, the occasional court appearance. It had served its purpose the day before for Victor Madrigas's funeral. Now it was pulling job-interview duty.

It was an odd interview that moved a lot faster than I expected. It had been eighteen years since I last looked for a job. Maybe that was how they were now. Everything's faster in the information age.

"So, when can you start?"

I hesitated. I had barely sat down and exchanged a few introductory pleasantries. Not only was he assuming that I wanted the job, he was already offering it.

Sitting across from me was Jimmy Hungerford, proprietor of A-Plus Investigators. Jimmy was all of maybe twenty-six years old. Maybe. I could be his dad, assuming that I had started procreating a lot earlier than I actually had. Jimmy's hair was sandy blond and military short. He had an eager face, staring at me with wide blue eyes. His right leg bounced in a distracted jackhammer under the desk. He sat on the edge of his chair, his whole body radiating a nervous energy that I suspected I could hear humming if I leaned in close enough.

"Slow down, Jimmy," I said. "You don't even know me yet."

But I already knew a bit about him. The most relevant bit was that his father, Nate Hungerford—of the Hungerford, Reilly and Osman law firm—had purchased A-Plus for little Jimmy after Jimmy's discharge from the army. The former proprietor of A-Plus was a seasoned old PI named Dan Wachs. Wachs had agreed to stay on the books in name only so that Jimmy could apprentice under him for the required three years before he could claim his own investigator's license. But Wachs was long gone, currently sipping rum runners on a beach somewhere in the Abacos. Enter the presently unemployed Mike Garrity.

Jimmy may have been the new boss of A-Plus Investigators but neither he nor his father knew Jack about investigating. Nate had made some calls to contacts in the Orlando Police Department and someone slipped him my name and highlights from my résumé. He had Jimmy call me and set up this "interview." However, I doubted I would see Nate today. Jimmy needed to establish the appropriate air of proprietary authority. But I was pretty sure that I knew who was really calling the shots, at least according to my buddies at OPD who had given me the heads-up that Jimmy would be calling.

"Sure I know you," Jimmy said, blinking. "I did some of my own investigating on you. Standard background stuff. Y'know. Seventeen years at OPD. A tour at MBI. Detective. Homicide for a while. A lot of closed cases. A big mafia bust. Good stuff, Mike. Seriously. Good stuff." I nodded. Some of his own investigating. All this was information fed directly to his father from my friends on the job. But at least it was accurate. "I also know," Jimmy continued, "that you quit when you got sick. Now listen to this . . ." He leaned forward conspiratorially. "A-Plus has an arrangement with a local law firm that we do a lot of work with. We piggyback on their benefits plan. Full medical with no preexisting-condition restrictions. Full medical, dude. You're not gonna get that at any other company our size. Seriously."

He sat back with his eyebrows raised and nodded his head for emphasis. That last bit of info was clearly meant to be the deal closer, and Jimmy had obviously been prompted to use it by his father. His delivery was clumsy and too soon in the discussion to seem anything other than forced. I pursed my lips and nodded back at him, to signify the respect I gave his "seriously."

"What's the typical case load?" I asked.

"Y'know. It varies. We do some insurance stuff. Workman's comp. Some domestic stuff. Cheating husbands. The usual. A lot of witness-background stuff for court cases. That's most of what we do here at A-Plus. Y'know, specialize in legal support. But I'm really interested in branching out. Pick up some more-challenging stuff to spice it up. Surveillance. Undercover. I just got some kick-ass new gear—cameras in cigarette packs, hidden mikes, the works—so we're all hooked up. I just need a guy like you with the experience to make it happen."

I nodded again. Oh, brother. What could I say to this kid? He wanted to play James Bond and Daddy bought him a great big dress-up set called A-Plus Investigators. Now he was inviting me to play, too. Did I want this headache?

Headache . . . an appropriate expression. It had been a little more than three months since my brain tumor had been removed and the question of health insurance was no small matter. While by then I had a good chunk of change in the bank from a freelance gig I'd picked up during the summer, I was still draining my savings, thanks to the giant COBRA payments I had to make each month. And, more important, now that I was sitting there, alive and—at least for the moment—cancer free, I wasn't sure what to do with myself when I got out of bed each morning.

I knew I didn't want to go back on the job. I burned out as a cop long before cancer gave me an excuse to walk away. But I didn't know how to do anything else. I was, however, able to rekindle some of my old fire during the freelance investigation last summer, tracking down a missing member of one of Orlando's popular boy bands. So, when Jimmy called the other day about possibly joining A-Plus Investigators, the general idea held some appeal. I could still use my skills and experience but in a completely new context.

The idea of starting my own firm just seemed like too much work. I had never been particularly entrepreneurial. Conversely, joining a big corporate shop seemed too much like going back on the force. Working in someone else's small outfit seemed the proper fit for me at that point in my life. Let someone else deal with accounts payable, marketing, and payroll. Maintain a certain level of autonomy. Recapture some purpose in my life.

And there *was* that small issue of health insurance.

For all the other negatives associated with brain cancer (a painful death not being the least), add exorbitant expenses to the list. My treatment was now well into six figures and only rising. Although he was no longer around (I hoped), like yet another ex-wife, I was still paying for the lifestyle to which my tumor, Bob, had grown accustomed.

Yeah, I named my tumor Bob. Don't ask. Like with my ex-wives, Bob and I had a complex, dysfunctional relationship. I suppose we still do.

So, as flippant as I was immediately inclined to be, Jimmy's deal closer about health insurance hit home. And working in a small shop might allow me the flexibility I needed for doctor's visits. The big question was whether or not I could put up with a steady diet of Nate Hungerford's legal scut work and Jimmy Hungerford's delusions of espionage.

Jimmy and I talked for another twenty minutes or so. For my first job interview in eighteen years, I guess I did okay. He offered me a salary of sixty grand plus a percentage of anything I brought in. Less than my salary at OPD but not bad considering the position. A-Plus covered all expenses, including mileage and a laptop computer. I'd get my own office in that lovely downtown high-rise, just three short floors below the law firm of Hungerford, Reilly, and Osman. Full medical, he repeated. With no preexisting conditions. Got it, Jimmy.

We shook hands and I promised to let him know in a day or two. Although in my head I was pretty sure that I already knew what my answer was.

CHAPTER 3

When the doctor told me that I had a malignant tumor in my brain, I was definitely surprised. On a scale of one to ten, that was a nine. Not quite a ten. I was seeing the doctor for a reason, after all. The headaches. The dizzy spells. I knew something was causing them, although I never suspected that the source was terminal cancer. So, let's just say I was "very surprised."

However, *this* surprise was off the chart. On that same scale of one to ten, this landed somewhere around twenty. Maybe thirty. For the first time in my life, I was literally speechless, unable to utter a sound for more than a full minute.

Cam stared at me, her brow crinkled in concern. "Michael? Did you hear me? Are you okay?"

I managed a nod and blinked my eyes. We sat across from each other in a dark corner of an Italian restaurant in Thornton Park, one of downtown Orlando's trendy, revitalized neighborhoods. I picked up my wineglass and gulped the rest of my pinot noir.

"Are you sure?" I croaked.

"Oh yeah."

"But how? I don't understand. . . ."

Cam twisted her lips in mock disdain. She spoke to me as she would to a small child: "Well, Michael, see, God gave men and women different parts for very special reasons. . . ."

"No. I mean . . . My chemo. The radiation. That wipes every-thing out. It just isn't possible."

"I know math was never your best subject, but I think you can count to three."

"That's how long?"

Cam nodded and played with the stem of her wineglass. I noticed that she hadn't sipped a drop.

"You're kinda freaking out here, you know," Cam said.

"Yeah, well. It's just . . . Y'know. We're divorced."

"Apparently, our legal status was irrelevant."

"I have *cancer*."

"No, you *had* cancer," she said emphatically, almost angrily. But I didn't think she was really angry at me. Cam had reacted that way more than once—as if she could force my cancer into permanent remission with the passion of her convictions. "The doctors took it out."

"You know the odds. You know it's probably coming back, probably worse than before."

She reached across the table, took my hand, and blinked at me with her golden-brown eyes. "Michael Garrity. Sometimes things happen in life that you could never predict or expect. You, of all people, should know this. Sometimes they're good things and sometimes they're bad things." She paused, tears welling in her eyes. "I don't know if you think this is a good thing or a bad thing, but . . . but, if you think this is a bad thing, it's going to break my heart. Because I think it's the most wonderful thing that's ever happened."

I squeezed her hand gently and bushed a strand of her styled blond hair back over her ear. "It's a good thing," I said and kissed her knuckles.

She laughed with relief and swallowed a sob. Then she pushed her wineglass across the table to me. I took a large swallow.

I, Michael William Garrity, forty-two years old, unemployed, twice divorced, with a daughter in high school and cancer in my head, was about to become a father again.

Yeah, that was a genuine kick-between-the-eyes stunner. After dinner I hugged Cam good-bye and walked over to downtown Orlando's centerpiece, Lake Eola Park. The evening was still warm in early October and the balmy weather had brought out the usual assortment of joggers, couples strolling, dog walkers, and homeless guys claiming their benches for the night. The fountain in the center of the lake was illuminated with red and blue lights, and two or three plastic swan boats floated across the reflection on the water. I put my hands in my pockets and ambled along the sidewalk that circled the lake.

Cam and I had been divorced for a few years. My daughter, Jennifer, idolized Cam and her trendy fashion sense. And it didn't hurt Jennifer's impression that Cam was younger than Becky and I by eight years. That only added to the cool factor. But the marriage had been doomed, more my fault than Cam's. By the end, I had lost all fire for my job and pretty much everything else in life. I was just going through the motions at work, at home, inside my own head. There was only so much that Cam could give without getting anything back.

However, after our separation, in a strange way Cam and I had become even better friends. Despite her occasional flings with other, usually younger, guys, we always seemed to end up back in each other's orbits. Every couple of months we found ourselves sleeping together, drifting back apart for a while, and then coming back together again. After Bob showed up—my brain-tumor diagnosis— Cam latched on to me in a way she had never done before. We slept together a few times more than usual, and apparently one of those events had been the jackpot winner.

After my operation at the end of June, I had endured a three-month regimen of radiation and chemotherapy follow-up treatments.

It was a brutal and aggressive strategy to eradicate any remaining cancer cells that the surgeons had missed. Bob had found himself a nice comfortable spot in an inconvenient part of my cerebellum. As they say, "location, location, location." Because of Bob's neighborhood in my skull, I was told that there were even odds that I could be a vegetable from brain damage caused by the tumor's removal. But there I was, three months later, walking and talking and thinking mostly coherent thoughts. However, the postoperative treatment was no picnic. When I wasn't puking, I felt like I was just about to puke. Loads of summer fun. One of the many treatment side effects I suffered was sterility, not that I was in much of a mood to practice fertility.

So there was Cam's magic number three. Three months since we'd last slept together, right before my operation and the medically induced sterility. She had waited that long to tell me for a couple of reasons, the first being the general wisdom to wait until the end of the first trimester in case of miscarriage or other complication. But the larger reason was a desire to let me focus on my treatment and recovery without the shock and distraction of news of such magnitude. Although I protested her delay in telling me, she had been absolutely right to do so. I had been a mess for the past three months and needed to focus all my energy and attention on my treatment.

I found a bench along the sidewalk and sat. One of the lake's genuine black swans trundled by and pecked at a discarded potato chip. So what did this mean for me and Cam? Remarriage seemed pretty unlikely. She had made that crystal clear in the past. Did a baby change things? Unlikely. Besides, after two unsuccessful attempts, I wasn't so sure that marriage was a good idea for me. However, I would definitely be a part of the baby's life, both physically and financially. Cam and I would both ensure that. Assuming, of course, that I lived a little while longer. I would strive to do a better job than I had with Jennifer, who was raised almost entirely by her mother.

I then noticed that behind the swan were three little babies, following their mother to the water's edge. One after another they plopped onto the lake and paddled beside the shore. I looked around for the swan father but didn't see him. I chose to believe that he was out there somewhere, maybe stuck in traffic or working a double shift to pay for all those babies.

A baby. Good Lord.

So I was in an especially paternal frame of mind the following Monday morning, when I went to visit Mr. Ben Madrigas at his office. I'm not sure what the company was—some software outfit in the Research Park by the University of Central Florida. It was a fairly new one-story building set among the simulation and training companies that dotted the landscape of east Orange County. Nice reception area. Frosted glass. Chrome desk. Leather couch. Trade magazines on the coffee table. But there wasn't time to get comfortable. Madrigas didn't keep me waiting long.

"Mr. Garrity, thank you so much for coming," he said, leading me into his office and gesturing to one of two guest chairs in front of his desk. He closed the door and took the other chair, both of us on the same side of the desk. He had pictures of his family next to his keyboard. A World's Best Dad blue ribbon was affixed to the bottom corner of his computer monitor.

"I'm surprised you didn't take some more time off," I said, before lamely adding, "considering."

He nodded. "Perhaps. But I need to keep my mind off it. I need to keep busy." I noticed a slight Spanish accent that I had missed at the cemetery. "I would just make things worse at home. We have some of my wife's family staying with us and that's keeping her busy. That's good for her. And my other children. But the best thing for me is to work. If I just stay busy enough, I can go a minute or two without thinking about Victor. If I just read enough e-mails, draft a project report, have a teleconference, then maybe I can stretch that minute or two into three or four. Eventually, somehow, I'll get through another day. At home, I wouldn't be able to manufacture enough distractions. It would be too hard."

I nodded, indicating that I understood. But how could I? How could anyone understand what he was going through unless he had been through it himself? I really felt bad for the guy. I took a deep breath.

"Look, Mr. Madrigas," I said. "I know this is a very difficult time for you, and the last thing I want to do is make it worse. I really think you'd be wasting your money on a private investigator. No one wants to believe that a loved one would harm himself. But it's a big problem all across the country, especially with teenaged boys. Trust me. I've seen it before."

Madrigas fixed me with his weary eyes, but he said nothing. I looked away, my prepared little speech a lot harder to deliver than I'd anticipated, but I plowed forward. "A lot of times, there are no outward signs. No warning of what would happen. Which just makes it that much harder to accept afterwards. But that's exactly what families have to do. My advice? Just do what you're doing. Move on. Talk to a counselor. I could even get some names for you, if you like. But please don't waste your money on an investigation. It'll just cause you more, unnecessary pain. It'll simply confirm the police report and, more important, it won't bring your son back."

This last line felt kind of harsh once I'd said it aloud. It had seemed a lot less insensitive when I rehearsed it in my truck on the way over. I had originally intended to say that "it won't bring Victor back," but I felt that using his son's name was too presumptuous. I didn't know him. It would be a kind of . . . violation, I guess. So I backed off slightly, but it still felt almost cruel as it crossed my lips. My intention was to be honest and spare the guy a lot of pain later, not to be an asshole. But that's how I felt.

Madrigas remained silent for a long, awkward moment, still gazing intently into my eyes. His expression was inscrutable. I couldn't tell if he was upset, relieved, pissed, or all the above. Finally, after an eternity of heavy silence, he spoke.

"Are you Catholic, Mr. Garrity?"

I blinked at him, thrown by the question. "Uh . . . sort of. I guess."

"Sort of?"

"Yeah, well, y'know. Raised Catholic. Altar boy. Sacraments. I'm sort of lapsed at the moment."

He nodded at me. "Do you go to Mass?"

I hesitated. I wasn't sure where it was going, but I was pretty sure that it was none of Ben Madrigas's business. However, given his loss and state of mind, I cut him some slack and answered.

"Yeah. Sometimes. I didn't go for years, but I've started going again lately. Once in a while." This was true. When I learned that I was the proud owner of a malignant brain tumor, I fell into what you might call a spiritual abyss. But I met a priest while I was in the hospital and he'd been helping me to climb my way out. Nothing overt or proselytizing; just a subtle, almost invisible encouragement. It's a cliché, I know, but a brush with death sure gets you thinking about God and the afterlife. Given the choice between believing that there is a perfect, eternal afterlife and believing that when we die we do nothing but decay, the former sure sounded a lot better to me. Since I had no idea either way, I figured that might as well choose Door Number One, which had the better payoff.

Madrigas sat back in his chair. "Then you know. You were raised Catholic."

"I know what?"

"Mortal sin. Suicide."

"Right." Now I understood. "I don't think an investigation is gonna change—"

"It's about knowing the truth, Mr. Garrity. The thought of my son . . . *suffering* now because of his last act on earth . . . it's a torment." He paused for a moment, collecting himself before the emotions welled up and spilled over. "Right now, my prayers for his soul are all about finding him eternal peace. But in my heart,

I just don't believe he could have done that to himself. I can't reconcile the prayers I must offer with my own knowledge of Victor." He sat forward suddenly. "Did you know he had been accepted to three different universities?"

When he paused and fixed me again with his eyes, I realized that he wanted an answer. "No, I didn't."

"He was seriously considering the priesthood as a vocation. Why would he apply to these universities, why would he make plans, specific career plans, if he planned to kill himself? It doesn't make any sense." He sat back again, weariness washing over him like an incoming tide. "I just, I just have to know the *truth*. Not what's most convenient for the police report. The *truth*. If Victor really did commit suicide, then, okay, I'll learn to live with that. I'll pray every day for his forgiveness and that I will someday . . . see him again . . . in the presence of our Lord—" He rubbed his eyes, the emotions getting the better of him. Breathing heavily, he sat up again, reenergized, and grabbed the armrest of my chair. "But, if he did *not* kill himself, if it was some kind of an accident, or, or whatever, then don't you see? That changes *everything*. I'll *know* where he is now. It changes *everything*."

He held my gaze with an almost, but not quite, wild intensity in his eyes before another wave of weariness pushed him back into his chair. He produced a handkerchief from his pocket and wiped his nose. I said nothing, not sure what I could say that wouldn't sound empty and flat.

"You're a father, Mr. Garrity," Madrigas continued. "I know Jennifer. She's a lovely girl." *Yeah*, I thought, *no thanks to me*. But I kept my mouth closed. "You understand what I'm saying. I'm asking you, one father to another, to help me. Tell me the *truth*. Whatever it is, at least I'll know."

As a father. And now as a father-to-be. The timing of Victor's death and Cam's pregnancy wasn't lost on me, as if there were some sort of cosmic balance sheet somewhere that always needed to have the credits equal the debits.

If I had been sitting in Madrigas's chair, I doubt that I'd have been as worried about the repose of my child's soul, but I understood his anguish. I had nearly lost Jennifer during my search for the missing band member and had become unhinged at the prospect of her suffering and being murdered at the hands of some wiseguy thugs. For a few brief moments, I had lost all connection with my rational self, falling into a chasm of violence, pain, and vengeance. So, I more than empathized with Madrigas's personal agony. And the prospect of my impending new fatherhood had stirred up my paternal emotions to an unexpected degree. Witnessing Madrigas's emotional torture conjured up a lump in my own throat. There was no way I could just get up and walk out without doing something.

"Okay," I said, sighing. "I'll see what I can find."

He reached out and gripped my forearm, but said nothing, his nostrils flared, his eyes locked on mine in triumphant gratitude. He managed a slight nod.

Madrigas walked me out of his office and I emerged into the harsh sunlight of a cloudless October sky. Seventy-six degrees. A chamber-of-commerce day, as they say. He shook my hand and offered whatever assistance he could for my investigation. It wasn't until he said good-bye and disappeared back into the building that I realized we had never discussed my fee.

No matter. Let me see what I could find. My plan, which was quickly coalescing in my mind, was to talk to the catching detective, find some speck of reasonable doubt, some hairline crack that I could feed Madrigas to allow him to believe that his son hadn't actually committed suicide. I hoped that would be enough to give the guy some peace. If I could scrounge up even a small grain of hope, then maybe that would be worth something. Madrigas would probably even feel better paying for it—it could justify his hunch about Victor and provide him the satisfaction of taking action to clear the stain from the boy's soul. And, if I took the job, I'd have something to offer Jimmy Hungerford to help justify my new employment.

I felt oddly off-balance by the whole meeting. It reminded me of my tumor-induced dizziness, before the headaches had gotten too bad. The news of Cam's pregnancy had knocked me sideways and I was struggling to find an emotional purchase to hold on to and right myself. Madrigas's exposed pain knocked me back again, and I felt not just figuratively wobbly but, to a certain extent, literally unsteady.

I sat in my truck and took several deep breaths. Just a few months earlier, I might've blamed my uneasiness on Bob, the overwhelming presence who resided in my brain and controlled my life. But Bob was gone now. I hoped. However, there was always a chance that a few lingering cells remained, waiting to grow back into Bob Jr., or Son of Bob, even after the aggressive radiation and chemotherapy. In fact, as the doctors continually reminded me in what I presumed was a cover-your-ass strategy for managing expectations, given the awkward location and type of tumor Bob was, the chance of lingering cells was pretty high.

The unsteadiness passed and I forced my thoughts away from Bob, away from the erroneous and involuntary mental image of my brain with a big chunk missing, as if someone had dipped into it with an ice cream scoop. I instead thought about Victor Madrigas. Focus on the case. Try to help his father, who was left behind in agony. Discover the truth, good or bad, about poor Victor's death.

CHAPTER 4

I was folding socks when the phone rang. I never was much of a sock folder. At the various times in my life I've been single, I tended to just dump them into the drawer. But, as part of the new, postcancer Mike, the impending-fatherhood Mike, I was trying out a more responsible domestic routine. Like most of my life's resolutions, I expected this one to last the usual three weeks and then fizzle away.

"Hello," I said into the phone. There was no immediate reply. I heard someone on the other end, but there was a long pause. I put down the socks. "Who's there?"

"Mike?" A woman's voice. "It's Debbie." She didn't say any more.

"Hi, Debbie. Is everything okay?"

"I—I don't know." Her voice caught. "No. I don't think so."

"What's wrong?"

Her breathing was labored, as if she was trying, unsuccessfully, to compose herself. "I'm at my doctor's. I just got out. I— There were some tests. Some results." I remained silent, letting her calm down, tell the story at her own pace. "It was bad news, Mike. The worst. I—I don't know who I should call. I'm sorry. I shouldn't have called you."

"It's okay, Debbie. What did the doctor say?"

"There's just—there's nothing he can do." She let out a choked sob. "There's nothing more he can do."

I sighed. Closed my eyes. "I'm sorry, Debbie. I really am."

"You're the only person that I've talked to about my cancer. I . . . I don't have anyone else to call. No one else understands."

I let out a long, slow breath. Shit . . . What can you say to someone who has just been told that she will soon die? What words would make any difference? Words were wholly inadequate, ephemeral. Uttered and then gone. Vapor. They never consoled me. They just felt like a social construct, people following some prewritten script. The friends who tried to offer me comforting platitudes comforted only themselves. After their words had drifted away, I still had cancer in my brain. That's all that really mattered.

"Do you want to talk about it?" I asked.

"I don't know. I don't know what I want to do."

"Where are you now?"

"Outside the doctor's office. On a bench. I—I don't want to get into my car. I don't want to drive home by myself, be in my dark house." She hesitated, breathing hard. "I can't make myself get up."

"I'll come get you."

"No. You don't have to." Then: "Okay." Her reflex was to protest, to say no, that I didn't need to go out of my way. But why lie? Her new circumstances meant that we were way past pretense. She wanted me to come pick her up, so that's what I did.

It took about twenty-five minutes to get there. She sat by herself on a park bench in front of a medical building next to the cancer center. She was dressed in blue jeans and a green top, like she was getting ready to shop at Target instead of receiving a death sentence.

I parked the truck in the circular driveway that fronted the building's lobby. I got out and sat next to her on the bench. She didn't say anything, barely looked at me. Once I'd settled in next to her, she buried her head in my shoulder and sobbed.

I put my arm around her and held her, not saying anything, not wasting my breath on useless words. She cried for several minutes, then slowly sat back up and wiped her nose with a tissue from her purse. Had I been more thoughtful or a better gentleman, I would have brought a handkerchief.

"C'mon," I said. "I'll take you home. We'll get your car later."

"No." She stared straight ahead, her eyes puffy and red. "No. I don't want to go home. I don't want to be there alone. I can't do it."

"I'll stay with you."

"No. I don't want to be there. I don't want to go home. Act like everything's normal. It's not. Nothing's normal. I don't want to pretend. I can't do it." Her voice pitched up a little higher, slightly more agitated.

I nodded my head, trying to reassure her. "Okay. Is there somewhere else? A relative or friend?"

"There's no one." She looked at me. "Take me to your home. I just want to be somewhere safe. And—and different." Her eyes pleaded. "Please, Mike."

"Okay."

I helped her into the cab of my truck and we drove in almost silence all the way back to my crap hole of an apartment complex, her gaze fixed blankly out the passenger's window. I was reluctant to reveal my shabby accommodations, evidence of what two divorces, one tumor, and several years of simply not caring can produce. I hoped I hadn't left anything too disgusting in the sink.

We ascended the exterior stairs and stepped into the apartment. It was a two-bedroom rental with worn gray carpeting and secondhand furniture. If Debbie was put off by the borderline squalor, she had too much class to comment—or even to react. Of course, she was a bit preoccupied at the moment.

Without asking, I poured two stiff drinks. While I poured, Debbie perused a stack of CDs by my Wal-Mart stereo and popped one in. It was something smooth and jazzy, I wasn't sure exactly what. It was obviously one of Cam's, left there by accident. Or maybe on purpose. With Cam you never knew. But it was nice and the mellow music helped take the edge off the palpable anxiety in the room.

"Here," I said and handed her a strong vodka and orange juice. She took it without comment and drank several large swallows. We both stood there for a moment, sipping our drinks, looking out the sliding glass doors to the parking lot below and community pool beyond. The drink warmed me and I felt the heat work its way out from the center of my body, radiating to my arms and legs, my neck, my fingers. The music flowed gently from the stereo, filling the room, washing over us like a soft incoming tide. Debbie placed her glass on the scratched coffee table.

"Would you hold me?" she asked. She looked smaller, diminished somehow. Her vulnerability was like a veneer, coating her from head to foot. She almost looked cold.

I nodded and put down my drink. I wrapped my arms around her, swallowing her with my chest and shoulders. She didn't cry. In an attempt to be comforting, I rubbed my hand slowly over her back, feeling the tiny ridges of her spine through her shirt. I also felt the smooth horizontal line of her bra and I thought, incongruously, that it must clasp in the front. I closed my eyes, silently chastising myself for never advancing past a tenth-grade maturity level.

Her arms tightened around my waist and I realized that we were swaying gently to the music. When had we started doing that? I felt Debbie's hands rub my back in turn. The vodka had reached my brain, glazing it in a warm, alcohol bath.

Debbie tilted her head up, opened her eyes. She held me for a moment in a penetrating, inscrutable gaze. Then she kissed me on the mouth. Not a chaste kiss. It was a kiss with heat and intention. I returned the kiss, but then pulled back.

"Debbie—" My heart pounded. "I don't think this is a good idea."

"I don't care," she said, her voice an intense whisper. "I don't care anymore about good or bad, right or wrong. All I care about is right now. This moment. This is all I have. And I need to feel alive, to know that I'm alive. I'll worry about tomorrow when it gets here. This is all that matters. This room. This day. This moment."

She kissed me again, a desperate, passionate kiss filled with defiance and fear and aggression. I hesitated for a half second, wondering if this would cause more harm than good, before surrendering.

We clutched at each other, our mouths pressed together, our hands groping, and stumbled into the bedroom, tearing at each other's clothes. We fell awkwardly onto the bed. Debbie pushed me down and straddled me, her breathing fast and anxious. We made love in a desperate, wild frenzy, with a passion that I hadn't mustered in a very long time. It wasn't exactly loving, but, in its own way, it was life affirming. Through this one physical act we could show Death that he didn't have us yet. We were still alive, damn it.

Afterward, we collapsed gasping onto the sheets and Debbie put her head on my chest. A few minutes later, I both felt and heard her crying again. Sex was only a temporary escape. The very vitality of the act placed her circumstances into greater relief, accentuating the cruelty of her prognosis. It all descended back onto her. I held her again, stroking her head. She had never removed her kerchief. I could feel the smooth, hairless skin through the fabric. We stayed like that until the sun set and the room darkened.

It was there, in my bed, lying naked in the darkness, that Debbie asked her big question, the one that started all the trouble.

"I lied to you," she said.

"Oh?"

"About having kids. That wasn't true." She lay on her back, looking up at the ceiling as she spoke.

"So you do have kids?"

She closed her eyes. "When I was sixteen, I got pregnant. I was dumb. I wasn't careful. I was sixteen." That was explanation enough. "I went through with the pregnancy, but I gave the baby up. That was my one and only child." She paused, the memory obviously painful. "It was arranged through a private lawyer, a friend of my father's. The other couple came to the hospital. They even paid for the medical bills. As soon as the baby was born, the nurse took it away. I couldn't even hold it." I heard the tears in her voice, the emotion bubbling up into the dark room. "They weren't even supposed to tell me if it was a boy or a girl. They didn't want me to get attached. They said it would only make it harder. But one of the nurses told me. It was a boy." She turned over and looked at me, her wet eyes catching the moonlight from the bedroom window. "There's no way to *not* get attached. It's impossible. He was inside my body for nine months. He's part of me. Taking him away doesn't change that."

I stroked her hair in an attempt to comfort her. "I'm sorry," I offered, not knowing what else to say.

"For a long time—years—I called him Jacob. It was only in my own head. I didn't know what the other couple named him, his real name. But I always liked the name Jacob. It's a good name, isn't it?"

"Yeah."

"I always wondered what happened to him. How he grew up. What he's like. Y'know? You can't switch that off. You're a parent. You know how it is. It's always there, the worrying, the wondering."

"Yeah. I know."

"So, a few years ago, I called my father's friend, the one who handled the adoption. He wouldn't give me the parents' name or phone number, but he did promise to tell them that I wanted to talk to them. If they wanted to, they'd call me. A couple of weeks later, they called." She paused again, controlling her breathing.

"They wouldn't let me talk to him, but they told me all about him. Everything. They were so nice. They really understood." She swallowed, took a breath. "He's a good boy. Graduated from high school. Never got in trouble. Lots of friends. Went to a local community college where he studied computer networks. Polite. Good manners. Likes video games." Her voice caught. "His name is Jonathan." She swallowed again and exhaled a deep breath. "That's a good name, too, isn't it? It's not too different from Jacob."

"Yeah," I said. "That's a good name, too."

"His mother told me that he just got a job in Orlando, working for the city. That's why I moved here three years ago from Fort Lauderdale. Not to stalk him or anything—I don't think the mom, the *other* mom, wanted me contacting him. I just wanted to be in the same city, read the same newspaper, feel the same weather, breathe the same air. Even if I never met him, I would at least know a little bit about what his life was like by living in the same city. Y'know? Does that make sense?"

"Yeah. Sure it does." I thought it sounded a little extreme, but who was I to judge?

"That was the only time I ever spoke to the parents. When I got sick, I looked up his number and tried calling him. But he moved and quit his job. I don't have the parents' number. I don't know how to find him." She reached over and gripped my forearm, her grasp tight and trembling. She took a deep breath. Then she asked the question: "Will you find him for me, Mike? I've been thinking about asking you since last week, when you told me you were a private investigator. Now, after today—after what the doctor said—I *need* to find him. I need to meet him. Hear his voice. See his face. Hold his hand once. Before it's too late. I need to meet him. I can't die without seeing my son's face. Will you do it, Mike? Will you find him for me?" Her voice trembled with emotion, the tears simmering just below the surface.

How could I say no? It was Ben Madrigas all over again, putting me in a position where I couldn't refuse. Except that this time it was Debbie coping with death—her own. There was only one answer I could give, of course. I knew my line, and I delivered it admirably.

"Okay. I'll find him."

CHAPTER 5

I took the job, of course. I called Jimmy Hungerford the next day, and, upon hearing the news, he informed me that he was "so totally stoked." I also told him that I already had two cases and gave him the general outline of what I was doing for Ben Madrigas and Debbie Watson. Jimmy thought that it was "frickin' awesome" that I already snagged two cases. He offered to help, to "pull out some of his smokin' new surveillance gear," but I politely declined and told him that I had it covered.

Although I tried to refuse, Debbie had insisted on paying me. So I took a five-hundred-dollar retainer and thought about my first move. The kid's name was Jonathan Dennis. He was twenty-two years old and, until recently, was employed by the city of Orlando as an IT administrator. A quick Internet search gave me his most recent address and phone number.

When I tried it, the phone number was disconnected. So I took a drive to his apartment. It was a middle-range complex, not a tenement but far from luxurious. A neglected pool sat across the parking lot next to the office. I knocked on Jonathan's second-floor door and a middle-aged black woman opened it.

"Can I help you?" she asked.

"Yeah. I'm looking for Jonathan."

"Who?"

"Jonathan Dennis. He lives here."

"Don't no one named Jonathan or Dennis live here."

"Are you sure?"

"I know who lives in my own damn house, don't I?"

"You mind if I come in and look around?

"Hell yes, I mind." She slammed the door in my face.

I had a pretty good feeling that she was telling the truth. All the same, I wandered back down the stairs and across the parking lot to the office.

As I suspected, Jonathan Dennis had broken his lease, paid a penalty of a month's rent, and promptly moved out about three weeks ago. The manager told me that he had rented Jonathan's place again right away. There was no forwarding address.

Okay . . . This had all the signs of a quick escape. Why was he running? Low on cash? Moving in with a girlfriend? Got a deal on a new place? It could be anything.

In my mind I backtracked over the information I had. A name. An employer. He worked for the city of Orlando. It wasn't much, but it was more than enough. Given that information, my next move was pretty obvious.

I had to go see Sally.

She was waiting for me, just like in the old days, sitting on the same concrete planter holding the same oversized purse, with a lit cigarette dangling from her puckered lips. She didn't look like she had aged at all since I had last seen her, but I didn't recall Sally ever looking anything except what could best be described as "weathered." So, in that regard, she was ageless. Leathery, overtanned skin hung loose and crinkled on her bones. Her dyed blond hair was teased up into a wild bird's nest on top of her head. Thick makeup spackled her face. She spotted me, shook her head ruefully, and blew out a chimney's worth of gray smoke.

"Well, lookee lookee," she rasped in her gravel voice. "The prodigal son returns."

"How's my girlfriend?" I asked as I sat beside her.

"Ha!" she barked and erupted into a laughing/coughing fit

that made me both smile and worry at the same time. "You wish, honey. You wish."

Sally Anderson was the mayor's office manager. She had been the mayor's office manager for a long time. Some said that she had been the mayor's office manager for as long as Orlando had had a mayor. Although three administrations and two political parties had come and gone, Sally remained. Her longevity made her arguably the most powerful person in city government.

I had gotten to know her fairly well during a brief stint as a police liaison for a city councilman. When my councilman lost his seat, I went back to catching bad guys. But I tried to keep in touch with Sally. She was a good person to know and I genuinely liked her. Underneath her tough, leathery exterior beat a kind, leathery heart.

Every other month or so I'd pick up a sack of turkey subs and two Diet Dr Peppers and meet her there on the concrete bench that also served as a planter in front of City Hall. The Clean Air Act had driven all the smokers down to the plaza, and everyone knew that was Sally's bench. We'd eat the subs, drink the sodas, and watch the lawyers and tourists wander by in front of the giant glass asparagus that served as Orlando's version of modern public art.

"So, how you doin', honey?" she said, her eyes flicking up to my hairline.

"Good, Sal. Tumor's out. The doctors think they got it all. I finished my chemo and radiation. All systems are go."

She patted my knee. "God bless ya. When I heard you had a brain tumor . . ." She shook her head.

"Yeah. Me too." I blinked the smoke from my eyes. "So how's Donny?"

She released a big sigh. "Rehab. Maybe the fourth time will be the charm."

Sally's thirty-one-year-old son, Donny, was an addict. Pills, coke, booze. It didn't really matter. If it was mood altering, Donny would swallow, shoot, or snort it. I had once caught Donny buying drugs on the seedier stretch of Orange Blossom Trail. Once I saw his ID, I knew who he was. Rather than arrest him, I called Sally. She drove down and picked him up. Since that time, Sally and I had always had a peculiar unspoken bond. She was grateful to me for sparing her son. Although I told her she didn't owe me anything—I truly believed that Donny would be better served by a rehab facility than the county lockup—she nevertheless provided me with small favors and bits of information that proved to be very valuable during various investigations.

"He can beat it, Sal," I said. "Maybe this is the one."

She took another long drag and blew out another plume of smoke. "He takes after his father. Gerald was a drunk. God bless him. Still is." Sally had been married at least four times that I knew of. She never lacked for suitors, but was coy about sharing the details, which was fine with me.

I handed her a sub and a Diet Dr Pepper.

"You remembered the extra pickles," Sally said, opening her sandwich wrapper. "God bless ya, Mike. You remembered my pickles."

"Yeah. How could I forget?" I winked at her and took a sip of my soda. We chewed for a few moments before Sally squinted up at me and smiled.

"So, what's on your mind, Detective?" she asked.

"I'm not a detective anymore. I quit, remember?"

"You quit the department. But I hear that you've been talking to a private firm. I hear that you might be a private detective."

I smiled and shook my head in amazement. "Is there anything you don't know?"

"Sure, lotsa things. That whole theory-of-relativity thing is a little over my head. And I wish I knew how to fix the Dolphins' quarterback problem. But, if it happens within the borders of this city, I'm gonna know." She took sip of soda. "So, what's on your mind, hon?"

"I took the job this morning. You're probably getting an e-mail about it right now."

"Probably."

"I have a case. More of a personal favor than a case, really. I need to find a guy named Jonathan Dennis. Until recently, he worked for the city as an IT administrator."

"Is that his last name, Dennis?"

"Yeah. Do you know him?"

"Nah. But I can find out. Gimme a day or two. Would that work?"

"The sooner the better. Time is an issue."

"Okay, hon. Lemme see what I can do. You gonna eat that pickle?"

"You can have it."

Sally snatched the pickle spear from the edge of my sandwich paper and crunched a big bite. She smiled at me.

"It's good to have Mike Garrity back doing detective work," she said.

I couldn't argue with her. I never could.

Late that afternoon, I pulled up in front of the Madrigas home and considered it for a moment before getting out. It was a nice enough place, an unremarkable middle-class ranch house in a sprawling neighborhood of nearly identical homes. This was one of the innumerable new housing developments sprouting up all over the greater Orlando area, vast acres of palmetto scrub and pine forests being plowed under and replaced by thousands of off-the-rack track homes in preplanned, usually gated communities. The growth was especially explosive in east Orange County, where Madrigas lived. The trees were all young and thin, offering almost no shade, but casting long skinny shadows in the late afternoon sun.

Mrs. Madrigas let me in. She was polite and even offered a wan smile, but she looked like she had been sucked dry of all bodily fluids. Her face was gaunt and pale, and her skin didn't seem to fit her properly. Grief wafted off of her like an odor.

The house was full of people. Other kids—Victor's siblings, I presumed—along with cousins and friends sprawled across the couches and carpet. Relatives were bustling about, picking up toys, washing dishes, cooking dinner in the kitchen. It looked like rice and chicken and something that smelled of roasted garlic. It made my mouth water. The house had wide, sliding glass doors that opened onto a small kidney-shaped swimming pool. However, despite the windows, the house seemed unusually dark. The late-afternoon sun seemed to fall at just the wrong angle.

Ben Madrigas shook my hand and walked me through the family room. I picked up a few surreptitious glances from the other adults. These weren't so much curious "hey, who's that guy?" glances as "so that's the guy" glances. They probably knew who I was and why I was there.

Ben led me down the hallway and stopped at a closed door next to the open door of the pool bathroom. He reached for the doorknob but then dropped his hand.

"I . . . I can't go in," he said. "Not yet. Is that okay?"

"Sure," I said. "I understand. I just need a few minutes."

He nodded and walked back down the hall toward the rice and the chicken and the roasted garlic. I turned the handle and went in.

The first thing that I noticed was that there wasn't much to notice. The room was mostly tidy, not the landfill decor of the typical teenaged boy. There were a couple of space photographs on the wall that looked like something produced by the Hubble telescope. An amateur telescope sat on a tripod in the corner. I sighed, stepped into the room, and closed the door behind me. A small pewter crucifix hung over the door.

The room looked untouched from the day Victor had died: a small pile of dirty clothes in one corner; half-finished homework on the desk; bed unmade. It looked as if he had just gotten up to use the bathroom and would be back at any moment, except for the darkened computer monitor on the desk.

I started in the closet. It was filled with the usual teenager's wardrobe. American Eagle sweats, jeans, sneakers. There were also some dressier clothes, including a decent pair of wingtips. A baseball glove and a half-deflated basketball were wedged into a back corner. In a box were some old papers and schoolwork, along with a few birthday cards from relatives and friends. Some old childhood board games were stacked on the top shelf. Stratego. Risk. Battleship.

When I was Victor's age, the area under my bed would have been like an archaeological dig; but there wasn't anything under his bed, save for a few dust bunnies and a nickel. I lifted the mattress. There was no sign of any of the three mattress *p*s: no *p*ot, no *p*ills, no *Playboy*s. There wasn't any cash either.

The dresser drawers revealed nothing, so I turned to the desk. There were some school notebooks and papers piled on the corner, some group photos of friends in the top drawer, and the usual desk junk of pens, Post-it notes, and paper clips strewn about. I searched through it but unearthed nothing of interest or that would reveal anything about his death. I flipped through the schoolwork.

Victor appeared to have been a pretty good student. His test scores and the written feedback from teachers on papers indicated an A student. There were more papers than I could look at in a reasonable amount of time, and I didn't relish the idea of camping out at the Madrigas house in the middle of their personal heartache. So I packed the papers under my arm and walked back down the hallway.

I passed again through the garlic-scented kitchen and Ben escorted me out the front door. He gave me permission to take the papers. He also had Victor's cell phone, which he ceremoniously handed to me as if it held all the answers. Maybe it did. We finally got around to the subject of my fee and I quoted him an hourly rate plus expenses. I didn't plan on actually billing him for many of the hours, but I was keeping up appearances. He agreed without any negotiation. He shook my hand, thanked me again, and disappeared back into his shadowed, sad house.

I stood for a few minutes under the darkening sky, looking at the clouds painted orange and red by the setting sun. I had dinner planned with Debbie. It seemed almost like I would be traveling back in time, from recent death to impending death, taking the clock a few ticks backward. One minute you're here on earth, a living, breathing person, watching TV, eating cheesesteak sandwiches, and the next you're gone. That one minute makes all the difference in the universe. Hell, one second. The difference between life and death is the difference between one second and the next. The time between biting the sandwich and swallowing.

Even though Bob was now gone, unceremoniously excised from my brain, my buddy Death continued to show up from time to time. I seemed to run into him everywhere, like that co-worker you always see at the grocery store. Maybe he had grown used to me and didn't know what else to do with himself, even though I was no longer on his watch list.

Of course, maybe Bob wasn't completely gone. Maybe I *was* still on the watch list.

Regardless, whether I liked it or not, I knew that Death would be waiting for me when I arrived for dinner at TGI Friday's with Debbie. Her incurable cancer would be too much for him to resist. Maybe if I ordered him some potato skins he'd back off. It was worth a try.

CHAPTER 6

When I ordered the potato skins I remembered to ask about the sour cream. And the cheese. I even remembered to ask about the bacon bits. But when it came time to order my entrée, I drew a blank.

"I want one of those, you know . . ." I stammered. I had the picture in my head; I saw it clearly. "You know. Round. Bread and meat."

"A sandwich?" the waiter asked, his eyebrows going up in disbelief at my stupidity.

"No. Not a sandwich. I know what a sandwich is." I was getting annoyed. It was right there on the tip of my tongue. I could picture it exactly. "Cooked meat. On round bread. With lettuce and pickles. You know . . . on a bun. That's it—a bun."

"A hamburger?" the waiter asked in an unsure voice.

"Yeah. A hamburger." I tried the word on like a pair of shoes. It fit. That was it. "I want a hamburger. Medium rare. A hamburger."

The waiter took down the order and slinked away. Debbie looked across the table at me, not saying anything.

"Well, that's new," I said.

"Are you okay?" Debbie asked.

"Yeah. The doctors told me I could have some . . . what did they call them? Mental lapses. I could have some mental lapses due to damage from the brain surgery. I wonder what else they scooped out of my brain with the tumor. . . ."

"You couldn't remember what a hamburger was?"

"No. I knew *exactly* what it was. I just couldn't remember what it was called. Weird." I sipped from my glass of beer. "I was told if something like that happened, I'm supposed to call this occupational therapist who'll work with me."

"Do you want to leave?"

"What? No. I'm hungry." I took another sip and looked seriously at her. "How are you?"

"A little better. I guess. I keep crying. I can't help myself. I had another doctor's appointment today." She looked off out the louvered window. "They aren't talking about treatment anymore. Now they want to talk about comfort. Pain management." She wiped her eye. "Hospice care . . . I don't want to talk about it anymore." I couldn't blame her.

"I started looking for Jonathan today." The change of subject seemed to help her focus away from the thought of impending death. This was a topic she was interested in. I told her about trying to call him. About the visit to his apartment. My conversation with Sally.

"How long do you think it'll take to hear back?" Debbie asked.

I hunched my shoulders. "With Sally, who knows? Maybe a day or two."

"I can't tell you what this means to me, Mike. Finding my son. It's like he was dead and you're bringing him back to life."

I thought about Sally's greeting earlier that day. "The prodigal son. He was lost but now he's found."

Debbie nodded. "Right. Except it's reversed. I'm the prodigal mother."

The potato skins arrived and we dived in. I looked up in midbite. For the first time all day, I didn't feel Death hovering over my shoulder. Debbie's condition meant that he was never very far away, but perhaps his attention was elsewhere, maybe on some poor bastard at another table about to wreck his car on the way home. I popped the last potato skin into my mouth and drained my beer.

My round meat patty with two buns had arrived.

Hamburger.

Goddammit. Hambuger hamburger hamburger.

I walked Debbie to her car after dinner.

"Are you sure you don't want some company?" I asked. "Just to hang out? Not be alone?"

She put her hand on my cheek. "Thank you. That's sweet. I'm better today. Really. I'll be okay." She kissed me gently on the lips and slipped into her car. "I'll call you tomorrow. Thanks for dinner." She drove off.

The prodigal son. That's what my father used to call me. It had been his standard greeting whenever I hadn't seen him in a while. *Well, look at this. The prodigal son has returned. And me without my fattened calf.* Liturgical humor. Thanks, folks, I'll be here all week.

My father was an ex-Catholic priest, so I cut him some slack. He didn't know anything else. He had fallen in love with one of his parishioners—my mother—and married her. Apparently it was quite the scandal at the time. He left his diocesan life to become a high-school English teacher, and I was the sole child of their union.

He never quite articulated it, but throughout my childhood I felt an unrelenting pressure to "be good," whatever that meant. Maintaining proper behavior in school, being an altar boy during Mass, paying dutiful attention to my parents, having a successful and meaningful career—they were all wrapped up into a homogenous stew of Catholic guilt. Being his only child, I had the sense that my father looked at me as the ultimate rationalization for leaving the priesthood. I had better be worth it—my life as justification for the scandal and shame.

Unfortunately, I never quite lived up to expectations. And being a cop was never what he'd had in mind. We had unresolved issues when colon cancer claimed him during my first year on the job. So now that familiar Catholic guilt remained repressed somewhere deep within me. If only the doctors could go in and remove it like my tumor.

Pondering my Catholic guilt got me thinking about poor Victor Madrigas and his tortured father. The following morning I would take the next step in my investigation of Victor's suicide. I didn't look forward to where that step might take me.

The detective assigned to investigate Victor's death was named Boyd Bryson. He agreed to meet me the following morning, but there was a catch. There's always a catch. It was his day off and he was heading out onto Lake Toho in his bass boat, so I had to meet him at a roadside truck stop at six a.m. This, as you might imagine, was quite a bit earlier than I was used to getting up in my recent state of unstructured unemployment.

I had never met Bryson. He worked for the Orange County Sheriff's Department, while my years on the job were spent primarily with the city of Orlando. But we had some mutual friends, and the report on me had apparently passed whatever litmus test he needed to justify talking to me about one of his cases.

Surprisingly, I arrived at the truck stop before he did, the first sliver of pink sunlight crowning over the crest of the horizon. I grabbed a booth and wiped something sticky from the table with a napkin. A young, tired-looking waitress, clearly on the tail end of an all-night shift, poured me a cup of coffee. Before she could ask for my order, Bryson walked in.

He looked exactly as he had been described to me. A former lineman for the University of Alabama, he was at least six-four, 250 pounds. But, despite his imposing size, his appearance was softened by a remarkably boyish face, scrubbed pink by an early-morning shave. He was dressed casually for fishing, topped with a camouflage baseball cap. In his giant, mittlike hand was a manila envelope. I caught his attention and waved him over.

We exchanged hellos and chatted briefly about a mutual friend at the sheriff's office who was in the middle of a particularly nasty divorce. Bryson's voice was surprisingly gentle and colored with a deep South accent that was becoming more and more rare in Central Florida. We ordered coffee and breakfast from the tired waitress. With his bulk, I expected him to request a three-egg omelet, but all he asked for was a bowl of oatmeal. I ordered the same.

"So," he said, pouring a pack of artificial sweetener into his coffee. "You want to talk 'bout Victor Madrigas."

"That's right."

"Why?"

"His father. He's having a hard time accepting the fact that Victor committed suicide."

Bryson nodded. Took a sip of coffee. "I understand. I have some questions of my own."

"Really?" I put down my coffee mug. "What kind of questions?"

"Well, nothin' concrete. Just a funny feeling, y'know? Don't get me wrong, everything supports a suicide. That's the only conclusion we could've come to." He took another sip. "But, you were on the job. You know how it is. You ever have a case where there were a couple of little things, loose ends, that you just didn't have time to wrap up? My lieutenant wanted this closed. We needed the name off the board. So, we came to the only conclusion that the evidence supported. But I can't help but wonder, what if I just kept digging. . . . What would I find? Probably nothin', right?"

The waitress returned with our oatmeal and we ate silently for a few moments. This was not at all what I'd expected to hear. He was being amazingly honest. What he was telling me was far from the public departmental line about the thoroughness of all investigations.

"What sort of loose ends are you talking about?" I asked between bites.

"Like I said, nothing big. Just inconsistencies. Like . . . He had been applying to colleges and had already been accepted into three. He had prospects. A future. He was popular at school. He had friends. There was no suicide note. With all that . . . potential, why would he swallow a bottle of pills?"

I nodded. "Unfortunately, that could describe a lot of teen suicides: 'What a shock. We had no idea.' "

"Right. I know. That's true. But there were some other things, too. The ME found a lethal amount of alprazolam in his system. Y'know, Xanax. Antianxiety drug. He had no prescription for it. Neither did either one of his parents. Neither did any of his friends that I could find out. They had no clue where Victor would've scored the drugs. He just wasn't the type to have a connection or a network for a hook-up or a fix."

I nodded again. "You're right. That's pretty thin."

"See? It's nothin'. Just speculation. But, as a professional, I'd like to tie this stuff up before I close a file. I'd like to know how he got the drugs. I'd like to know that there was some warning sign somewhere, an offhand comment about killing himself, giving his possessions away, somethin'. Y'know, tie up the loose ends. Then I don't sit around wondering afterwards. I'm sure that, with a little more digging, I'd find out that the suicide conclusion was a hundred percent correct. But I didn't, so I'll never know more than ninety-nine percent."

I thought about poor Ben Madrigas sitting in his office, trying to string together two consecutive minutes where he wasn't tormented by the thought of his son's immortal soul in hell. "Is there anything that I can offer his father that would give him enough reasonable doubt to believe that it was an accident? Anything that could help him find some peace, even if it's only in his mind?"

Bryson scooped a mouthful of oatmeal and chewed thoughtfully. "You gotta be careful there, Mike. Extra careful. See, there were an awful lot of meds in that boy's body. An *awful* lot. You see where I'm gettin' at here? Too many to be an accident. He wasn't just tryin' to get high or lose himself a little and then accidentally went too far. I've seen that before. So have you, I bet. This boy had somethin' like thirty times more than the minimum lethal dose in his body. This was intentional." He leaned across the table and locked eyes with me. "So if you go back and tell that boy's father that it wasn't suicide, just what exactly *are* you tellin' him?"

I sat back. "Oh, brother . . ."

"Oh brother is right, brother. And you know what would happen then. No father would let that lie. The last thing the sheriff needs is some grieving parent goin' on TV and squawkin' about how we didn't do a thorough job and demanding that we reopen the investigation. That case is closed. So says my LT, and that's the next best thing to God and the sheriff."

"What would your lieutenant say if he knew you were sitting here talking to me about this?"

Bryson looked down and a rueful, inward smirk crossed his lips. "Let's just say it would be best for all concerned if he didn't find out."

I drained my coffee. "So, then why *are* you talking to me?"

"It's that one percent. I can't spend my time chasing smoke. Tyin' up loose ends unsupported by evidence on an open-and-shut suicide. I'd be crucified." He finished the last spoonful of his oatmeal. "But you can. You don't answer to my LT. When you called, I figured, *Why not?* Maybe you can tie up the loose ends and I won't have to wonder anymore. Make it a hundred percent." He slid the manila folder across the table to me. "Here are some of my case notes, the summary from the ME's report, some contact info. It should get you started." I took the envelope. "But here are the rules: you keep this quiet. My LT finds out and I can make it bad for you. *Bad.* You give me everything you find. And, I'm sorry to say, you can't tell the kid's father it wasn't a suicide."

I opened the envelope and flipped through the papers. "And, suppose . . ." I said casually, pulling out a printed photo from the scene, Victor's eyes open and lifeless, staring at me almost plead-ingly. "Suppose I find out that it really wasn't a suicide?" I looked up from Victor's eyes to Bryson's eyes.

"If you find that," he said, sitting back and crossing his arms, "then I'd appreciate as much notice as you can give me so I can hide under my desk. 'Cause the shit is really gonna start flyin'."

CHAPTER 7

When I walked into the office, Jimmy Hungerford looked like he was being scolded. He sat in his desk chair, hands clasped between his legs, looking up at a man in an expensive suit. The man stood over him, wagging a finger and shaking his head. The man was older, midfifties, with gray temples and a slightly expanding waistline.

Jimmy's father.

They both turned to me when I walked in.

"Dude," Jimmy said. I assumed that it was a greeting.

I nodded. "Jimmy."

Nate cocked his head, eyeing me. Then his face registered recognition. He smiled and held out a hand.

"You must be Mike Garrity. Jimmy's told me all about you." We shook hands. "I'm Nate Hungerford, Jimmy's father. The agency does a lot of business with my law firm upstairs."

"So I've heard," I said.

"We were just discussing a recent case. And the importance of actually serving papers to the people who are supposed to receive them." He looked pointedly at Jimmy, who returned a tight-lipped smile.

"Thanks for the tip," I said.

Nate hiked up a trouser leg and sat on the edge of Jimmy's desk. "I hear that you've already brought in two cases."

"Yeah."

"I'm impressed. How are they going?"

"Fine. It's early in both."

"What are the cases?"

"A missing person and a suicide investigation."

Nate nodded. "Who are the clients?"

I hesitated. Chewed the inside of my cheek. I tilted my head at Jimmy, then turned back to Nate. "Client confidentiality prevents me from discussing the details with anyone but Jimmy." In my peripheral vision I saw Jimmy's eyes brighten.

"Well," said Nate. "We're all family. I won't divulge anything. Attorney-client privilege, right?"

"Sorry," I said.

"I have a vested interest in the success of this agency. I like to know what's going on. In fact, I have a *right* to know. Hell, my money pays for most of this agency's caseload."

"Maybe. But not these two cases."

A flash of something not altogether nice passed over Nate's face before vanishing behind a slick grin.

"Well," he said. "I see you're a man of integrity. That's to be commended." He checked his watch, made a vague statement about having to get back upstairs, and left the office. Jimmy wheeled around to me in his chair.

"Dude," he said, breaking into a wide, toothy smile. "That was so awesome. My dad's not used to people saying no. He hates it. *Not these two cases.* Ha! Awesome . . ."

"I was serious about client confidentiality. The worst thing that can happen to you, other than getting arrested or killed, is to pick up a reputation that you can't keep a secret. A PI firm should be a vault for information. People come to private investigators with their lives' most dirty little secrets and suspicions. You need to be like a priest."

"A priest. Right. Except for the no sex, though."

"Yeah. Except for that." I sat in one of the guest chairs, hoping that the vow of poverty was also exempted. "You said I need to fill out some paperwork?"

"Right. I am so pumped that you're coming on board. Totally pumped." Jimmy retrieved the human-resources paperwork that I needed to complete. A-Plus contracted all HR functions to a separate company. I sat at my new desk and filled out an impressive stack of forms. The health coverage was as good as Jimmy had promised.

"Okay," I said when I was done. "As the agency principal, you really do have a right to know the status of all the active cases." I filled him in on both the Victor Madrigas and Jonathan Dennis investigations.

Jimmy pursed his lips and nodded his head. "Gotcha . . . gotcha. What can I do to help?"

I had anticipated the question and was ready. "I need a picture of Jonathan Dennis. They might have something in the computer downtown for his city ID badge, but I think they purge the pictures when you no longer work there. Jonathan went to West Orange High. I need you to get me a yearbook photo." Jimmy's brow creased but his head kept nodding. That was his thinking face. I suspected that while interested in the assignment, he had no idea how to actually accomplish it. I helped him out: "I'd probably start by going to the school. They usually keep archive copies of yearbooks in the office. Maybe you can get a scan or a photocopy of the picture." The brow uncreased a little. "Class of '04."

"Cool," Jimmy said. His eyes narrowed in thought.

"No disguises, Jimmy. Or secret cameras. Just a straight-up retrieval."

"Yeah, I knew that."

But he couldn't hide the disappointment on his face.

"Okay, Mike, I want you to point at each picture and tell me what it is."

She was young. Too young to tell me what to do. Midtwenties, I'd guess. Her name was Megan and she was my brand-new occupational therapist. Megan had raven-black hair, a pale complexion, and a single silver stud in one ear. She also had just a little too much cleavage popping out of her black knit top. Thanks to a last-minute cancellation, I was able to get a morning appointment to start figuring out why I couldn't remember how the hell to say "hamburger."

I sighed. "Okay. That's a car. A train. A duck." A large binder full of pictures of various items was open before me. By me pointing at images and saying what they were, the therapist would be able to determine the severity of my memory loss. I felt like I was three years old.

A is for apple. B is for brain damage.

I thought I did okay. I identified all but three pictures. As soon as Megan told me what they were, they immediately popped back into my memory, little pegs finding empty holes in my brain and plugging themselves in. Mouse, shovel, and cake: that's what I couldn't remember. How could I forget cake, for God's sake? Each was just as frustrating as the Hamburger Incident of last night.

"Your brain suffered some trauma from the operation, Mike," Megan said.

No shit. Try plucking a malignant growth out of your cerebrum and see if you can remember "mouse." But that's not what I said.

"Yeah," I said instead.

"Your brain needs exercise."

"Exercise?" I pictured my poor wrinkled brain with the scoop taken out running on two little legs on a tiny treadmill.

"Sure. You need to use it. Get the synapses firing again. Make new connections. Use it or lose it."

"Okay . . . So, what do I do? I can't exactly do brain-ups."

"Sure you can, figuratively speaking. Read a book. Do a cross-word puzzle. Memorize the Preamble to the Constitution."

"We the people."

"There you go. What's the rest?"

"Hell if I know."

"Figure it out, Mike. It'll be good for you. Use it or lose it." She looked at me seriously. I forced myself not to look at her cleavage.

I left the therapist's office and got into my truck. *We the people* . . . The two cases I was currently working on were forcing me to think more than I had in a long time. That had to be good for my now Bob-free brain. I could start reading again, too. I wonder if *Sports Illustrated* counted.

As I pulled out of the parking lot, I realized that I actually knew a little more of the preamble than I'd thought. I had memorized it in fifth grade and the doctor's brain scoop had obviously missed some of it. *We the People, in order to form a more perfect union, establish something and promote the something with liberty and justice for all. As it was in the beginning, is now, and ever shall be, world without end. Amen.* Okay, I didn't really know much more than the first few words, and I may have mixed it up a bit with the other chunks of childhood knowledge sloshing around in my brain gumbo. But if I could've just remembered it, I'd have turned around and run back into the building so I could shout it at Megan.

I vowed to learn the rest of it. And then I'd come back and recite the whole damn thing.

The report confirmed everything that Boyd Bryson had said. After seeing the therapist, I returned to my apartment and laid the files out on my scratched coffee table. The medical examiner determined Victor's cause of death as an overdose of alprazolam, commonly known as Xanax, a popular antianxiety drug. It required a prescription, but it was easy enough to score on the street or in the hallways of a large suburban high school. Although such transactions were usually for small quantities, not the large amount of drugs Victor had apparently swallowed. Bryson had spoken to at least a dozen of Victor's friends and his interview notes were solid. He was a good detective, very thorough. However, the kids offered no leads and none had any idea where Victor might have gotten the pills.

No behavior skeletons in Victor's closet, either. He was an altar boy. Literally. He helped serve Mass every week at St. Joseph's. Of course, given my personal experience in the rectory as a kid, some of the meanest, most twisted individuals I had ever met were altar boys. And that includes my seventeen years as a cop.

But Victor was also a volunteer youth minister, a service I couldn't claim in either my youth or my adulthood. He helped teach religious education one night a week. He was a straight-A student in school. No discipline problems. No steady girlfriend, but a tight group of close friends. He played saxophone in the jazz band. None of his friends had ever been in trouble. Bryson's notes didn't list even a detention.

Victor had been accepted early into three colleges, two state universities, and a private Catholic seminary out of state. By all accounts, Victor was good kid, a kid who had things together, who was going places. There were three eight-by-ten photos in the envelope: two sterile shots of Victor's lifeless face and a color yearbook portrait. The yearbook picture featured a smiling, optimistic young man, looking slightly up past the camera, grinning with gleaming teeth that had recently had their braces removed, his bow tie a little askew. His brown hair was an inch or two longer than in the ME's photos, and his dark eyes seemed to hold wonder and humor and even optimism. But I was probably reading too much into it. Juxtaposed next to the two images of his open-eyed death gaze, the yearbook picture took on more meaning than it would have alone.

"Why, Victor?" I muttered aloud, holding the yearbook picture in one hand and the death gaze in the other. Looking back and forth between the two, I couldn't reconcile them. I understood what Boyd Bryson meant. There was just a funny feeling about it.

Certainly nothing in the evidence suggested anything except suicide. Regrettably, there are plenty of kids just like Victor all across the country—good kids, kids with prospects, who swallow a handful of pills. But usually there was some warning sign somewhere. It might be subtle: a teacher noticed him being quieter the last few days; friends claimed that he refused invitations to the movies; parents noticed a loss of appetite. Victor presented none of these signals.

Again, there was plenty of precedent for cases just like Victor's. A complete shock for friends and family. No good explanation. A tragedy. If we only knew.

Still . . .

That one percent was nagging at me. If he had just left a note, explained why he felt suicide was necessary . . . But he didn't. I could definitely see Ben Madrigas's angst. He simply couldn't believe that his son was capable of killing himself. Based on Detective Bryson's notes, Ben Madrigas wasn't alone in thinking that.

I shoved all the files back into the envelope and pushed it aside. I decided that I had read enough. I needed to do some interviewing of my own. And I knew exactly who I was going to interview first.

CHAPTER 8

"Tell me about Victor Madrigas," I said.

My daughter, Jennifer, stopped walking and looked at me. She was on a break from her new after-school job at Copy King, which called itself a document-service shop but looked to me like a poor man's Kinko's. We were walking across the strip mall parking lot to a Starbucks on the other side.

"Is that why you came to see me?" she said. "To ask about Victor?"

"That's one reason. I'll get to my other reason in a minute. What can you tell me about him?"

"Why are you asking about Victor?" I explained that Victor's father had asked me to look into his suicide, to see if there was any evidence that it could have been an accident. Jennifer nodded and slowly began walking again. I stepped in beside her. Finally, she said, "*Was* it an accident?"

"I don't know. Probably not. I don't know if we'll ever know. What do you think?"

We reached the door of the Starbucks and she stopped. "I just can't picture Victor doing that. He couldn't. . . ." Her eyes filled with tears and I gently pulled her away from the door, where she was blocking a group of patrons from exiting. I continued to hold her arm in what I hoped was some sort of comforting gesture. Despite the crucible we'd gone through during the summer, when she was abducted, we still didn't have what you might call a "close" relationship. The fact that we were now able to speak in civil sentences was epic progress in our father-daughter interactions. But a hug just wasn't a natural response for me here.

"I'm sorry," I said. "It's too soon to be asking you questions like that. I didn't realize that you and Victor were so close."

Jennifer produced a tissue from her purse and wiped her nose. "We weren't really. I mean, he was Carrie's brother, so y'know, we kinda knew each other." I nodded, recalling that Carrie was one of Jennifer's core group of school friends. "But he was so *nice*. He was always protecting things. He found this stray cat once and it took him, like, five hours to catch it. But he did and brought it to the shelter. He even paid for its shots. He'd make the football players stop picking on nerdy guys in the hallway. He even told me and Carrie that if anyone bothered us, he would take care of it." She wiped her eyes, but the tears were streaming again. I stood quietly, giving her a moment to collect herself. It was hard to watch my daughter in such distress. "Why would he kill himself? Why would he do that?"

"I don't know, honey. Unfortunately, these things usually don't make very much sense." I gave her arm a squeeze. "C'mon. I'll buy you a double mocha frappalatte thing with extra whipped cream."

Jennifer attempted a smile and blew her nose. We made our way into the shop and ordered our drinks, the whipped mocha concoction for her, a cup of strong black bean for me.

"So what's the other thing?" Jennifer asked as we sat at a small table.

"Other thing?"

"Yeah, you said there were two things you wanted to talk to me about."

"Right . . . right. Yeah, see, I've got some news. Nothing bad. Nothing about the cancer. But it's big. I'm just not sure how to say it."

"Okay."

"Well, it's just that, I know it'll seem weird, but . . ."

"I'm gonna be a big sister."

My bugged eyes and slack jaw informed her that, yes, indeed, she *was* going to be a big sister.

"How did you . . ." I managed to mutter.

"It's, like, so obvious." Jennifer blinked innocently before admitting, "Cam told me."

"Cam—"

"Don't get mad. We went to lunch the other day and she, like, had to get up twice to puke and three times to pee. So she told me why. She said she was doing you a favor, anyway. She said you'd be all squirmy and uncomfortable trying to tell me."

"She was right."

"Yeah." Jennifer managed a chuckle. "You shoulda seen your face." She took a long pull on her drink. "So, are you guys gonna get married again or what?"

"Probably the what. It's complicated."

"Well, I think it's totally awesome. I can't wait. I can help babysit and pick out clothes and toys and everything. I think I can even change a diaper." She made an icky face at the thought. "Maybe."

I breathed a very large and literal sigh of relief. Jennifer and I were just forging a new and improved relationship, so the last thing I needed was to introduce a new baby and the elements of jealousy and resentment into the mix. I wasn't exactly the world's greatest father to Jennifer growing up, and she might not be too thrilled with the prospect of my getting a parental "do-over." But, so far, she seemed genuinely excited. That was a good start.

"And you know what's the best part?" Jennifer asked, leaning conspiratorially across the table. "When she hears, Mom is gonna totally *freak*."

Jennifer was right. Becky freaked.

When I spoke to her from my apartment the next day, she had six hundred and twelve reasons why my being a father again was a terrible idea. I had cancer. Cam and I were divorced. I was a crappy father the first time around. I was too old for a baby. I was irresponsible. My career was in tatters. I was colossally selfish (she actually used the word *colossally*). They were all valid reasons. They were certainly all true. But I trumped them all with the simple statement that Cam was having the baby anyway and I was going to be a father again in spite of all the reasons amassed against me. Then I smiled and calmly pressed the End button on my phone.

While there is generally nothing good about divorce and I wouldn't recommend it to anyone, I will admit that one positive consequence is the fact that I was no longer forced to listen to Becky's crap. When I was diagnosed with cancer, Becky turned off the sourpuss-ex-wife routine and became nothing but supportive and sad. Now that it looked like I might actually survive, at least for a while, the sourpuss was back. Even with her new husband to focus on, judging me was still her favorite hobby. But divorce and a terminal illness had provided me with Teflon shorts. Becky could judge all she wanted. I couldn't care less.

As soon as I hung up, the phone rang again. I pressed Answer.

"Look, Becky," I said. "It's none of your business."

"Who the hell is Becky?" answered the raspy voice on the other end.

With my finely tuned investigative skills, I realized that in fact it was not Becky calling back to continue our argument.

"Sally?" I asked.

"So who's Becky and what's none of her business?"

"My ex-wife. And pretty much everything."

"Believe me, after four husbands, I understand."

"What have you got, Sal? Good news for me?"

"I got news. You decide if it's good. The kid, Jonathan, up and quit without notice almost three weeks ago. If you want details, go see his ex-supervisor. Name's Ed O'Malley. Works in IT. You know where that is?"

"Yeah. Can I mention your name or will O'Malley be happy to see me?"

"No need to mention me. O'Malley may not be happy to see you, but he'll help if he can. Just tell him your name."

"Thanks, Sal. I owe you one."

"I'll keep that in mind the next time I get divorced."

It was late morning when I walked into Ed O'Malley's downtown office. O'Malley was about my height and carrying a few pounds too many. He was in his mid- to late thirties but was clearly trying to appear at least ten years younger. He had a little brown soul patch on his chin and was dressed in a shiny purple shirt with a monochrome tie. The look might have suited an NBA point guard, but it didn't even come close to working for him. O'Malley's few extra pounds stretched the stomach buttons on his shirt more than style dictated. From a fashion standpoint, his reach far exceeded his grasp.

"Ed O'Malley?" I said from the doorway.

He didn't look up from his computer screen. He breathed heavily through his nose. His fingers flew across the keyboard.

"I prefer Edward," he said.

"Can I talk to you for a minute?"

"I am quite busy. It seems the city of Orlando is the target of a very nasty worm. Very nasty indeed. I am protecting our servers as we speak."

"That's good. But I'll only take a minute." I seated myself in one of the office guest chairs.

O'Malley was still focused on his computer screen, not looking at me as he spoke. "Please make an appointment and return at a future date. I will be pleased to converse with you at that time."

"Normally, that would be fine. But I'm under a bit of a deadline. I don't have time to make an appointment."

"Will I have to call security to escort you from my office?" He continued to stare at his computer, typing furiously.

"I hope not. Look, my name's Mike Garrity and I just have a couple of questions—"

At O'Malley's head finally popped up and his dark, hooded eyes zeroed in on me. He stopped typing.

"Mike Garrity, did you say?" He pursed his lips and absently scratched the soul patch.

"Yeah."

"Tell me, Mike Garrity . . . tell me why the mayor himself, a man I haven't spoken to more than twice in my life, called me today and told me to assist anyone named Mike Garrity who might ask for help."

"Gosh, Edward, I'm not sure. Did that really happen?" Good old Sally.

"Yes, indeed it did, Mike Garrity. Indeed it did. You are the Mike Garrity he referred to, are you not?"

"I am indeed."

"Well then, let's get this over with as quickly as possible," O'Malley said and clasped his hands over his shiny tie. "What are your queries?"

"Do you know where I can find Jonathan Dennis?"

"I do not."

"When did you last speak with him?"

O'Malley pointed at my chair. "When he walked into this office and sat in that very seat to unceremoniously resign without notice. The height of unprofessionalism."

"When was this?"

O'Malley turned back to his computer and clicked something, typed something, then clicked something else. "Nineteen days ago, at two forty-five in the afternoon."

"Do you have a photo of him? Maybe from an ID card?"

O'Malley pushed his brown caterpillar eyebrows together. "I don't know."

"Think you could print one for me?"

O'Malley wasn't sure about this. I gave him my most disarming smile, which felt like a pained grimace to me.

"I think not," he said. "I don't have access. You would have to get that from Security. Or Human Resources." He scratched his soul patch again. "Is there anything else?"

"Almost done. Where did you send Jonathan's last check?"

"To the address on file."

"Which is . . . ?"

O'Malley paused. "That is confidential personnel information. I cannot divulge it."

I pulled out a piece of paper. "Okay. Just tell me if it's different from what I have." I read Jonathan's address and phone number. O'Malley consulted the computer again.

"We have the same data."

"What about a cell phone? I'm sure you guys have each other's cell numbers. Y'know, in case of a worm attack on a Saturday or something."

"I do."

"May I have it, please?" Another charming grimace. "I'll be sure to tell the mayor how cooperative you've been."

"I suppose . . . It's not in the personnel records. But I have called it three times in the past two weeks and he never answers and never returns my calls." O'Malley read me the cell number. "Why do you want this information?"

"A relative is looking for Jonathan. He just got an inheritance."

"How wonderful for him," O'Malley said flatly. He made a show of looking at his digital watch.

"One last question—"

"Is that a promise?"

I ignored the sarcasm. "Did Jonathan have any close friends that you knew of? Either here at work or maybe outside work that he talked about?"

O'Malley leaned back in his desk chair, the springs creaking loudly. He looked up at the acoustic tiles in the ceiling and pursed his lips in an affectation of thought.

"Friends . . . Only one that I can think of," he said. "He sometimes ate lunch with a gentleman from the press office. Steven.

Steven Schumacher, I believe." O'Malley tilted forward again in his chair and gave me the dead eyes. A not-so-subtle signal that he was done.

"Is Steven Schumacher here now?"

"I haven't the slightest idea. His office is two floors up."

"Yeah. Okay. Well, thanks, Ed. Sorry—Edward. I appreciate the help." I stood. "I'll be sure to tell the mayor."

O'Malley was already turning back to the computer screen. "Good-bye, Mike Garrity."

"Hope you catch that worm."

But Edward O'Malley said no more. His only reply was the rapid clicking of computer keys.

I wandered upstairs and poked my head into the public-affairs office. I asked a cute brunette behind the lobby desk where Steven Schumacher's office was.

"Do you have an appointment?" she chirped.

"Nah. I was just in the neighborhood and thought I'd stop by."

"So he's not expecting you?"

"Not exactly. I'll only be a minute."

"Why don't I call him."

I had to restrain all my old cop impulses, which were urging me to barge past the brunette and start poking my head into offices. But I was a private citizen now. I had to play by different rules.

"That would be great," I said and offered her the charming grimace.

"Your name and affiliation?"

"Affiliation?"

"Who are you with? Media? Advocacy group? Private industry?"

"Mike Garrity. Private industry."

She punched a number on the phone, mumbled something, and hung up. She smiled and told me that Mr. Schumacher would be right with me. I plopped myself into a chair and thumbed through an old issue of *Florida Trend* magazine.

"Mr. Garrity?"

I looked up and saw a good-looking young guy, sandy-blond hair, clean-cut, wearing a blue shirt and yellow tie. Steven Schumacher extended a hand. I stood and shook it.

"So," Schumacher said. "How can I help you?"

"Do you mind if we talk in private?"

"Of course. My cubicle isn't exactly private, but the conference room is open."

He walked me to a small but neat conference room and we took seats across from each other. I folded my hands and looked at him. He smiled and raised his eyebrows in interest.

"I'm looking for Jonathan Dennis," I said.

Schumacher's face didn't change. The smile and expectant eyebrows remained frozen for a second. A beat too long to be natural. I could tell that he was trying to be nonchalant; but by trying, he wasn't nonchalant at all.

After the prolonged moment, the eyebrows came down. "Who?" he asked.

"Your friend. Jonathan Dennis. I need to find him."

"Who said we were friends?"

I made a bemused face. "Are you kidding? You guys have lunch all the time. Are you saying that you *aren't* friends?"

"No." Schumacher swallowed. "I was just curious."

"So, can you tell me where to find him?"

"And who are you again?"

"Mike Garrity." I shot him the charming grimace. "Private industry."

Schumacher nodded, but he wasn't really responding to what I had said. The wheels in his head were spinning. His eyes were looking at me but his mind was elsewhere. "I see . . . And this doesn't have anything to do with the mayor's office?"

"No. So, may I please have Jonathan Dennis's phone number and address?"

"No. I mean, I don't have it."

"You don't know where he lives?"

"No. He moved after he quit." Schumacher scratched his chin. If I were a poker player, I'd called that a "tell."

"What about his phone number?" I asked.

"It's not in service."

"How about a cell phone?"

"I don't think I even have it."

"You don't think? You mean you might have it?"

"No. I don't have it. We mostly talked on the office line during work. We actually IMed more than we talked." I knew from my daughter that IM stood for "instant message."

"When was the last time you saw him?" I asked.

"I don't know. The week he quit."

"And you haven't spoken to him since?"

"No."

I sighed. "Look, Steven. I don't know why you're lying, but I'm not here for any bad reason. I was just asked to find Jonathan by a family member who wants to talk to him. That's it. I swear."

"If it's a family member, why doesn't he have his number already?"

"They do. They did. But, as you said, Jonathan moved and his phone was disconnected. They can't find him." Schumacher didn't say anything. I could tell that he was thinking again. The guy had no hope ever to move up the ranks and become the mayor's press secretary. He couldn't lie for shit. "Where is he, Steven?"

"I don't know."

"Steven . . ."

"I don't know. Seriously." Somehow, Schumacher's "seriously" seemed less sincere than Jimmy's "seriously."

"Why did he quit his job?"

"I don't know."

"Why did he move so suddenly?"

"I don't know."

"What's two plus two?"

"What?"

"I'm trying to figure out what you *do* know. How about two plus two? You know that?" I thought it was pretty funny but Schumacher wasn't laughing. No accounting for taste. "Okay. Look . . ." I wrote my name and number on a small piece of notepaper. "Please have Jonathan call me. I'm not here to hassle him about anything. I just want to talk. Okay?"

I slid the paper across the table. Schumacher looked at it as if it were covered with anthrax. Finally, he palmed it and slipped it into his pocket.

"If he calls me," he said.

"Exactly. It's important, though, Steven. Be sure to tell him that I don't have a lot of time."

"If he calls me," Schumacher repeated.

"Of course." We didn't say much more after that. Schumacher quickly escorted me to the lobby and then disappeared back into the cubicle maze. I had no doubt that before I reached the elevator, he would already be on the phone with Jonathan.

CHAPTER 9

I had Jonathan's cell phone number. I didn't want to do this by phone. In person was better. But Schumacher was probably already talking to him, so I figured that I would go with the one lead I had. I punched in the number.

I got a message.

"Hi. This is Jon. I can't answer the phone right now. Leave your name and number and I'll try to call ya' back. Later." I waited for the tone.

"Hello, Jon. My name is Mike Garrity. I'm a private investigator. Could you please call me back? I have a client who would very much like to speak with you. It's nothing to be concerned about, but it is important." I left my number.

"Who was that?" Cam asked. I sat next to her in the waiting room of her ob/gyn.

"No one. A case I'm working on."

She closed the *People* magazine she had been flipping through and turned to me. "How do you like your new job so far?"

"Hard to tell. I haven't even been doing it a week yet."

She smirked at me. "You like it, though. I can tell. You were a good cop and you'll be a good private investigator."

I returned the smirk. She squeezed my hand. There was a lot of meaning in that squeeze: *Thanks for coming with me today. Can you believe that we're going to be parents? I'm a little scared. I'm so glad you took a job—it means that you're fighting to live.* Of course, she didn't actually say any of this. But I knew.

A nurse poked her head through the hall door. "Camilla?"

We followed her to an exam room and Cam slipped into a paper gown. Out of decency I averted my eyes, although you would think that several years of marriage and one impregnation might have earned me a peek. However, things somehow felt different now, like we'd entered some new phase of our complicated relationship. Added to the new vibe was the fact that I had recently slept with Debbie. Should I tell Cam? She probably wouldn't care. She told me about *her* boyfriends. But I figured this wasn't exactly an appropriate place or time for a quasi-confession. Plus, there was no sense in testing a pregnant woman's hormones.

'   The doctor entered the room and greeted us. She was tall, African American, perhaps in her late thirties. Her hair was short, but her thin, tapered face had a flawless complexion and beautiful almond-shaped eyes. Her name was Dr. Laura Ugabe.

"So, how are we feeling?" Dr. Ugabe said. Her voice was colored with an exotic, musical accent; not quite Caribbean, probably African. She may not have been African American, after all. I think she was African African.

She examined Cam and asked what I assumed were all the usual questions. I don't ever recall attending a pregnancy appointment with Becky when she was expecting Jennifer. My uncomfortable presence in the exam room was tangible evidence of my personal growth. At least that's what I told myself.

Before I realized what was happening, Dr. Ugabe had placed a small radio device on the table next to Cam and was positioning a tethered microphone on her abdomen. *Whoosh-whoosh-whoosh-whoosh.* A rapid, staticky noise blared out of it.

"Is everything okay?" I asked. "What is that?"

"That," said Dr. Ugabe, "is your baby's heartbeat."

Heartbeat . . . After several days with Debbie—hell, with my tumor, several months—and near total immersion in the pool of death, it was a shock to my system to be confronted with this very real confirmation of *life*. My baby's heartbeat. It literally pushed me back into my chair. Growing inside Cam at that very moment was a living person. It was no longer simply an abstract concept. The audible heartbeat made it a reality. I swallowed and exchanged a look of wonder with Cam. Her eyes were wet.

"Would you like to see him—or her?" Dr. Ugabe asked.

Unable to speak, we both nodded.

Dr. Ugabe wheeled a portable ultrasound to the table and applied lubricant to Cam's abdomen. Then she positioned the wand on Cam's belly and turned on the monitor so that we could see.

"There it is," Dr. Ugabe said. "Your baby."

There it was. A black-and-white blob on the screen. But a blob with a head and appendages. And a heartbeat. I couldn't speak. I couldn't move. I could only stare. Cam held her hand out and I took it, mesmerized by the floating fetus in the monitor. I didn't recall feeling that way when Becky was pregnant. Things were different sixteen years ago. I was the macho cop with the short fuse. Invincible. Unemotional. I don't think I ever saw an ultrasound of Jennifer. Maybe a fuzzy printout. My fight with cancer had tempered me, had made very clear to me what a miraculous gift a simple heartbeat was.

"Can you tell the sex yet?" I asked when my voice returned.

"Still too early," Dr. Ugabe said. "A few more weeks."

"Does everything look okay?"

Dr. Ugabe smiled at me. "Everything looks perfect."

I couldn't have agreed more.

Cam and I ate dinner together and tried valiantly not to gush and blubber over our food. I elected not to tell her about Debbie; it just didn't seem right. When we were done, I walked her to her car, kissed her on the cheek, and watched her drive off. It occurred to me that I had done almost the exact same thing with Debbie two nights before.

I walked over to my truck. As I did so, I realized that I was literally across the road from the very spot where Victor Madrigas's body had been discovered. Victor was found sitting in his 1998 Honda Civic in the parking lot of a local SuperTarget. According to the medical examiner, he had been there for several hours before a passing shopper unloading a cart full of groceries bothered to notice him and called 911.

So I drove across the street to the SuperTarget and parked in the general area described in the police report. I sat in my car and watched the shoppers pour in and out of the big-box store like ants crawling on a nest. It occurred to me that SuperTarget was one of the few places on earth where you could buy pants, a bicycle, and thinly sliced roast beef all at the same register. I wasn't sure if that was a good thing or a bad thing.

I closed my eyes and tried to get a vibe about Victor's death. Why had he done it? Why the SuperTarget? The place was crowded with high-schoolers and undergrads from the nearby University of Central Florida. It was probably one of his hangouts. Maybe it had some significance for him. Had he taken the pills and then driven here, sitting quietly in the car waiting to die, watching these same shoppers scurry back and forth?

Not so long ago, I suppose I wasn't that different. When I was diagnosed with cancer, I quickly resigned myself to letting nature take its course. I figured that the universe was sending me a message and I'd just go with it. So, for a few months, I did much the same thing as Victor had done—I sat and watched and waited to die.

But things had changed. I had decided to let the docs saw off the top of my head and perform a Bob-ectomy. I hadn't become a drooling vegetable like they'd feared. I had a renewed relationship with my sixteen year-old daughter. I had a new job. And I had just heard the heartbeat of my unborn child.

What had been going on in Victor's life that swallowing a bottle of Xanax and sitting in his car was the best alternative? A stunning blond girl sashayed past my windshield in tight, low-riding jeans and a midriff-baring tank top. I watched her stroll by with what I realized was a bit too much interest. I blinked and looked away, convincing myself, I hoped, that she must have been at least eighteen. Involuntarily ogling a legal adult didn't feel quite as smarmy.

This was very likely the same view that Victor had seen as the night closed in around him. A whole world waiting for him beyond high school, a world filled with sashaying blondes and college and endless possibilities. Why hadn't he seen it? Or had he? Despite what Detective Bryson had said, was this just some sort of terrible accident? Had Victor just wanted to get high and hang out, not knowing what he was doing?

But when I considered the accident angle, the funny feeling was still there. Most kids, unless they're serious addicts, don't get high and sit by themselves in a parking lot. Getting high or loaded is almost always a social activity. And, by all accounts, Victor had been far from a serious addict. In fact, nobody could recall seeing him take any drugs. Ever. Maybe this had been the first time, which might explain an overdose due to ignorance, but I wasn't buying it. Even a first-time user knows that you don't swallow the whole bottle of pills.

Nope. I decided that Detective Bryson was probably right. My girlish intuition was telling me that this had been no accident. It was either exactly how it looked, a tragic suicide, or . . . or what? A murder? Was I seriously considering the possibility that Victor had been murdered, despite the absence of any motive or physical evidence?

Well, that's what Ben Madrigas was paying me for. If I was going to really look into his son's death and any possibility that it hadn't been a suicide, then I had to at least peer down this road, even if I ultimately decided not to pursue it. *Okay, Garrity . . . start with the basics for all cops and journalists: who, what, where, when, why, and how.*

I knew what and where—at least where Victor had been found. Right there, under the halogen glow of the SuperTarget parking-lot lamps. I knew when. I even knew how: a bottle of antianxiety pills. If it really had been murder, then the how would indicate the who—probably somebody close. Pills imply intimacy or at least close contact. Even if he or she had secretly dissolved the drugs in a drink, the killer would have had to get close. And Victor would have drunk it. So, unless this was just some freakish, random killing, the do-er would probably have been known to Victor. But the big question remained without even a glimmer of an answer: why?

That's probably because there was no answer. Boyd Bryson would agree that ninety-nine times out of a hundred, things pretty much were how they looked. And this looked exactly like a tragic teen suicide. I glanced out my side window. An overweight soccer mom loaded three kids under five years old into a maroon mini-van, followed by a brigade's worth of grocery supplies. I watched her slide the side door shut and suddenly realized that I was wasting my time.

I was getting no vibe about Victor's death. This was a dumb-ass idea. Returning to the scene of the crime is a Hollywood fantasy. What was I doing? I spent a career closing cases by sheer hard work and perseverance. Feet on the street. I don't think I ever got a single piece of evidence or witness testimony by visiting the crime scene and trying to feel a "vibe." Damn, was I out of practice. Is this what I was supposed to be teaching Jimmy Hungerford? I turned the ignition of my truck.

And then I got a vibe. Specifically, in my left front pocket. My cell phone was ringing. I pulled it out and flipped it open.

"This is Jonathan Dennis," came the voice on the other end. "Who is this?"

CHAPTER 10

"This is Mike Garrity," I said.

"You're the PI who called me?" Jonathan replied.

"That's right."

"Okay. No face-to-face meetings. Not yet. Your *client* will have to wait."

"All right." I blinked my eyes. This didn't feel quite right. "Do you know why I called you?"

Jonathan chuckled tersely. "I have a pretty good idea."

"Why don't you tell me?"

"Nice try, Sherlock. I have a few more arrangements to make. When I'm done, I'll call back and tell you what to do. But, trust me, we won't be talking any details on this line."

"Look, Jon. I don't know what you're talking about. I have a client, someone from your past, who just wants to talk to you."

"Right. And I'll be happy to talk. I look forward to it. But not yet. I'll call you back when I'm ready. Later."

Click. He was gone.

I tried calling back but he didn't pick up. I didn't like the feeling I was getting from Jonathan Dennis. This wasn't right. He didn't sound like he was talking about the same thing that I was talking about. He sounded like he might have been talking about something shady. Perhaps this had something to do with why he had suddenly quit his job and moved out of his apartment.

There was no way I'd be able to go home and go to sleep with my mind churning over the mysterious Jonathan Dennis. So, instead, I wandered into the SuperTarget and bought a pair of binoculars. Then I returned to my truck and called Jimmy.

"Yeah?" Jimmy answered.

"Jimmy, it's Mike Garrity. Were you able to get that picture of Jonathan Dennis?"

"Totally, dude. I way got it."

"Good. Do you have it with you?"

"Sure. Right in the front seat of my car."

"Okay. Tell me where you are. I'll be right there."

Jimmy gave me directions to a pizza place near downtown. I made it in just over twenty minutes. I found Jimmy inside, sitting at a checkered table with another guy. A half-eaten pizza was on a pedestal between them. As I stepped up, I noticed that the other guy had sandy-blond hair and was young—younger than Jimmy. I also noticed that he had Down syndrome.

"I got it, man," Jimmy said, standing. "The secretary lady at the school gave me a hard time, but I kept workin' on her and workin' on her until she was just, like, take it, take it and go away." He grinned at me.

"That's great, Jimmy. Good work." My eyes drifted to Jimmy's dining companion.

"Oh, sorry, dude," Jimmy said. "This is my kid brother, Richie."

Richie stood and held out his hand, a coached behavior.

"Nice to meet you, Richie," I said, shaking his hand. The kid sat back down with a smile.

"I kinda look after him," Jimmy said. "You know how it is."

I nodded but I had no idea how it was. This tiny glimpse into Jimmy's personal life was surprising. I didn't picture him with the maturity to care for a sibling with special needs.

"So," I said. "The picture?"

"Right. Here—" From a manila folder he produced a good black-and-white photocopy of Jonathan Dennis's yearbook picture. It was a little small, but it was clear enough for an ID, which was all I needed. Jonathan looked like a million other young men. Stringy dark hair, thin face, wispy teenage mustache, greasy smile. Put a better smile on his lips and he didn't look all that different from Victor Madrigas's yearbook picture.

"Thanks," I said. "Good work."

"You're on the case right now, aren't you?"

"Not really. Just following up on some stuff."

"I could help you, dude. I could come with you."

"What about Richie?"

"He's cool. He can come with us. He likes to sit and listen to books on tape. I got Harry Potter on the iPod. He's a good kid. He won't be any trouble."

I couldn't help but smile. "Thanks, Jimmy, but there's no need. I'm just doing research. If I need backup, though, I'll be sure to call. Okay?"

Jimmy shook my hand by clasping thumbs, like we were a couple of gangbangers on a street corner. I waved good-bye to Richie and slipped out the door. Once I was back in my truck, I turned to my cell phone and googled the address for Steven Schumacher, Jonathan's lying friend from the mayor's office. I knew that if I got lucky with the traffic lights, I would make it to Schumacher's apartment in another twenty minutes.

I got there in exactly twenty-two minutes. Not too bad. Schumacher lived in an older apartment complex on the northern edge of the Orlando city proper. It was a flat-topped two-story place painted a pus yellow. The amber halogen glow of the streetlights didn't help its aesthetic appeal.

Schumacher lived in a ground-floor unit at the front of the building—the street side. I pulled into a Kentucky Fried Chicken parking lot across the street and grabbed the SuperTarget bag from my front passenger seat. I yanked the binoculars from their box, rolled down the driver's-side window, and settled back in my seat. I couldn't count the number of surveillances on which I had sat vigil. Although, I was decidedly more comfortable on this one than on any during my former career. Usually it was me and Big Jim Dupree, my former OPD partner, teamed together. Back in the day, sitting there in our unmarked car, we couldn't have been much more different physically. Where I was white, he was black. Where I was average size, he was gargantuan. Big Jim was six foot five and 270 pounds. I was considerably less. I loved Jim like a brother, but it could get pretty cramped in the front seat of a car wedged in with a guy like that.

So I stretched out a bit and put the binoculars to my eyes. I could see both the apartment door and the front window. And neither one showed me anything for more than a half hour.

After sitting for almost forty minutes, my bladder was telling me to visit the inside of the KFC. But just as I put my hand on the truck's inside door latch, I saw Schumacher's apartment door open. Then I saw Schumacher step outside.

Then I saw another guy follow him out of the apartment. The other guy was a little shorter than Schumacher and his dark hair was longer. They locked the door, turned, and then walked right at me.

I dropped the binoculars and ducked down below the dash. But not before I got a good look at the other guy. It was dark, and he was older now than in Jimmy's photocopy, but there was no doubt that Schumacher's companion was Jonathan Dennis.

Once I was sure that they were past my truck, I sat up and peeked out the back window. I saw Schumacher and Jonathan inside the KFC, sitting together in a booth, hunched over a couple of fried chicken legs. They seemed to be talking a lot. Schumacher shook his head a couple of times, refusing or disagreeing about something. I watched them for a while, until my bladder felt like it would literally burst. Then I casually slipped out of my truck and walked into the restaurant.

When I was done in the men's room I washed up and went back into the dining area. Jonathan and Schumacher were still at their table. I ordered some chicken strips and a Coke. Then I sat a few tables away in the nearly empty dining room, making sure that I was at Schumacher's back so he wouldn't see me. Their conversation was hushed and hard to hear, so I didn't get much of what they said. I did observe that Jonathan seemed to be doing most of the talking. Schumacher mostly just looked at the table, picking absently at his food.

"The sooner the better," I heard Schumacher say. "That's all I'm saying."

They stood and pitched their trash. I put my head down as they passed me on their way out of the restaurant.

Jonathan said, "Don't worry, man."

Through the big front windows I saw them cross the street and slip back into Schumacher's apartment. I sat long enough to finish my chicken and Coke. It gave me time to think.

I had no idea what Jonathan and Schumacher were up to, but it smelled like old socks. Whatever it was, it had forced Jonathan to go into hiding and Schumacher to lie. These weren't exactly the actions of innocent people.

There might have been a legitimate explanation for the picture I was seeing—maybe a crazy ex-girlfriend, maybe too much credit-card debt—but I quickly realized that I didn't care. Although it would have been nice to ferret out Jonathan's mystery before talking to Debbie, so that she had some idea of what her son was up to, I didn't think I should take the time. I knew that Debbie cared more about contacting him before it was too late than she did about whatever trouble he might be in.

All the same, I pulled out my phone and punched in a familiar cell number.

"What's up, G?" came the deep, baritone voice of Jim Dupree, clearly reading the caller ID on his cell phone.

"Big Jim," I said. "How you been?"

"No, the question is, how *you* been? You beat that shit yet?"

"The tumor's gone—for now anyway. Except for some scattered memory issues, I seem to be back in the saddle."

"Memory issues, huh? Like maybe you forgot how to call your old partner and tell him you took a job as a dirty PI?"

"Dirty?" I said. "Now, is that a nice thing to say?"

"For me it is. You should hear what I really wanna say." I could hear him sucking his teeth. "Why don't you come back home where you belong? We got plenty of real cases to work. Why you runnin' around chasin' cheating husbands and peepers? C'mon, G . . ."

"This is the right thing for me now. If I change my mind I'll let you know."

"Yeah, you do that. So, what favor you lookin' for?"

"Favor? What are you talking about? Can't I call an old friend and just catch up?"

"Don't bullshit a bullshitter. What do you want?"

"I'm hurt. I really am. How are Lydia and the kids?"

"They're great. Nathan broke his finger playing ball. Well, it was great catching up, old buddy. Let's get together real soon, okay?"

"I want to run a name by you."

Jim paused. "I'm listenin'."

"I'm working a case and I'm getting a funny feeling. Does the name Jonathan Dennis mean anything to you?"

"Which is the first name?"

"Jonathan."

"Never heard a' him."

"Anything in the case database?"

"Look at the clock. What time is it? After ten. What makes you think I'm sitting in my office at all hours just waitin' around for you to call me? I got a life, you know."

"Sorry. I wasn't thinking. I just got caught up in my own stuff. I'll try to call you back tomorrow."

"Yeah, well, try not to be so selfish."

"Okay. I'm sorry."

"There ain't nothin' in the database anyway."

"You *are* at work, you son of a bitch!" I actually pointed at the phone with my free hand. One of the KFC workers looked at me from the register.

"Yeah, but I *shouldn't* be. That's the point." He sighed a big sigh. "I'll ask around tomorrow when all the slackers are back at work."

"Thanks, Jim."

"Last time I did you a favor, we ended up with a headless body, a kidnaping, and a major scandal in the police department. *This* case ain't like that last case, is it?"

"I hope not."

"I hope not, too. For your sake."

I got back into my truck and made one more call on the cell.

"Hello?" Debbie sounded tired.

"Did I wake you?" I asked.

"No. Not really. I'm just beat. It wasn't a good day. I didn't feel good."

"I'm sorry. Is there anything I can do?"

"No. I'll be okay. I just need to rest."

"Okay. I'll let you go. I'd like to take you out tomorrow, if you're up for it."

"Sure. That would be nice."

We said good-bye and I hung up. I thought I might tell her about having seen Jonathan, but with the way she sounded, it didn't seem right. Tomorrow would be better. Tomorrow I would deliver her son back into her life; the one who had been lost but now was found.

I thought about the baby growing inside Cam. A second child for me, a second chance at parenthood. I neither expected nor deserved it. The story of the prodigal son is a story of second chances. This baby was the ultimate second chance. So now I had become the prodigal son. My father's voice echoed in my head and I pictured him looking up at me with a wry smile. *Well, look at this. The prodigal son has returned. And me without my fattened calf.*

It may be an excuse, but I never quite learned how to be a father from him. He loved me, I'm sure, but he always maintained a sense of pastoral distance. All he knew was his prior life in the rectory, and his habits were ingrained by the time I showed up. He wasn't publicly affectionate with me or my mother. So, due partly to his example and partly to my own personal failings, I screwed up my first chance at parenthood. I hadn't done a very good job with Jennifer. Whoever she had become was due entirely to genetics and Becky's parenting. I had been absent both physically and emotionally. The failure of my marriage to Becky had also created an awkward distance between my parents and my daughter, something that each side resented.

But now here I was, with a second chance to get it right. It was too late either to reunite Jennifer or introduce my new baby to my parents. But there was still some good I could do. I could bring Jonathan back into Debbie's life, the truth about Victor Madrigas to his father, and my unconditional devotion to my unborn child.

Of course, plans have a funny way of not turning out quite the way you hoped.

CHAPTER 11

Death was in the room while Debbie and I ate dinner, but he had the good manners not to hover directly over us, instead checking out the dinner selections of nearby patrons. He circled at the edges of our conversation, neither of us acknowledging him directly.

Debbie felt a little better, although she still appeared tired. There were dark circles under her eyes and her movements seemed slower and more deliberate. But she was in decent spirits and otherwise looked quite pretty in jeans and a powder-blue shirt. She asked once about the search for Jonathan, but I ducked the question.

I felt confident from actually being able to order a chicken picatta entrée without forgetting how to speak and excited with the knowledge that I had found Jonathan. While waiting for the right moment to bring it up, I was hit with sudden inspiration. Maybe it was the two glasses of wine. Maybe it was the swirling mix of parental thoughts in my head: Jennifer and the baby; my father and his perpetual disappointment; Debbie and her missing son. I still had a chance to do some good. Whatever the reason, it was a crazy, spontaneous idea—the kind of idea that the old Mike Garrity would have rejected immediately. The new Mike Garrity decided to roll with it.

I suppressed a stupid grin as we piled into my truck and I pulled out of the restaurant parking lot. After a few minutes of driving, Debbie turned to me.

"Where are we going?" she asked.

"I need to make a stop before I take you home."

This appeared to satisfy her, at least for the moment. She looked out the window, her mind on other matters. Several minutes later I spotted the Kentucky Fried Chicken restaurant. I parallel parked the truck directly in front of Steven Schumacher's apartment.

"Come with me," I said as nonchalantly as I could. She followed me up the sidewalk and we stopped at the door. I raised a fist, poised to knock. "Are you ready?"

"For what?" Debbie said.

"To meet your son."

I grinned at her and pounded on the door. I saw the blood actually drain from Debbie's face.

"You mean here?" she gasped. "Now?"

"I do."

"No—" She shook her head, stepping back off the path. "No no no . . ." She took three steps backward, panic contorting her face. "I can't—"

"Debbie—"

"No . . . Why didn't you tell me?" Breathing heavily, she turned and sprinted several yards, ducking down behind a nearby ficus bush.

"Who is it?" I heard a male voice call from inside the apartment. My head swiveled from Debbie to the door and then back again. "Who's there?" the voice called again.

"Uh" . . . "Is Steven Schumacher here?" The door opened not quite halfway. Jonathan Dennis stood there in a T-shirt and cutoff sweats. The light of a television flickered in the room behind him, casting the apartment in an eerie blue strobe.

"Steve's not here," he said, narrowing his eyes at me. "Who are you?"

"Steve said . . ." I mumbled, thinking quickly. "Steve said that we could talk tonight, off the record, for a story I'm writing on the mayor's office."

"So you're a reporter?"

"Sort of. Freelance. You know."

Jonathan looked me up and down. "Well, like I said, Steve's not here. You got a name you want me to give him?"

"No. That's all right. I'll call him at the office and arrange something. Thanks anyway."

Jonathan gave me one more hard stare before shutting the door. I heard the deadbolt and chain sliding into their places.

I stood there on the stoop for a moment, with no idea what I should do next. I was sure that Jonathan was watching me through the door peephole. That's what I would have been doing. So I didn't want to stroll directly over to Debbie. I walked back down the front path to the street. As I passed near the ficus bush, I called out the side of my mouth.

"Stay there. He's probably watching. I'll circle the block and then come back."

And that's exactly what I did. I got back into the truck and drove in a big circle around the apartment complex, my mind racing. Clearly, I had made a tactical blunder. How could I have been so stupid? The new Mike Garrity was clearly dumber than the old one. Of course this had backfired. Even if Debbie hadn't been dealing with a terminal illness, the prospect of confronting the son she had abandoned at birth would be enough to freak out even the most prepared person. And I had sprung it on her like a thoughtless kid jumping out from behind a door.

I pulled the truck to the curb near the ficus and Debbie hustled into the passenger seat.

"Debbie. I'm really sorry—"

"Don't speak to me." Her lips were tight and she stared straight ahead out the windshield. "Take me home."

"Okay."

We drove in absolute silence for eighteen minutes, an excruciatingly long time. Debbie lived in a decent but aging two-bedroom bungalow on the edge of downtown. I parked in her driveway. She pulled the door handle and stepped out. I followed.

"Don't," she said. She still wasn't looking at me, hadn't looked directly at me since she left the ficus bush. I froze. "I know you meant well. But you should've told me."

"I know. I'm sorry."

"So am I."

Without a backward glance, she turned and marched into the house. I lingered for a moment, jingled my keys absently, and decided that the best thing I could do was remove myself from the premises.

I drove home, brushed my teeth, threw on a T-shirt, and crawled into bed. I forced my eyes shut. I tried to breathe deeply and evenly. No use. My brain was still on overdrive, refusing to let me off the hook for my epic blunder. So I did what I always do when faced with an emotional challenge.

I had a drink. Specifically, I had three fingers of bourbon with a splash of water.

I drank it quickly, sitting in my shadowed living room in my boxer shorts. After a few minutes I felt the liquor warming me, compelling my muscles to relax, my mind to slow down. My breathing slowed. I closed my eyes.

I saw myself in a doctor's office, standing in my boxer shorts and holding my tumbler of bourbon. I walked down a hallway past examination rooms, the ice in my glass clinking as I moved. Each room held a bald, pregnant woman in a paper hospital gown. Each woman offered me a knowing smile as I passed by. From inside the rooms I heard the *whoosh-whoosh-whoosh* of fetal heartbeats. The door at the end of the hallway was open and I wandered in. An anonymous doctor in a lab coat stood with his hands clasped behind his back, looking at a brain scan tacked up on a wall light box. I had seen hundreds of brain scans. I knew them well. Somehow I understood that I was looking at my brain. The doctor turned and gave me the same knowing smile. Then he pointed at the scan. There was a dark, malignant blob in the center of my brain.

There, he said. *The prodigal son has returned.*

My eyes snapped open and I jerked upright, knocking the empty glass to the floor. I took long, deep breaths, controlling my rapid breathing. I swallowed dryly and looked around. I was still in my living room. Through the darkness I could see the digital clock on the microwave in the kitchen: 2:46.

I pulled myself up from the recliner and stumbled through the dark to the bathroom. I splashed water on my face, looked at my haggard expression, and knew that there was no way I would get back to sleep. Rather than go to bed and toss and turn until the sun came up, wallowing in my guilt, I threw on a pair of pants, grabbed my keys, and headed down to the parking lot. I told myself that I was just going for a drive. To clear my head. Think things through.

But, deep down, that was a lie.

I knew exactly where I was going.

I got a cup of coffee at a twenty-four-hour Krispy Kreme and parked in the same spot at the Kentucky Fried Chicken (which was now closed). After a few sips I again produced the binoculars and settled in for . . .

What?

What exactly was I doing there? I suppose I wanted to uncover Jonathan's story: why he had quit his job, moved suddenly, and was hiding out with a friend who lied about it. Maybe I'd be able to figure it out and spare Debbie whatever pain I could.

I focused on Steven Schumacher's front window, which was black and still. I scanned the cars parked on the street and in the apartment lot to the side. I should've found out what car Jonathan drove. A stupid oversight. I'd ask Jimmy to look it up online later in the morning. It occurred to me that, coincidentally, both my old partner and my new partner were named Jim. However, Jimmy Hungerford and Jim Dupree couldn't possibly have been more different in both appearance and personality.

I trained the binoculars on the apartment door and focused. I felt a tingling on the back of my neck. Something was amiss.

I blinked my eyes and placed them back on the binoculars. It was night, so it was hard to see clearly, but it looked like the front door was ajar maybe six inches.

Why did that bother me? Jonathan was hiding out. I had heard the chain and deadbolt on the door earlier in the evening. It didn't seem likely that he had simply left the door not just unlocked but open. I took one more sip of coffee and stepped out of the truck.

I approached the door carefully, making as little noise as possible. There were no lights on inside the silent apartment. Not an unusual situation at three thirty in the morning. It was too dark to see anything through the gap in the open door. I knocked lightly on the door frame.

"Hello?" I said softly. "Anyone there?" I put my palm on the door and pushed gently. It swung into the apartment. "Hello? Your door is open."

The light from the streetlamp spilled into the place and I saw a cheap couch and a projection TV. At the far end of the room were a kitchen counter and a darkened hallway.

"Hello?" I repeated. "Steven?" I took a tentative step into the apartment. "Jonathan?"

There was no answer. I saw a stereo and a wallet on a shelf beside the door. The place clearly hadn't been robbed, although I saw some open drawers and an overturned end table. I opened the wallet. Inside were Jonathan's driver's license, some credit cards, and maybe forty bucks in cash. A set of car keys lay nearby.

This meant that Jonathan was probably home. The last thing I needed was him stumbling out of bed, finding me poking through his wallet, and ventilating my spleen with buckshot. I put the wallet back on the shelf and stepped backward out of the apartment. I fished for my cell phone and dialed Jonathan's number.

From somewhere inside the apartment I heard a Coldplay ringtone. The music was relatively near, not coming from the shadowed hallway. I let it play for a minute or two before I disconnected. Then I tapped the Internet and found Schumacher's home listing. I dialed that and heard a loud, electronic warble echo through the apartment.

I let the phone ring until the answering machine picked up. I didn't leave a message.

Damn.

Stepping back into the apartment, I flipped on the living-room light and called out loudly, "Hello? Anybody home? Your door was open! Hello?"

There were more drawers open in the kitchen and the floor was littered with pens, paper, and utensils. I liked neither the look of the place nor the cold feeling I had in the pit of my stomach. I made my way down the hallway off the kitchen. There appeared to be two bedrooms and a guest bath. Both bedroom doors were just ajar but revealed nothing of the rooms beyond. I called out again with continued silence the only reply.

I knocked on the first bedroom door and it creaked open. I hit the light switch and saw a pigsty. An unmade double bed sat in the center of various pieces of clothes strewn all over the room. The drawers had been dumped and the closet emptied. But, as far as I could tell, the room was unoccupied.

I moved across the hall to the other bedroom. I pushed the door open and it caught halfway into the room on a pile of clothes. This room was also a mess. I turned on the lights and saw the extent of the mess. Even worse than the other room.

I also saw the occupant: Jonathan Dennis, lying serene and still on the bed. He looked like he was sleeping, eyes closed, lips slightly parted. The picture of peaceful slumber.

Except for the several red puncture holes dotting his bare torso and a single gaping slice across his neck from ear to ear.

And the blood. Good Christ, there was blood everywhere.

I stood motionless for a second, taking in one of the grislier homicide scenes I had ever witnessed, and that was saying something. I lifted my phone. But before I could dial 911, I heard footfalls and the jingling of keys behind me.

I whirled, preparing myself for a fight. Steven Schumacher stood with a furrowed brow, clearly wondering what I was doing there. He couldn't see past me yet into Jonathan's room.

"You?" he said, stepping toward me. "What are you doing here?"

But then he looked into Jonathan's room. The blood was still pretty fresh, crimson splashes all over the room. Schumacher's mouth dropped open.

"Oh my God . . ." he said. "Oh my God!" He turned and sprinted out of the hallway, through the kitchen, and, I presumed, right out the front door.

It was then that I knew I was in for a very long night.

CHAPTER 12

The cops arrived pretty quickly, within ten or fifteen minutes. The first on the scene was a uniform patrolman with a crew cut. He was young, freshly minted from the academy, and I didn't know him. I sat on the front stoop, waiting for him, like a kid expecting Dad home from work.

"Hey, sport," I said.

He was nervous and not in a chatty mood. "Hands on your head. Face down on the grass."

"That's not necessary. I'll cooperate. Give you a full statement."

He removed his sidearm and pointed it at me. "I won't ask again. Hands on your head. Face down on the grass. Now."

I sighed and complied. He pounced on me, driving a knee into my spine and jerking my hands behind my back. He locked cuffs onto my wrists.

"You have anything in your pockets?" he barked.

"No."

"Where's the knife?"

"I don't have a knife. I didn't kill him."

The cop frisked me roughly, pulling my pockets inside out and grabbing me in places where only very special women had ever grabbed. This grabbing was decidedly less pleasant.

The next thing I knew, several more patrol cars screeched into view, their lights flashing in a blinding strobe. Cops swarmed out.

Someone yanked me upright and my arms felt like they might pop from their sockets. The cuffs tore into my wrists.

"This him?" a deep voice said. I couldn't tell who had spoken in the staccato illumination of the lights.

"That's him." I recognized the second voice: Steven Schumacher.

"Holy shit," someone else said. "It's Garrity."

A fiftyish sergeant named Tully, whom I had known for years, leaned down. His gray hair and mustache blinked blue and red in the flashing lights.

"Garrity? Is that you?"

"Hey, Tully. How's Denise?"

"What the hell are you doing here?"

"Wrong place, wrong time."

"No shit. You know you're gonna be the lead story in the news today, right?"

"Anything you can do to help me there?"

Tully shook his head. "The vic worked for the mayor, Mike. The witness still does. You do the math. Murder plus mayor equals ratings. Man, you're in it deep."

"Who's the primary?" I asked.

"I dunno. I think Joey V is on tonight. Lucky you." Joe Vincent. A good homicide detective but an asshole human being. Great. "He'll wanna take your statement himself. Sorry, Mike, we gotta put you in the back of the car until he gets here."

"I understand. Just have the guys take it easy. I'm not gonna resist."

"Sure."

"I didn't do it, Tully. I don't know who did."

"Whatever you say, Mike."

Two uniforms escorted me to the backseat of their squad car, where they unceremoniously locked me in. I closed my eyes and leaned back in the seat, trying unsuccessfully to get comfortable with my wrists locked behind my back.

Through the window I saw more cops arrive, along with crime-scene technicians and local news vans. Then I saw Joe Vincent's pinched face as he peered in through the side window, like I was an exotic toad in a terrarium. He examined me with disgusted curiosity, but he didn't say anything. He walked off and I saw him. disappear into the apartment.

Joey V and I had some history. Going back to my days on the job, I had been the lead investigator on a gambling sting that netted a number of organized-crime figures in Florida and New York. I had made the papers, been interviewed on CNN, and even been immortalized in a Discovery Channel reenactment of the case. Joe Vincent had been involved in the investigation, but not to the extent that I had. So, much to his chagrin, he had been excluded from the case's resulting publicity. He'd dealt with his disappointment by concluding that I was some sort of egomaniacal glory hound. My take was that he was just jealous. So, the last couple of years on the job, my relationship with Joe Vincent had been one of him doing every little thing he could to knock me off my supposed high horse. Then, last summer, Joey V had been assigned to a murder that involved my freelance investigation. He had tried his best to pin it on me, concluding far too easily that I was capable of decapitating someone for a contract. But the case couldn't stick, which didn't help him within the department. In the case of Jonathan Dennis, I would get no benefit of the doubt from my old colleague Joe Vincent.

While Joey V was gone, the news crews jockeyed for position, their bright white camera lights cutting through the darkness and colored flashing police lights. They pointed their video cameras at me. I didn't look at them, but I also didn't look away. I had done nothing wrong and I would not act as if I had.

Joe Vincent returned and put his face close to the car window.

"You're one sick fuck, you know that, Garrity?" he shouted through the glass. Then he stood and spoke quietly to two uniforms standing nearby. When Joe was done talking to them, they slipped into the front seat of the car I was sitting in and started it up.

I knew where we were going. I had been there a million times in the past eighteen years. However, this trip would be a first for me.

I had never entered the Orlando Police Department in handcuffs before.

They put me in an interrogation room and chained me to a metal table bolted to the floor. I knew the room well, just as I knew most rooms in that building. I knew that on the other side of the large wall mirror was an observation room, likely filled to capacity with both official members of the homicide-investigation team and curious rubberneckers. My presence in the room would be an irresistible novelty for the department gossips and busybodies—cops and staff alike.

They made me sit for a long time—it felt like more than an hour—before anyone bothered to poke a head in. Finally, the head that poked in was that of Joe Vincent's partner, Gary Richards. His gaunt, melancholy face was serious.

"Hey, Mike," he said.

"Gary."

"You okay? You want a coffee or something?"

"Yeah. I could use the caffeine. What time is it?"

"Almost five. I'll be right back."

I had always liked Gary. He was a few years younger than I and carried himself with a quiet dignity, and even more so since the untimely death of his wife to breast cancer a few years earlier. His fine, straw-colored hair was now tinged with gray, but he didn't seem any older. His demeanor had always been studious and quasi-professorial, even as a uniformed rookie in a patrol car.

Gary returned in a few minutes with my coffee and a sour-looking Joe Vincent. Joe, on the other hand, was closer to my age and was the brash yang to Gary's quiet yin. He was about average height, but solid, with muscle just starting to go a little soft. He sported a thick shock of salt-and-pepper hair that looked like he had recently added some extra pepper from a bottle of Grecian Formula. Joe sat across from me without greeting, placed a yellow notepad in front of him, and clicked a pen.

"Here you go, Mike," Gary said, placing a Styrofoam cup of black coffee in front of me. He stepped to the side of the room and sat in another chair.

"Thanks," I said and took the coffee with my free hand—the one not cuffed to the table.

Joe twisted his lips and stared at me flatly. I gave him a smile and a wink, then toasted him with my coffee cup as a greeting.

"You think this is a joke, Garrity?" he said.

I sipped the hot coffee. It was just as I remembered it: strong and terrible. I really missed it.

"C'mon, Joe," I said. "You know I didn't do that guy. I have no idea who did. Let me give you my statement so I can go home. I'm exhausted."

"You ain't goin' anywhere. I'm supposed to just take your word for it? Oh, Mike says he's innocent. That's good enough for me. Fuck you."

Gary cleared his throat. "You know the drill, Mike. We gotta ask you some questions."

I took another sip. "So ask."

Joe and Gary exchanged looks.

"Tell me why you were in the apartment tonight," Gary said.

I put the Styrofoam cup down. Took a deep breath. "You guys probably know I just took a job as a PI." Their faces told me that they knew. "Well, I have a client. She gave up a son for adoption twenty-two years ago and asked me to find him. The vic in the bed is the son."

"Jonathan Dennis," Gary said.

"Right."

"So you were in the guy's apartment at three thirty in the morning for that?" Joe said. "You had to go there in the middle of the night?"

"No. Something was hinky with the kid. He quit his job, abandoned his apartment. He was hiding out with Schumacher. I went there to see what I could find out. I saw the front door ajar. I knocked, called out, even tried the phone. When no one responded, I went in."

I could tell that Joe wasn't buying it. "Schumacher said you came to his office looking for Jonathan Dennis."

"That's right. I heard they were friends."

"The neighbors said they saw your truck in front of his apartment earlier tonight."

"Yeah. I tried to reunite Jonathan with his mom, but she got cold feet."

Joe opened a manila folder and found a page. "You called Dennis's cell phone both tonight and the other day." It was a statement.

"Yeah. Like I said, I was looking for him."

Joe checked the page again. "Dennis called you back. You guys talked for a couple of minutes."

"Yeah."

"About what?"

"Nothin'. I told him I wanted to meet him. He said 'not yet.' I never got a chance to ask why."

Joe sat back, slouching in the chair. "Come on, Garrity. You can do better than this. If you're gonna make up a story, at least make it a whopper. Put some space aliens or ninjas or something in it. This is pathetic."

"Screw you, Joe. I'm telling the truth."

Joe sat forward suddenly, and anger colored his words. "Why were you stalking this guy? Who wanted him whacked?"

"This is ridiculous. You're gonna force me to ask for a lawyer."

"Yeah," said Joe, his voice dripping with sarcasm. "*That's* exactly what an innocent man would do."

"Mike," said Gary in a calm, even tone. "Why don't you tell us about your client."

So I did. I told them about meeting Debbie Watson at the support group. About her leukemia. About her request to find her son so that she could meet him before she died. I left out the sex. I told them about going to the mayor's office (but I omitted Sally's role). I told them about talking with Ed O'Malley and then with Steven Schumacher. About surprising Debbie and how that had backfired. Then I went through the whole, detailed sequence of the night's events that had led me to the interrogation room.

"You have Debbie Watson's phone number?" Gary asked.

"It's in my cell phone. You guys have that. It's her cell number." I also described where she lived.

"Okay, Mike," Gary said, standing. "Give us a few minutes."

Gary and Joe exited the room, leaving me alone in the bright fluorescent lights. I glanced at my now empty coffee cup and immediately realized that I should have asked to use the men's room.

By the time they returned almost thirty minutes later, I was close to having an embarrassing accident in my shorts. They escorted me through the stares of the bullpen to the restroom and then paraded me back through my former colleagues like a big-game trophy. They returned me to the room and locked me again to the table.

"So where's the knife?" Joe said. I rolled my eyes and sighed. "Don't make this any harder than it has to be, Garrity. Tell us where the knife is."

"It's up your ass. With your head," I said.

Joe pointed his finger at me. "You're goin' down."

"Here's the thing, Mike," Gary said. "You have a prior history of asking about the guy. You talked to him on the phone. You've been seen lurking around the apartment. Your fingerprints are all over the inside, including on the guy's wallet. You were found standing in the room with the victim at three thirty in the morning."

"Gary," I implored. "I explained all that—"

"Yeah, I know. But I've been calling the cell number you had for Debbie Watson and there's no answer."

"She's very sick," I said. "She might have the phone turned off. She was pretty upset last night, too. She could have the phone off to avoid me. Try her land line."

"I thought of that. But there's no Debbie Watson listed in the phone book."

"What?" I blinked. "I dunno . . . Maybe— She might just have a cell."

"Yeah," said Gary. "Maybe. A lot people are doing that now. Getting rid of their home phone and just using a cell. So, I sent a couple of uniforms out to the address you gave me. They knocked and did a walkaround but no one was home."

My mind started spinning up into overdrive. Where would she be? It was early, but . . . "She might be at work," I offered. "She works for a lawyer downtown. A private practice."

"Who?" Gary asked.

That was a damn good question. Who *did* she work for? Had she told me? I was pretty sure that she had, but I couldn't remember it. Hell, I couldn't even remember the word *hamburger*.

"I don't remember," I said.

Joe shook his head and grimaced. "Yeah, okay. We'll get right on that hot lead. What were you looking for in the apartment? It was torn up pretty good." I closed my eyes. I could block out his snarling face, but not his voice. "Where is the *goddamn knife?*"

Joe was hopeless. I opened my eyes and turned to Gary. "C'mon, Gary. Give me a chance to find her. She'll tell you."

"Mike," he said, looking even more thin and melancholy. "If there's anything you want to tell us, now would be the time. I can help make it easier."

"Gary . . ." I was aghast. I had even lost Gary.

"It doesn't look good, Mike. I've gotta be honest."

"You can't possibly believe it was me."

"Well," Gary said. "There's more. See, while we were out of the room, I talked to Jonathan Dennis's parents." Gary took a breath and fixed me with his eyes. "Jonathan was not adopted."

CHAPTER 13

In that instant, I could have sworn that I felt the floor tilt. I gripped the table edge to steady myself.

"What?" I asked.

"He wasn't adopted," Gary said gently. "Your story just has too many holes." He pulled his chair up next to mine and leaned in, talking quietly. He put a reassuring hand on my forearm. "Look, I've always liked you, Mike. You were good to me when Sarah died. And I was glad to hear you were doing well after your operation. I can help you. I want to help you. I can make this a lot easier. Let me do that for you. Just tell me where the knife is. Just talk to me and let me help you."

I stared down at the pitted surface of the table, mottled gray and brown from years of abuse and coffee stains. I didn't look up at either Joe or Gary. Somehow, Debbie had gotten the wrong information. He was the wrong guy.

"I want a lawyer," I said flatly.

"I told you!" Joe barked in triumph, jabbing a finger at me. "I told you he'd lawyer up."

Gary sighed and leaned back, his narrow face drooping with disappointment. "Okay, Mike."

I thought about calling Nate Hungerford, but I didn't know him well enough and didn't get a good vibe from him when we'd met in Jimmy's office. Instead, I told Gary to call Mark Lindemann. Mark was an ex-FBI agent turned defense lawyer. He had given up chasing bad guys a few years ago to cash in on the lucrative business of defending them. He and I had worked together on some cases when he was still with the feds and I was detailed to the local, three-county Metropolitan Bureau of Investigation.

Mark arrived within an hour and we were given a private place to talk, a small, windowless conference room. Mark was in his late forties, African American, with short, thinning hair that gave him a high forehead. He still looked like a fed, with his shiny shoes and excellent posture. Once a fed, always a fed. He was in good shape, with a runner's frame, and looked sharp in a pressed white dress shirt and conservative, dark silk tie. He was all business, which I appreciated. He didn't want the whole story—at least not at first.

"We need to focus on getting you out of this building," he said. "Joey V desperately wants to arrest you."

"Yeah."

"As we speak, they've got at least two teams combing the crime scene looking for physical evidence to incriminate you. When I say combing, I mean literally *combing*. The carpet, the grass, everything. They probably already have a search warrant for your apartment to look for the knife. My guess is that they're pawing through your underwear right now. I just hope they used the house key they took from you and didn't barge in with the battering ram. You know how they like to use their toys."

"Yeah." I pictured my front door splintering off its hinges, followed by ten cops tearing my place apart. "Do they think I killed him, took the knife home, then came back?"

Mark hunched his shoulders. "They're leaving no stone unturned. At the moment, nailing you is the city of Orlando's number-one priority. Their plan is to hold you here for as long as they can until they get as much evidence as possible. Then they'll officially charge you and book you. They want murder one."

"Why haven't they arrested me yet?"

"The DA is being cautious. They think they have enough for an arrest, but this is high profile, involving one of the mayor's staff. They don't want to blow it. They have two immediate problems. One: the murder weapon. They really want to find that knife. They're looking everywhere in and around the vic's apartment. Bushes, cars, rocks, sewer grates, everywhere. The chief himself sent every available body down there to help. If they don't find it, they'll probably grab all the knives in your kitchen and ask the ME if they match the cuts on the vic." Mark took a breath and leaned forward onto the conference table. "And, two: the actual room where the victim was found. Although your prints are all over the apartment—light switches, doorknobs, the wallet, you know—they haven't found anything actually in the room where the body was. With so much blood everywhere, they think that's where he was killed. But they haven't found anything yet to place *you* in the room."

I nodded. "So, are they going to release me or arrest me?"

Mark shrugged again. "It could go either way. Joe Vincent is arguing that your experience as a cop—a detective—means you know how to cover your tracks. If Schumacher hadn't come home when he did, you would've had time to wipe up the fingerprints and make a clean getaway."

"Mike Garrity: supercriminal."

"Something like that."

"Does Joe have a theory for motive? Why does he think I'd kill him?"

"Not yet. Right now they're just looking for rock-solid physical evidence. They figure they'll get enough physical evidence to lock you up without bail, go on TV and tell everyone they have someone in custody, then start interviewing to figure out why. They think someone hired you to do it and you messed up the apartment to make it look like a robbery. But, like I said, Schumacher came home unexpectedly, before you could grab the wallet and DVD player."

"I didn't mess up the apartment. It was like that when I got there."

"I just wish you hadn't touched so much. It makes things harder."

"What about Schumacher? What's his alibi?"

"He says he was at his girlfriend's. We'll worry about that later. That has nothing to do with getting you out of here."

As I sat there for the next hour and a half, Mark excused himself a couple of times to talk to the detectives and prosecutors. They had to let me go, right? I had never been in Jonathan's bedroom. I didn't have the knife.

Or did I? The way things were going, I wouldn't be surprised to learn that they'd found a bloody knife in the bed of my truck, dropped there by someone—Schumacher?—to set me up. It had been a very bad night and day. I didn't even know what time it was. I just knew that I was hungry, exhausted, and my back ached. I could have used a shower and a shave. And a stiff drink.

Mark happened to be in the conference room with me, chatting on a cell phone with his office to reschedule his day's appointments, when Jim Dupree stepped into the room. Jim's bulk filled the small space, displacing the air itself, compressing the atmosphere, the pressure pushing against me. Jim did not sit. He just looked down at me, his large, dark eyes considering my innocence or guilt.

"Tell me the truth, G," he said. "Did you do it?"

Mark snapped his phone closed in midsentence. "Do not answer him. Do not talk to him." Mark turned to Jim. "Get out, Jim. Joey V is the primary. You shouldn't be in here."

"Tell me the truth, G," Jim repeated.

"Say nothing, Mike," Mark said.

I looked up at Jim's wide, brown face. His expression was genuinely troubled. I looked over at Mark. His expression was angry. He shook his head for me to keep my mouth shut. I looked back at Jim.

"No," I said. "I didn't do it."

"Dammit, Mike!" Mark said.

Jim nodded once. I saw his body relax. That was all he needed. "Remember when you asked if we had any cases related to Jonathan Dennis?"

"Yeah," I said.

"Well, we do now."

"Thanks."

"If they book you," Jim said, "I'll try to get you put in your own cell." He shook his head ruefully. "Watch your ass, partner. Joey V is on a rampage. He wants you in the electric chair."

I nodded but didn't know what to say. How does someone re-spond to information like that? Jim said good-bye and left the room.

"Don't do that again," Mark said. "I can't help you if you don't listen to me." Then he, too, left the room. I understood why he wanted me to keep my mouth shut. Nothing I could say would help. But Big Jim was different. He was my partner, my friend. I needed him to know that I was innocent. He needed to hear me say it. And that was all it took. Jim asked me to tell the truth and he knew that I would, good or bad. I knew that he would now do everything he could to help me.

After another hour or two—I had lost all sense of time—Mark finally returned with Joe Vincent and Gary Richards. Joe looked extremely pissed. That was probably a good sign. Gary unlocked the handcuff from my wrist.

"Come on, Mike," Mark said. "You're going home."

Except I didn't go home.

After Mark walked me out to the parking garage, directing me in a path that would expose me to the fewest television cameras, he drove me back to Schumacher's apartment, where my truck still sat. He handed me my keys and told me to go home, eat some-thing, take a shower, and get some sleep. It was two thirty in the afternoon by the time I slid into the cab of my truck.

I pulled into the drive-through of the KFC across the street and ordered a chicken sandwich. Then I immediately drove to Debbie's house.

It would be an understatement to say that I had a lot to tell her. Not only was Jonathan Dennis not her son—or so the police claimed—he was now dead, carved to bits in the very apartment I had dragged her to last night. Oh, and, by the way, the cops think I did it. Whatever trouble Jonathan was mixed up in, the trouble that forced him to quit his job and abandon his apartment, had caught up with him. And swept me up in it.

I assumed that the police had not yet gotten to her. If at all possible, I really didn't want her to hear all this from Joe Vincent. It was going to be hard enough for her without having to endure Joe's inevitable browbeating. However, it was also quite possible that the cops were no longer actively looking for her. After having attempted to follow up on my story and not finding immediate success, it was probably filed away as yet more evidence of my guilt, a desperate grasp for a fictitious alibi.

I wished I could remember the name of the lawyer she worked for. She was probably at work, not at home now, in the middle of the afternoon. But, since I couldn't recall the lawyer's name, I decided to try her house. With her illness, she sometimes stayed home. I might catch her there. I preferred to talk to her in person, but if she wasn't home, I would call her cell phone.

I pulled up to her house and parked in the same spot in the driveway as I had approximately sixteen hours earlier. There was no other car in the driveway. She probably wasn't home.

But I got out of the truck anyway and walked up the front steps. I pounded on the door. After a silent moment I pounded again, a little more loudly. As I suspected, still no answer. I stepped to the side of the door and peered into the living-room window. With the sun's glare on the glass, I couldn't see inside. I cupped my hands around my face and pressed it close to the window. It looked dark and still inside.

I returned to the front door and knocked again. Finally, I

accepted that she wasn't home and turned away from the door. When I did, I saw an older gentleman standing on the sidewalk, watching me. He held the end of a leash attached to a small gray Scottish terrier. They stood quietly watching me, each with a droopy gray mustache framing his mouth.

"They're gone," the man called.

"Yeah," I said, stepping off the porch. "I guess she's not home."

"No," he said. "I mean, they're gone. I saw 'em last night, loading up a big van. I think they moved out."

I blinked at him. "What? Moved out?"

"That's what it looked like."

"When?"

"Like I said. Last night."

"No," I said. "When last night?"

"Pretty late, I guess. I was walking Rufus here. I usually take him out around eleven thirty, so probably about then."

I shook my head, trying to clear it. It wasn't making any sense. "Are you sure? Maybe we're not talking about the same person. Do you know the woman who lives her?"

"Not really. I've just seen her around since they moved in a month or so ago. I do know the landlord. Looks like he'll have to find another renter."

"What does she look like, the woman who lives here?"

"Well, I don't know. She was pretty. In her thirties or forties, I guess. I'm not good at ages. It's impolite to guess a woman's age."

"What about her car?"

"A Toyota, I think. A Camry."

"What about her hair? What color was her hair?"

He pursed his lips, thinking. "You know, I'm not sure. She always had a scarf on her head. I never saw her hair."

I rubbed my hands on my face, feeling the rough stubble from two days of not shaving. Scarf on her head, Toyota Camry. That sure sounded like Debbie. But, moved out? It didn't make any sense. The old guy had to be mistaken.

"Do you know her name?" I asked.

"No. We never really chatted. I'd just see her sometimes while I was out walking Rufus." He patted the dog on the head, who regarded his master indifferently. "I did hear her husband call her Carol once, though."

I froze. I tried to understand what he had just said, but I was obviously too tired, too shook up by the events of the last few hours. "Excuse me, did you say *husband*?"

"I assume he was the husband because he was living there with her. But, you never know nowadays. Could've been her boyfriend, I suppose. He loaded most of the boxes into the van last night. Big fella. Shaved head. Goatee beard. Or maybe a Van Dyke. Which one has the mustache and beard and which one is just the beard?"

The ground felt unsteady under my feet. I forcibly controlled my breathing and leaned over. I put my hands on my knees, to keep from collapsing onto the grass.

"Hey, fella," the old guy said. "Are you okay?"

I was not okay. I was very far from okay. I closed my eyes and breathed deeply. I finally understood what an idiot I was. A world-class, gold-star idiot.

I had just been used, played as a pawn in what I now realized was a gigantic scam.

CHAPTER 14

I went home. I didn't know what else to do. I was too tired to think straight, to process the mental whiplash from the events of the past twenty hours. The cops clearly had been there, but at least the place wasn't trashed. They had used my house key, thus sparing my door frame from the battering ram. My drawers had been rifled, but nothing seemed so out of place that I could complain. There might have been a knife or two missing from the kitchen. I had no idea.

There were at least fifteen messages waiting for me on my answering machine. Most were from the press, wanting interviews. Two were from lawyers, soliciting me as a client. The rest were from friends and family expressing concern and shock at seeing me on the local news that morning, sitting in the back of a squad car in connection to a grisly murder.

My first call was to Becky. But I didn't want to talk to her. The phone rang twice.

"Hello?" said a man's voice.

"Wayne," I said. "It's Mike. Please put Jennifer on the line."

"Mike, for God's sake. You're all over the news."

"I know that, Wayne. That's why I'm calling. Put Jennifer on the line." I heard Becky's raised voice in the background, uttering what I assumed was a shrill question. "Don't put Becky on the phone. I want to talk to my daughter."

There was a brief pause and I heard the rustle of the phone being handed off.

"Mike?" came the female voice through the receiver. I closed my eyes. It was Becky. "What the hell is going on?"

"It's a long story. Let me talk to Jennifer."

"I don't care how long it is. You better explain yourself."

After the night and day that I just had, there was no way on earth that I was going to explain it to Becky. "Not now, Becky. I can't. I'm too tired."

"I don't give a shit how tired you are. You tell me what's going on."

"Put Jennifer on the goddamn phone!"

There was an angry crack in my ear that I presumed was the phone being slammed down on the counter. A moment later I heard: "Dad?"

"Jennifer—listen to me—"

"Dad, are you okay?"

"I'm fine. Listen, I didn't do it. Whatever they said on TV, whatever your mom or Wayne says, whatever the kids at school say, don't listen to anyone but me. I didn't kill anyone. I don't know what happened, but I'm gonna find out. Just trust me, okay?"

"Okay . . ."

"Do you believe me?"

"I don't know what to believe, Dad."

"I'm innocent, Jennifer. I wouldn't lie to you. Tell me you believe me."

"I—I believe you."

Those were the words that we both needed to hear. I released a massive internal sigh of relief. I quickly wrapped up the call and said good-bye. I heard Becky reaching for the phone, I disconnected.

My next call was to Cam. It went about the same as with Jennifer, although she'd never doubted me for a moment. She told me that she already knew I didn't do it. She also told me not to watch TV. I wouldn't like it.

So, naturally, the first thing I did upon hanging up was flip on the television. I caught the local cable-news station. The current story was a weather update of Hurricane Lorraine. A new fore-casted path had been released, and, like a typical overseas tourist, she was headed straight for Orlando. It was now a category 3, with sustained winds of 120 mph.

Then the anchor came on and recapped the day's top stories. Guess who was number one? I saw my unshaven mug looking uncomfortable in the back of a squad car. My name was given and I was described as a former police officer brought in for questioning related to a grisly murder that had occurred in the apartment of a member of the mayor's public affairs staff. Neither the anchor nor any of the three on-the-scene reporters—one at the apartment, one at the police headquarters, and one who looked like she was sitting in another part of the studio set—told me anything I didn't already know. The cops hadn't released any details about our conversation. Good.

Although I was past bone tired—I was cellular tired—my brain was still on overdrive. I was still grappling with the fact that Debbie was gone. After trying to reach her on her cell phone twice while in my truck, I tried once more. No answer. I did not leave another message. What could I say? *So, Debbie, how's it going? Hope you're having a good day. Oh, by the way, why'd you lie to me and set me up for a murder rap? Call me back whenever you get a chance, 'kay?*

No, despite my exhaustion, there was no way I would be getting to sleep without artificial inducement. So, as I always do in a tough situation, I pulled out a bottle of bourbon, poured the last of it into a glass with a splash of water, and chugged it standing in my kitchen. I felt the booze working almost immediately. It overpowered the defenses of my overactive brain and soaked it in liquid relaxation.

I moved to the bathroom, where I washed my face and brushed my teeth. I tried not to look at myself, but I couldn't avoid it. My face was the stuff of nightmares: dark bags under my eyes, pale complexion, two days of gray and brown stubble, the sclera of my eyes more red than white. I stumbled into the bedroom, kicked off my shoes, and fell onto the bed face-first and fully clothed.

The new postcancer me was becoming a lot like the old precancer me.

My slumber was long, dreamless, and overdue. After so much happening in such a short amount of time, my brain checked out for about twelve hours, leaving me in blissful blackness, a deep, warm hole I didn't want to climb out of.

So I didn't. When I awoke in the wee, predawn hours, I refused to get up. I lay twisted up in my sheets in a gray no-man's-land between lucid and asleep, not quite awake, for a long time. I didn't know how long and I didn't care. It was great.

Eventually, however, a cacophonous pounding stirred me from the gray zone into the light. The noise was coming from my front door. I stood up, shuffled to the door, and peered through the peephole. I expected a reporter, whom I would promptly ignore. But it wasn't a reporter. I opened the door.

"Morning, Jimmy," I said in a hoarse waking voice.

"Dude," he replied anxiously. Then he shook his head. Words could not capture his emotions. So he repeated his greeting, except this time it was in a doleful tone: "Dude . . ."

"Yeah." I held the door open wider. "Wanna come in?"

Jimmy Hungerford nodded and trudged into my apartment. I put on a pot of coffee. He sat heavily at my kitchen table.

"I tried callin' you last night, but you didn't answer," Jimmy said.

"Yeah. I was pretty beat. I fell asleep and didn't get up until right now."

"Did you kill him?" He looked up at me like a kid asking if Santa was really a lie.

I sighed. "No. He was dead when I got there." I then proceeded to tell Jimmy the whole story. It helped me to go through it again, to lay out the facts. I had a feeling that I would be repeating it often: to cops, prosecutors, Mark Lindemann, Ben Madrigas. I realized that I hadn't yet spoken to Ben Madrigas. He was probably freaking out. I made a mental note to call him later that morning at a decent hour.

Jimmy didn't doubt me at all. He believed everything I told him, which made me feel good. For some reason, Jimmy's opinion really mattered to me. Where had that come from?

"So," he said. "What do we do next?"

That was a good question. "I don't like to be used," I said. "It pisses me off. I wanna find my friend 'Debbie' and figure out just what the hell is going on. If I can do that, I have a feeling that I have a decent chance of clearing my name. I'm pretty sure that the cops aren't looking for her. They already have their suspect." Jimmy looked at me expectantly. I could see the energy welling up inside him: like a puppy ready to be thrown a tennis ball. "You ready for some real PI work?"

"Fuckin' A."

"Okay. We need a woman to make some calls for us. Hire a temp if you have to." I gave Jimmy the date that I'd picked Debbie up from the cancer center, the day she'd received the bad news about her prognosis, which had led to her sleeping with me. Was that a lie, too? I shook it off. No time to dwell on that now. I told Jimmy to compile a list of every oncologist in the building and in the surrounding buildings. The woman was to call each one and claim to be Debbie Watson. She was to tell the receptionist that she needed to verify her recent appointment for her insurance company. Could they please confirm that she'd had an appointment that day?

Because of the new HIPPA patient-privacy laws, I was pretty sure that neither Jimmy nor I would be able to get that information from a doctor's office. I wasn't sure that it was actually privileged information, but I wasn't taking any chances. If the offices thought that they were speaking with Debbie and she already knew the appointment date, they would probably give her a yes or no. I expected all no's. I had a sinking suspicion that we wouldn't be able to find a single doctor who could confirm Debbie's appointment. But I needed to know for sure.

Jimmy nodded and promised to get right on it. "What are you gonna do?"

I wanted to follow up with Steven Schumacher. I didn't trust that guy. He'd lied to me about Jonathan's presence in his apartment. People usually lie for a reason and that reason was likely what had gotten Jonathan carved up like a Christmas ham. But things were too hot around Schumacher and his apartment just then. Between the cops, the media, and the mayor, there was no way I'd get near him. Plus, I might get arrested if I did. It might be seen as threatening. But I couldn't send Jimmy to talk to Schumacher. I needed to do that myself. I'd wait a day or two, see if the frenzy abated, and maybe resume my surveillance.

In the meantime, I'd see if I could figure out just who Debbie Watson was. And who was the live-in guy who had loaded her belongings into a van at eleven thirty at night.

CHAPTER 15

I called Ben Madrigas at his office. As I'd suspected, he was very concerned about what he had seen on the news. I explained that it was a misunderstanding related to another case and that I was innocent of any wrongdoing. However, I offered to resign from his case. If he wanted someone else to investigate Victor's suicide, I would understand and turn over my notes. He refused my offer, wanting me to stay on the case. I thanked him for his confidence and hung up.

A quick records search told me that the landlord of the downtown bungalow where Debbie lived was a gentleman named Al Vilance. I looked up Al's home address and hopped into my truck.

Al lived a few blocks from the rental home. I rang the doorbell and a moment later a short guy with an unshaven face of gray whiskers squinted up at me. He wore baggy khaki pants held up over a wife beater tank top by black suspenders. A few wild wisps of white hair poked up from the top of his shiny head.

"Yeah?" he growled at me through one squinted eye. I couldn't help but think that I might have just found Sally's next husband.

I introduced myself and explained that I was looking for the woman who lived in the rental house around the corner.

"Oh yeah? Me too!" He jabbed a finger at me. "They up and left in the middle of the night. Can you believe it? Can you believe that? That's why we need security deposits. Now I gotta find a new tenant."

"You mind if I take a look at the place? I might be interested."

"Oh yeah?" His squinty eye opened. "Why the hell not? Just a sec." He disappeared back into the house for a moment and reappeared with a shock of black hair plopped on top of his head. Apparently, Al Vilance never left home without his toupee. It was a disconcerting look.

Of course, I wasn't really interested in renting the place. But I wanted to get inside and I figured that was the most effective way to do it. Al walked me down the street and around the corner, shuffling along the sidewalk in a pair of battered slippers. He jangled an impressive ring of keys as he walked, occasionally muttering to himself and adjusting his toupee.

"So, how many people lived there?" I asked as casually as I could, trying hard to avoid looking at his hairpiece.

"What?" he growled. "Did I live there? How the hell would I know? I only ever saw the two of 'em."

"They didn't leave a forwarding address, did they?"

He sneered up at me with a withering look that told me just what a moron I was to ask such an idiotic question. I nodded. *Got it, Al.*

We reached the house and Al somehow found the proper key on his metal ring. He popped the door open and we stepped in. It was a small, two-bedroom bungalow, probably built sometime in the 1940s. It was actually quite nice, with hardwood floors and a shady canopy of big, moss-dripping live oaks. But what I wanted couldn't be found there: namely, some clue about who Debbie Watson was.

The place was as anonymous and clean as a hotel room. Al informed me that the sparse, 1970s-style furniture was his and included in the lease. No pictures on the shelves. No bills in the trash. No food in the fridge. I wished I could get a few minutes to lift some fingerprints, but I'd need to persuade Joe Vincent to do that. An unlikely scenario. Besides, by the looks of the place, it had probably been wiped clean.

"What were their names?" I asked, while he walked me through the master bedroom. "The couple who lived here?" I glanced at the bed and flashed back to the grappling intimacy that Debbie and I had shared in my apartment. Had that been real? What about the bald guy with the beard? Did he know?

Al squinted at me suspiciously. "You wanna rent the place or not?"

"I dunno. It's nice. Lemme think about it."

"Yeah, right." Al might have been a grump, but he was no fool. "So . . . the names?"

Al sighed. "His name was Norman. Norman Fitchburg. He signed the lease. I'm not sure what her name was. Carol or Cathy or something." He scratched his chin stubble thoughtfully. "If you talk to 'em, tell 'em they're not getting their deposit back. They paid cash, but they broke the lease. I gotta keep it."

I took one last look around the anonymous home and promised Al that I'd pass it along.

I drove farther into downtown and parked in the garage for the A-Plus offices. When I got off on my floor, my stomach lurched as if I were still on the elevator. Standing outside the A-Plus office were a couple of uniformed patrol cops.

"Hey, fellas," I said as I approached. "Lookin' for me?"

They exchanged glances. Then they moved aside and one of them opened the office door. I passed through and saw Joe Vincent, Gary Richards, and three more cops boxing up computers and files.

"Well, look who's here," Joe said.

"What are you guys doin' here?" I asked, although I knew exactly what they were doing. They had a warrant to confiscate all electronic and paper files that might be related to my casework. They were looking for my motive for killing Jonathan Dennis.

"We gotta take the computers and records, Mike," Gary said. "You know the drill."

I nodded. "I'll save you some trouble. You won't find anything in any of that stuff. I only started working here a few days ago and don't have any records yet."

"We wanna look anyway," Joe said.

"If you want to be productive, I have a lead for you." Joe rolled his eyes and went back to the files. Gary raised his eyebrows for me to continue. "Norman Fitchburg. I'm not sure how he's tied up in this, but I have a feeling he is."

"Who's he?" Joe asked.

"I'm not sure. I think he's involved with Debbie Watson."

"Oh, your made-up girlfriend?" Joe asked. "Yeah, we'll get right on that."

"If you won't look for her, I will," I said.

"Well, you better look fast. 'Cause as soon as I have one more half an ounce of evidence, your ass is mine. And you know how the boys like ex-cops in the cell block. You won't last a week."

"You're wasting your time, Joe," I said. "Let me help you."

"You wanna help me? Tell me why you've been stalking Jonathan Dennis. I talked to a Kentucky Fried Chicken employee this morning who told me that he saw you sitting in your truck, watching the apartment across the street. He also saw you come into the restaurant at the same time Jonathan Dennis and Steven Schumacher were eating there. We already know you've been poking around for him at the mayor's office. And a neighbor saw your truck at the apartment earlier the same evening he was killed. You want me to go on? Why were you stalking him? Who were you working for?"

"I already explained all that—"

The office door burst open and Jimmy and his father charged in.

"See?" Jimmy said.

Nate Hungerford immediately inserted himself into the middle of the search. He reviewed the warrant and chatted briefly with Joe Vincent and Gary Richards.

"It's all in order," Nate said. "Collect what you need and then move on."

The cops were almost done anyway. They loaded the boxes

onto carts and wheeled everything through the door. Joe shot me one last malevolent glare before disappearing out the door.

"Mike," Nate said. "I'd like to talk to you, please." He walked into the small conference room off the lobby area. I followed him. He closed the door and remained standing.

"What will the police find in those files?" he asked.

"Nothing."

"Tell me the truth."

"I am telling you the truth. I haven't worked here long enough to even write up a grocery list."

Nate Hungerford sighed and trained his inquisitor eyes on me. "What happened in that apartment?"

"I didn't kill him, if that's what you're asking."

"Who did?"

"Dunno. But I'm gonna find out."

"I presume this is related to one of your two cases." Hungerford continued to look at me expectantly. I said nothing. "Tell me about the case."

I blinked at him. "We've already been over this. I don't work for you."

"I have a significant financial stake in this firm and that investment has been jeopardized by you being arrested for murder."

"I wasn't technically arrested. I was just questioned as a person of interest."

"A-Plus Investigations has already been mentioned in the paper and on television in connection to this homicide. It's not the kind of publicity we want or need."

"Look," I said, taking a step toward him. "I work for Jimmy, not you. I've already told him everything I know. I'm not telling you anything."

"You need a lawyer. Whatever you say will be protected by attorney-client privilege."

"I already have a lawyer. And I already told him everything, too."

"Who?"

"Mark Lindemann."

Hungerford nodded, more to himself than to me. He opened his mouth to speak, then closed it, thinking better. "Do you know what the police are looking for?" he asked, the arrogant tone in his voice morphing into something more akin to pleading.

I shrugged. "A motive? The murder weapon? The DA is making them work for it and they're fishing."

Hungerford's demeanor softened and he almost seemed to shrink a little. "Please keep me in the loop as things progress. It's important to me."

Without making any commitments, I turned and left him standing alone in the conference room.

"You okay, honey?" Sally said, her face obscured behind a cloud of smoke.

I nodded. We sat on a bench at Lake Eola Park, eating subs and sipping Diet Dr Pepper. The swans glided by on the rippling water. Mothers pushed toddlers in strollers along the sidewalk.

"Yeah," I replied, chewing.

"Boy, you sure brought a ton of heat down on the mayor's office. The reporters smell blood."

"They're bothering him?"

"Hell yeah. He keeps tryin' to talk about his downtown redevelopment plan. He even had a press conference about it yesterday. All the reporters did was ask about the dead guy."

"I'm sorry."

"It gets worse. Your old friend, what's his name, Joey V's been pokin' around."

"He's not my friend."

"Whatever. Anyways, he's on the trail. He talked to the kid's boss, O'Malley, who told him you came by asking a bunch a' questions. O'Malley told him about the personal call from the mayor ordering him to cooperate with someone named Mike Garrity."

"Uh-oh . . ." I saw where that was going.

"Damn right, uh-oh. So Joey V goes to the mayor to ask why the special treatment for Mike Garrity, who is suspected of murdering someone who used to work there. He starts hinting at words like *accessory*. He don't come right out and say it, but he gets his point across. He does this to the *mayor*. So the boss says that he doesn't even know you. He called O'Malley as a favor to one of his staff. Who? they ask. Sally Anderson, says the mayor."

"I'm sorry, Sal. . . ."

"So the cops, they come to see me. Ask why I asked the mayor to help you. What could I say?"

"Just tell 'em the truth."

"Yeah, well, I did. I just tol' 'em that you asked me if I knew where the kid was, so I asked the boss to help." She took a long drag on her cigarette. Blew the smoke out the side of her mouth, a courtesy for me. "And I always do anything Mike Garrity asks. I tol' 'em you didn't kill anyone and they should stop wasting taxpayer money on a bullshit investigation and go find the real murderer."

"You're a champ, Sal."

"Yeah, that's me. Muhammad Ali." She stubbed out her butt and wiped her mouth with a paper napkin. "Okay, listen. Schumacher isn't around. The boss gave him a leave of absence until all the nonsense dies down. His apartment is still a crime scene and, so I've been told, soaked in blood."

"Yeah," I said. "You were told right."

"So, Schumacher's staying with his girlfriend. Here's her address." She slipped me a piece of paper. "Now don't be stupid, Mikey. You hear me?"

I nodded. "Stupid is bad. Got it."

She slapped my face. It didn't really hurt, but it surprised me. "I'm not kidding. I care about you, you jerk. I'm giving you this information because you asked, and, as I said, I always do whatever Mike Garrity asks. But don't you do anything stupid. If Joe Vincent catches you sneaking around Steven Schumacher, that's all he'll need to haul you in. And, whatever you do, don't threaten the kid."

"Why would I threaten him?"

She gave me a look. "Don't help them arrest you, you hear me?"

"I hear ya, Sal." I kissed her on the cheek.

We both knew perfectly well that I intended to threaten him.

CHAPTER 16

I drove by Schumacher's apartment. I'm not sure why. There was nothing to accomplish by doing so. I was drawn there like a pilgrim to a shrine, compelled just to be in the vicinity.

The place looked deserted. No neighbors. No cops. Yellow police tape was still strung across the front door, sealing it up like a tomb, which it actually had been for a short time. I elected to follow Sally's advice not to be stupid and did not get out of the truck to peek in the windows. Instead, I flipped open my cell phone and called Jimmy Hungerford.

"No luck, dude," he said. "This Debbie chick wasn't a patient anywhere."

"Have you checked every office yet?"

"No, not all of 'em. But, like, thirty so far. We'll be done soon."

"Any problems getting the information?"

"No way, man." Jimmy chuckled. "It was easy. I got my friend Erin to make the calls just like you said. She tells them she's Debbie and the date she thought her appointment was. Then they just look it up on the computer and say, 'Nope, no appointment that day.' If they wanna get all helpful and start looking at other dates, Erin bails."

"Okay. Don't stop until you go through the whole list. I've got another one for you."

"Oh yeah?"

"Yeah. Did Dan Wachs teach you how to run a personal-information search—addresses, credit history, all that—before he left?"

"Sure. I do 'em sometimes for my dad's firm."

"Good. Find out everything you can on someone named Norman Fitchburg. Tell me if he's a real guy and if he recently rented a house in downtown Orlando." I gave him the address of Debbie's house. I thanked Jimmy for the help and signed off.

I next drove to my apartment. However, as I approached the complex, I spotted a navy-blue cargo van parked on the street. It was unremarkable and most people wouldn't have given it a second look. But I slowed down as I went by. As I suspected, it had a city-government license tag. I had spent a lot of hours sitting in surveillance vans just like that one, so its presence popped out at me. I pulled my truck up behind it and got out.

I pounded my fist on the van's back doors. There was no response. I pounded again.

"C'mon, guys," I called. "Open the door." I pounded again.

After a few seconds' delay, the back door opened a crack and a familiar face peeked out.

"Hey, Mike," said Ernie Yakimoro, a detective I knew. He looked tired. His dark hair was disheveled and there were visible bags under his eyes.

"Ernie. Good to see ya'. Who else is in there?"

"No one you know.'

"Sure, whatever you say. Listen, Ernie, I just want to save you guys a wasted night. I'm not staying here tonight."

"No? Where you going?"

"Nice try. You guys might as well go home. I promise I won't come back tonight."

"Well, Mike, if that's true, I appreciate the consideration. But you know how it is. We gotta stay for the whole shift."

"Yeah."

Ernie looked down, not quite sure how to end the conversation. "I heard about your surgery. How you feeling?"

"Pretty good, I guess. I'm not so thrilled about being accused of murder, but my head's a lot better."

"Good. Good." He avoided eye contact, instead glancing at my feet.

"Okay . . . See you around."

"Right."

He closed the door and I returned to my truck. The poor bastards were going to be stuck in that van all night.

True to my word, I did not return home that night. I drove from my place directly to St. Luke's. I parked the truck and made my way into classroom B, where I found Jerry setting up the room for one of his support-group sessions. When I walked in, he was adding a metal folding chair to a semicircle of other chairs. He looked up at me through his long hair and his mustache twisted in confusion.

"Hi, Mike," he said. "I think you have the wrong night. This is an alcohol-dependence group, not cancer."

Alcohol dependence? I should probably join that one, too. I wondered what other groups Jerry facilitated that might fit my problems. Athlete's foot? Halitosis? Golf slice? I could come and spill my guts to Jerry every night of the week.

"Yeah, I know," I said instead. "I just wanted to catch you for a minute to ask a couple of questions."

"Of course." Jerry sat in one of the folding chairs and gestured for me to do the same. I did so. "I saw you on the news."

"Oh yeah?"

"Rough night?"

"You could say."

"Are you okay?"

"Yeah. All things considered."

"Is it anything you want to talk about?"

"Not in the slightest."

Jerry smiled and narrowed his eyes at me. "All right. So, what's up?"

"How well do you know Debbie Watson?"

"Debbie Watson? From your cancer group? Not much at all."

"Tell me what you can."

"She's only been to a couple of meetings. Pretty quiet. Leukemia, I think. I never saw her talking to anyone except you. Why do you ask?"

I ignored the question. "How did she join the group—did she register or just show up?"

He thought about it for a second. "She just showed up. That happens sometimes."

"Did she tell you much about her cancer?"

"Not really. With her hair loss, I figured she was in the middle of or had just completed her chemo. Talking about it is what the group is for. It takes some people a few sessions to open up." He looked pointedly at me. "Right?"

"Yeah," I replied. "Right. Did she show you any medical records or provide a doctor's name or something that might verify the that she had cancer?"

Jerry's brow creased. "Verify? No, we don't require anything like that to join the group. You didn't have to provide anything. Why would we? We're talking about a cancer-support group. Nobody *wants* to be in that group." He considered me thoughtfully for a moment. "Are you suggesting that Debbie lied about her cancer?"

"I don't know. I think it's possible."

"Based on what?"

"I can't say. I'm just trying to find out what I can."

Jerry shook his head. "I don't believe it. Nobody would do that. Talk about tempting fate . . ."

"When's the last time you talked to her?"

"At the last session. We said maybe five words to each other. Like I said, she only talked to you."

"Yeah." I felt like a first-class rube. How could I have been so stupid? How could I have let myself be manipulated so completely? Jerry's voice cut into my self-recriminations.

"Did you hear about Andrew?" he asked, referring to the retired army military-police colonel from our group who had recently entered hospice.

"No," I replied.

"He died yesterday." Jerry must have seen the blood drain from my face because he quickly added, "I'm sorry. I know you two got along well."

I swallowed a hard lump in my throat. "We were both cops."

"I know."

Why would Andrew's death affect me so suddenly and emotionally? I didn't know him well—just conversations during our group sessions. But he wasn't that different from me. A little older and spunkier, perhaps, but he was a fighter. And I liked him. His death was sudden and swift. It was unfair. I hated the mental image of Death smirking, checking his watch, marking off Andrew on his ledger as a job completed ahead of schedule.

It suddenly occurred to me that if Debbie *was* lying about her cancer, the looming presence of Death that had been hovering over us couldn't have been for her. It must have been for me.

"Mike," Jerry said, looking carefully into my eyes. "Are you sure you're okay?"

"Yeah." I blinked away the thoughts that were distracting me. "If you happen to hear from Debbie, would you mind calling me? You have my number."

"Sure. I'll also tell her you're looking for her." Jerry shook his head. "I still don't believe it. I don't care what suspicions you have. What kind of sick person would pretend to have cancer?"

I made no reply. But that was exactly what I planned to find out.

Before leaving St. Luke's I checked in with Jimmy. His friend Erin had been through every doctor's office in a five-block radius of where I had picked Debbie up. Debbie wasn't a patient at any of them. Jimmy had also found nothing yet on Norman Fitchburg, confirming, so far, my suspicions that it was a fake name. Jimmy had found a few Norman Fitchburgs, but none so far matched our guy. I thanked Jimmy and instructed him to keep looking.

I made my way over to Cam's townhouse in Winter Park. She lived in an upscale condominium just off the trendiest stretch of pavement in Central Florida, a short walk from Ann Taylor and Williams-Sonoma. I rang the bell and Cam opened the door, looking somehow even more beautiful in sweatpants and a T-shirt. Maybe it's true what they say about pregnant women having a glow.

"Can I stay here tonight?" I asked.

Cam smiled wearily and opened the door wider. I gratefully slipped into the sanctuary of her townhouse. To her credit, Cam didn't ask me about Jonathan Dennis, didn't ask me to tell her what had happened. Instead, we made a pot of spaghetti and some garlic bread and ate it at the coffee table while watching *Jeopardy!* on TV. It was exactly the kind of evening I needed.

"How are you feeling?" I asked once Alex Trebek had announced the winner of Final Jeopardy.

"Being pregnant is weird," she said. "I get hungry and nauseous at the same time. I cried my eyes out the other day because my sock had a hole in it. I'm exhausted. I have to pee every five minutes. I'm happy. I'm scared."

"What are you scared of?" I couldn't remember Cam ever being scared of anything.

"I've had some cramps and spotty bleeding lately. The doctor tells me that sometimes happens. But it freaks me out. I may be younger than you, but I'm still older than average for a first-time pregnancy." She sighed and folded her legs under her on the couch. "Mostly I worry about the usual things. You know, ten-fingers-and-ten-toes sort of stuff. Will it be healthy? Will I be able to handle this whole parent deal?"

I nodded. "I'll help you."

She smiled and grasped my hand. I heard her sniffle. "See? I'm getting all weepy. It's pathetic."

I slid closer to her on the couch and put my arm around her. She snuggled in next to me and I held her tight for the next hour; while we watched some shark documentary on cable. It felt comfortable and good. I can't believe that I let our marriage slip away.

Eventually, we made our way to the bedroom, where we fell asleep leaning against each other. There was no sex, but the closeness of our bodies and the presence of the baby growing inside Cam generated an intense intimacy that enveloped us like a cocoon.

I awoke early, the sky still dark in the predawn hours. I sat up, my head throbbing in a familiar and terrifying rhythm. Bob the tumor was famous for awakening me with skull-splitting headaches that were so bad that they sometimes made me vomit. But Bob was gone now, removed by the neurosurgeons at Florida Hospital. *He's gone,* I repeated to myself. *Gone.*

The headache, however, reminded me of the painful truth that the odds of Bob returning were quite good. And if he did return, he would likely be a much more dangerous type of tumor than before. I thought about my recent dream in which doctor pointed at a dark tumor in a picture of my brain. . . . A premonition or a manifestation of my darkest fears?

I stood up and shook off the thought. It was stupid to dwell on the possibility of Bob's return. There was nothing I could do about it anyway. I shuffled sleepily into the kitchen and brewed a pot of coffee. Looking at the kitchen table, I saw my keys, wallet, and two cell phones. The first cell phone was mine. But the second one, I suddenly remembered, belonged to Victor Madrigas. I sat at the table with a steaming mug of coffee and flipped open Victor's phone.

I scrolled through his contact list and jotted down a dozen or so names and phone numbers of whom I presumed were friends. I would make arrangements to speak to each of them about Victor's death. It would have to be later, however. It was still too early to start calling people on the phone, especially high school kids.

I turned on my phone. There were a few messages: one from Becky that I wouldn't be returning anytime soon, and a few more from reporters that would also be ignored. There was also a message from Jimmy, confirming that he couldn't find anything on Norman Fitchburg. It was a fictitious name. My new friend Al the landlord had taken Debbie and Norman's security deposit in cash and had never bothered to verify anything.

I sighed. Debbie had covered her tracks well. No verifiable employer. A fake name. No forwarding address. I was wasting time chasing leads down blind alleys. But no more. It was time to focus my attention on the one lead that I knew had to have something to do with what had happened to Jonathan Dennis.

It was time to visit Steven Schumacher.

CHAPTER 17

As soon as the hour was decent, I hit the Krispy Kreme drive-through for a box of hot, delicious fat calories. I then brought them downtown to the A-Plus office as a thank-you offering for Jimmy's help the day before. He appreciated the doughnuts but said that they weren't necessary. He was "totally stoked" about the investigation. He called it a "real live murder case," unaware of the irony of the statement. But his passion was infectious. If I hadn't been the one under investigation for the murder, I might actually have gotten "stoked," too.

Although I questioned his experience and competence, I actually liked having Jimmy in my corner. He had done a good job, as far as I could tell, checking into all the doctors who might have treated Debbie, as well as doing a background check on Norman Fitchburg.

"How's Richie?" I asked.

"My brother?"

"Yeah."

Jimmy's face lit up. "You remembered his name."

"Sure."

"He's good, man. He's an awesome kid. Awesome. Most people don't understand Down kids. But Richie, he's amazing. He's always upbeat, always smiling. He wrote me an e-mail every day when I was in the army. He takes care of himself. Does his chores." Jimmy picked up another doughnut but held it absently instead of eating it. "My dad's always worked a lot, y'know? So he doesn't get to spend much time with Richie. Like I said, not everyone understands. So, me and Richie, we spend a lot of time together. We're buds."

I nodded, getting the picture. My guess: Jimmy probably raised his mentally challenged brother because his father couldn't deal with it. That made me like Jimmy even more.

"I need to see what I can find out about Steven Schumacher," I said. "There was a reason he lied about Jonathan staying with him. He knows more than he's letting on." I handed Jimmy the piece of paper with Victor's friends' names and phone numbers. I explained who they were. "I've gotta keep pushing on this murder case," I said. "But I don't want to completely neglect the Madrigas investigation. If you're willing, I could really use your help."

"Anything you need, bro. Name it."

"I want you to talk to each of these kids. Find out what you can about Victor. Were there any signs he might commit suicide? Where did he score the drugs? Did they think it might have been an accident? We're looking for anything we can tell his father that might give him some hope, no matter how slim, that Victor did not intentionally kill himself." I poured myself a cup of coffee from the office pot. "I was going to talk to them, but these kids are my daughter's friends. They're as likely to talk to me as they are the school principal. But you're closer to their age. You're not related. You might actually be able to get them to tell you the truth."

Jimmy was staring hard at the list of names, nodding seriously. "Maybe . . . maybe . . ."

"So, what do you think?"

Jimmy looked up at me, a purposeful glint in his eye. "I'm on it."

I grinned. "Awesome, dude."

Schumacher's girlfriend Carly shared a suburban house on an oak-lined street with two other young women. I pulled my truck along the curb a block or so away and settled in to observe. I saw a slim, young brunette in a dark business suit exit the house. She slipped into a Nissan Altima and drove off. A few minutes later, an attractive blonde in similar work clothes came out. She was quickly followed by Steven Schumacher, who was eating what looked like a Pop-Tart and wearing a pair of shorts and a T-shirt. The blond kissed Schumacher good-bye and zoomed away in a baby-blue VW Beetle. The girlfriend.

This Schumacher was really roughing it: sleeping late, avoiding work, and camping out with three hot postcollege babes. He watched the Beetle disappear around the corner and finished his Pop-Tart. Then he went back into the house. I watched the place for another twenty minutes or so, until Schumacher emerged again. His hair was wet—presumably from a shower—but his clothes were the same ones he had worn to say good-bye to his sweetie.

He hopped into a red Mitsubishi Eclipse parked on the street and started it up. I followed him through the quiet neighborhood and out onto a main commercial artery. A few miles down the road, on a corner containing a retail strip mall, Schumacher parked the Mitsubishi and sauntered into a Starbucks. I sat in my truck, waiting, watching.

Finally, wiping his mouth on his shirtsleeve, Schumacher came out the front door, holding his frothy cup of designer coffee, and got back into the Eclipse. I followed him at a discreet distance all the way back to his girlfriend's house. He got out of the car and strolled back up the front walk to the house. About halfway up the walk, the driver's-side door of a nearby black sedan—I'm not sure of the make—flew open and a guy stepped out. He moved quickly toward Schumacher, cutting across the grass. He wasn't running, but he was moving with a definite purpose—and it didn't look like the purpose was to sell cookies.

By the time Schumacher spotted him it was almost too late for him to react. I saw his eyes go wide over the top of the brew he was sipping. He took an involuntary step backward as the guy closed the distance.

The stranger was a big fella. Tall. A few extra pounds around his gut. Shaved head. Goatee beard and mustache. The exact description the dog walker had given me of Debbie's live-in roommate. Norman Fitchburg. He was a bit more muscle-bound than I had pictured. The size of his arms and set of his brow screamed *steroids.*

It appeared that Fitchburg didn't have a whole lot of respect for personal space because he jumped right into Schumacher's face. Schumacher took another step backward. Fitchburg grabbed his arm roughly to keep him from getting away and the coffee cup shook loose, splashing all over the sidewalk. Fitchburg leaned in even closer. Schumacher's face went white and he shook his head. Fitchburg nodded. Schumacher tried to pull away but was no match for the bigger man's strength. Fitchburg pulled Schumacher off the sidewalk and across the grass to the black sedan, which I had finally identified as a Chevy Impala. He shoved Schumacher unceremoniously into the passenger's seat and then slipped behind the wheel. In another moment, the Impala pulled past me and took off.

My truck was facing the opposite direction, so I had to turn around and get behind him quickly without being made as a tail. I waited until they turned a corner and then floored the accelerator, tires squealing across someone's finely manicured lawn—*sorry, buddy*—and tried to make up the distance before I lost him.

I raced around the corner after them just in time to see their red taillights turn another corner. I kept them in view, making sure that there were at least two or three cars between us. We went a few miles down the road, turning occasionally. Then Fitchburg accelerated through a fading yellow traffic light and the car in front of me braked to a stop, the sole driver in Central Florida not willing to run a red light. I stood on my brakes to avoid plowing into the back of the car. *C'mon, c'mon . . .* I said to myself, urging both the light to change and Mr. Cautious in front of me to move. I watched Fitchburg disappear around another corner.

An eternity later, the light finally turned green, and I was able to swerve around Mr. Cautious, becoming the kind of asshole driver I've always hated and vowed never to become. Oh well. Better than being convicted for murder.

I couldn't see the Impala anywhere. My heart sank with the dawning realization that I had lost them. I had no idea where to go. Damn Mr. Cautious and his goddamn traffic laws.

But wait—the neighborhood looked familiar. Why did I know it? Then it hit me. I was near Schumacher's apartment, maybe two blocks away, except I was approaching it from the opposite side from which I had previously come. Going with a hunch, I turned down Schumacher's street and slowly approached the apartment building.

There was the Impala sitting out front. And there was Fitchburg dragging Schumacher up the sidewalk to the front door.

I didn't want to be spotted so I pulled in to my new favorite hangout, the Kentucky Fried Chicken across the street. I wasn't sure what my next move was. Should I watch and follow? Maybe Fitchburg would lead me to Debbie. However, by sitting there doing nothing, I could have been allowing Schumacher to get whacked in the same room where Jonathan Dennis had bought it.

Fitchburg tore the single line of yellow police tape from the door and shoved Schumacher in front of it. Schumacher fumbled with his keys but eventually managed to get the door open. Fitchburg threw him in and shut the door.

That's when I made up my mind. If Schumacher was about to be murdered, I couldn't sit on my ass and let it happen. I leaned over and scooped my 9 mm Glock pistol from the glove compartment, shoved it into the back of my jeans, and hustled across the street to the apartment. Hunching over, I jogged up to the apartment's front picture window. I leaned around the hibiscus shrubs just enough to peer through the window and the open vertical blinds within. The window was cracked slightly and I smelled the pungent aroma of cleaning fluid wafting out. The crime-scene cleanup crew had been there to sanitize the room where Jonathan had died. They had obviously left the window open a bit to air the place out.

Fitchburg and Schumacher stood in the middle of the living room, Fitchburg clutching a handful of the younger man's shirt. I saw Fitchburg slap Schumacher on the side of the head, a nasty blow that staggered the kid. Through the open window I heard their muffled conversation.

"Where is it?" Fitchburg bellowed, raising his hand for another blow.

"I don't know!" Schumacher replied.

Instead of striking, Fitchburg reached into his pocket and produced a small black case. With the flick of his wrist, the case flipped open into a long, shiny blade. Schumacher's eyes widened in terror. Fitchburg tightened his grip on Schumacher's shirt and pulled him closer. He raised the knife.

I pulled the Glock from the back of my pants and tensed my muscles in preparation to spring. I decided not to charge through the front door. There were too many steps to reach it, and if Fitchburg was really going to cut the kid, by the time I got to the door it would be too late. Instead, I decided to pound on the window to get his attention and, if necessary, shoot Fitchburg through the glass.

But in the nanosecond before I sprang up, Schumacher caved.

"Okay!" he squealed, holding up a hand. "Okay!"

"Where?" growled Fitchburg.

Schumacher pointed at the kitchen. "The cabinet. Top left."

Fitchburg dragged the kid into the kitchen and kicked a dining chair into place. Schumacher made a move to climb up but Fitchburg shoved him back roughly.

"I don't think so," Fitchburg said. "You might have a gun hidden up there. Don't move." The big man stepped up onto the chair and then the counter. He opened the cabinet and peered in. "Where?"

"I—I'm not sure," Schumacher said.

"You better not be bullshittin' me."

"I don't even know what's up there. Jon just said not to tell anyone, not even the cops, if they ever asked. He put something up there, maybe in one of the coffee mugs. I swear I don't even know what it is."

Fitchburg made a sour face and reached into the shelves. He threw a couple of saucers and mugs to the floor, smashing the ceramic into shards. He swept his beefy arm through one shelf, sending stacks of bowls and plates crashing down. Schumacher winced. Then Fitchburg stopped. The disgusted twist of his lips curved into a sneering grin. I heard the faint tinkle of something small and light rattling inside a coffee mug. Holding a cup in his hand, Fitchburg hopped down to the floor.

"This what he put up there?" Fitchburg asked, showing the cup.

Schumacher peered in. "I guess. I never saw it."

"*Right . . .*" Fitchburg dumped the contents into his big palm and slipped it into his pocket. I couldn't see what it was. "Now, lemme ask you a question. You gonna tell anyone about our visit today?"

Schumacher shook his head. He was no idiot.

"Good," Fitchburg continued. " 'Cause if I hear that you told the cops about this, it would be bad for you . . . and your pretty girlfriend." Fitchburg suddenly raised his hand and slid the blade of the knife across the meaty deltoid of Schumacher's upper arm.

The kid yelped. Fitchburg pulled the knife free, the edge of the blade tinted crimson. Schumacher threw his opposite hand over the wound and took a terrified step backward. I saw blood seep between Schumacher's fingers. The big guy was much faster than I'd thought. And he was a cutter. He liked it.

In another instant, Fitchburg was on his way out the door. In my original plan, I'd thought I might follow him in my truck. He could probably lead me to Debbie. But the guy was moving too fast. He would be out the door in a second or two and I was still crouching in front of the window outside. I wouldn't have time to slip away and get back into my truck in the KFC parking lot across the street. As soon as he opened the door, he'd see me either standing there or obviously running away.

So, I made an instant decision. Instead of try to get away or hide, I hustled directly to the apartment's front door. I arrived at the door just as it opened. As soon as I saw Fitchburg's shiny bald head emerge through the opening, I lifted my pistol and pressed the muzzle into his ear.

"Hi," I said. "What's in the pocket?"

CHAPTER 18

The big man said nothing, but I saw his fingers twitch.

"Drop the knife," I ordered. He didn't move. "Drop it." The knife clinked on the concrete stoop. "Good. Now empty your pockets."

"Go to hell," he growled.

"That's original," I said. "What's next? *Go screw yourself? Eat my shorts?*" I pushed the muzzle of the Glock farther into his ear. My adrenaline was pumping hard and I was angry. I was afraid of what I might do. I shoved my hand into Fitchburg's front pocket— the one containing whatever had been in the coffee mug. I hoped it wasn't a hypodermic needle. My fingers closed around something small and smooth, like a decorative key chain.

I pulled my hand out and saw that it held a computer flash drive.

"What's on this?" I asked.

"Nothin'."

"Oh, come on, Norman. Really. You can do better than that. You could've said pictures of you and my sister or something. Anything."

"Fuck you."

"That may be the least original of all. You need some new material." I slipped the thumb drive into my pocket. "Why'd you carve up Jonathan?" No answer. "Where's Debbie?" No answer. "What's her real name?" No answer. "Aw, now don't be like that, Norm, or whatever your name is. Just because I criticized your material, don't pout and clam up. Get back up on that horse."

Fitchburg's fist suddenly shot up. Christ, he was fast. I twisted my head—enough to save me from a broken nose, but not enough to avoid the blow altogether. His knuckles cracked into my cheek, staggering me backward onto my ass and blurring my vision for a second. Fitchburg scooped up his knife and lunged at me.

I squeezed the trigger of the Glock, my vision still fuzzy, my aim random. Fitchburg halted in his tracks, his left arm snapping back, turning him slightly. I had hit him. I blinked my eyes and steadied my hand. I'd gotten him on the outside of his left bicep. At that range, if it hadn't hit bone, the bullet had probably passed right through and out the other side. Fitchburg grimaced and held the wound, blood leaking out between his fingers. The sight made me remember Steven Schumacher, who, I assumed, was at that moment behind us in the apartment, holding his own bleeding arm. He had probably called 911 by then. Good. The cops needed to have a conversation with Mr. Fitchburg.

"Don't move," I said, still sitting, pointing the gun at his head.

"You made a big mistake," Fitchburg said through clenched teeth.

"I wanna talk to Debbie. Where is she?"

"You don't get it. She's gone. Debbie never existed."

"Whoever she is, I wanna talk to her."

"Gimme the hard drive, Garrity. Give it to me now and I'll forget all about this."

"Now *that's* original. Much better. Very unexpected, considering I'm pointing the gun at you. The cops oughta be here any minute."

"I doubt it." Fitchburg raised the knife, but winced. The bullet wound must have hurt like hell. Good.

"Drop . . . the . . . knife," I said deliberately. I figured that it was the same weapon used to slice and dice poor Jonathan Dennis. With eyes like hot coals, Fitchburg backed away, taking a step down the sidewalk to his waiting car. "Hold it!" I barked. "On the ground!"

"You're gonna have to put me on the ground yourself and hold me there. Even with a hurt arm, I don't think you can do it alone. Or you can shoot me dead. But I'm not stoppin'."

He continued backing down the sidewalk. I realized that I couldn't shoot him like that. My cop training prevented me from gunning someone down who wasn't directly threatening me or someone else. If I wasn't going to shoot him, then I needed to call for backup. He was right: he was too big and too fast for me to take down alone. I needed a taser and a couple of other guys. But I wasn't a cop anymore. I was a PI. I was out there alone, on my ass and fuzzy-brained from a punch in the face. The only one I could call then was Jimmy.

Great.

Fitchburg didn't say another word. He just slipped into his Impala and sped off, tires squealing around the first turn. I slowly pulled myself to my feet, feeling my bruised face and already regretting the shiner that was brewing. I shuffled back into the apartment.

"Schumacher?" I called. There was no reply. I walked farther into the apartment. Then I saw why Fitchburg had said that he doubted the cops were coming. Schumacher had opened a bedroom window and kicked out the screen. He had obviously climbed out and hauled ass away. *Thanks, buddy.*

My predicament suddenly became quite clear. I had just engaged in a violent confrontation in front of the apartment. I had shot Fitchburg in the arm. Somebody had probably reported that gunshot. Cops would be en route. It definitely wouldn't help me stay out of jail to be caught shooting someone in front of the previous murder scene, while the guy who had fingered me fled bleeding out the window. That wasn't a picture I wanted Joe Vincent to see.

I quickly exited the apartment and jumped back into my truck. In another moment I was gone. If anyone was watching me,

I could have trouble. My physical description at the location, as well as the make and model of my Ford F-150, would be enough to send Joey right to my place with a pair of handcuffs.

In the distance I heard the sirens. I pressed my foot harder on the accelerator.

I drove straight to the A-Plus Investigations offices. However, when I tried to enter the office, the doorknob wouldn't turn. Locked. Jimmy was probably out at Victor Madrigas's high school, talking to his friends. Since most of the agency's work came directly from Nate Hungerford's law firm upstairs, there really wasn't much need for a receptionist. So, when Jimmy was out, the place was locked. Maybe his father had a key. I wanted to get in and use one of the nonconfiscated computers to check out the thumb drive.

I made my way upstairs to the Hungerford, Reilly, and Osman law firm and strolled into the lobby. It was what you might expect from a high-powered downtown law firm. All the signifiers of power and wealth were on display: cherrywood furniture, marble floors, expensive art on the walls. But the main thing I noticed when I walked into the lobby was the crowd.

There were a dozen or so people crowded around Nate Hungerford, who stood strategically in front of a painting of a Florida wetland scene. A short, balding guy in an expensive suit stood next to Hungerford, smiling broadly. Two news crews pointed bright lights and video cameras at them both. I recognized at least one of the reporters from the local TV affiliates.

"Well, of course we're pleased," Nate Hungerford said, a big smile on his face. "On behalf of Mr. Lawrence and the entire Lawrence Company, we would like to commend the city commission on their vote yesterday. They showed great leadership and great vision for the future of Orlando."

Reporters shouted questions at him. Nate pointed at one young woman—I think she was from the *Orlando Sentinel*—whom he called Glenda.

"Aren't you concerned about the eminent-domain issues?" Glenda asked. "There are a lot of people affected by this decision."

"Certainly we're concerned," Nate said, glancing at the balding guy and looking appropriately serious. "These are never easy choices. But the commission voted and the Lawrence Company is committed not just to following the letter of the law, but to making sure people are treated fairly. Everyone affected will be compensated more than fairly."

I leaned over to a young guy in a suit standing nearby. He might have been a junior associate or a paralegal for the firm. He eyed the red bruise blossoming on my cheek.

"What's all this about?" I asked.

"Don't you read the paper?" he asked.

"As a matter of fact, I don't."

"We represent the Lawrence Company," he said and paused, as if that explained everything. He nodded his head toward the short, balding guy. I blinked at him. "The city commission voted yesterday on that big Parramore redevelopment project. It's a go and the Lawrence Company got the contract for planning and construction. A hundred and ten million dollars, baby." The kid grinned. Definitely an associate. Only a lawyer at the firm would be that happy about the deal.

"Do you think Hungerford will be busy for a while?" I asked. Nate Hungerford was still holding court.

"I'd say he'll be busy for the next five years."

I nodded and wandered out of the office. I'd find a computer somewhere else. The cops had confiscated both the laptop that Jimmy had provided and the desktop computer in my apartment. But they hadn't yet touched anything in Cam's condo. And I knew exactly where she kept her laptop computer.

It was in her second bedroom, the one that currently served as a home office to support her job as a pharmaceutical sales rep. This was the bedroom that would soon be transformed into a nursery.

I had a hard time envisioning Cam as a mother: the glamorous, black-clad blonde in the Porsche Boxster. But when I looked around her home office, with its stylish chrome desk and minimalist leather furniture, I was struck with a fully formed vision of oversized plush Disney characters piled in a crib and wallpaper borders featuring bunny rabbits. It was as different from the current incarnation of the room as you could get, yet I saw it all and knew without a doubt that it would come to pass.

I shook off the vision and found the laptop computer. A minute later I had booted it up and logged in. While the computer hummed to life, I examined the flash drive. Why hadn't Steven Schumacher told the police about it after Jonathan was killed? Maybe he didn't realize its significance. Maybe he didn't want it in the cops' hands for some reason. I needed another chat with Mr. Schumacher. Another visit to his girlfriend's house was probably in order.

Whatever was on that little chunk of digital memory, it was hot enough to get someone killed. I considered calling Jim Dupree and turning it in. It just might be the evidence that would get Joe Vincent off my back. But I would be abdicating all control of my situation—what little I actually had—by turning it over at that point. Plus, I'd have to explain how I'd gotten it, and at the moment, that story could only hurt me. Joey V would use whatever I gave him to construct a case against me, not to clear me. Big Jim wouldn't be able to protect me. No, the risky, but smarter, play was for me to figure out just what the hell was going on and then hand it all over to the cops in a tidy little package.

So, with the computer fired up, I slipped the cap off the hard drive and plugged it into the laptop's USB port. Here we go . . . I heard a small beep as the computer recognized the new hardware. A message window popped up informing me that the system was searching for the proper program to use to read the files on the drive. It asked me what it should use. I selected to open a directory so that I could see the drive's contents.

Then another, smaller, gray window popped up asking me the

access password. Password? Hell if I knew. I typed "Jonathan" and clicked OK.

There was a beep and the password-entry box reappeared. Damn. I tried "Schumacher." Same result. I then tried "Dennis," "JDennis," "SSchumacher," and even "Carly" (Schumacher's girlfriend's name). None of them worked. I tried "Debbie," "Watson," "DWatson," "Norm," "Norman," "Fitchburg," "NFitchburg," "Fitch," and a half dozen other variations. It was hopeless. I had no idea what the password was. I was no computer codebreaker. I could barely check e-mail.

But I did know someone who could crack the password, a genuine hacker with more geek cred than a roomful of software engineers. He was also someone who wouldn't be put off by the quasi-illegal nature of the mission. In fact, that would be his favorite part. The only trouble was that, to get to him, I needed Cam's help. And Cam hated his guts.

CHAPTER 19

Cam looked at me with an expression that I hadn't seen since the last days of our dissolving marriage. She was wary, suspicious, and altogether not happy.

"Tell me why exactly you want to talk to Skip," she said. We sat in the living room of her condo, eating flatbread and hummus, washing them down with some sort of Chinese black tea. Staying with Cam was always exotic. In my apartment, if we had any snack at all, it would have been a bag of semistale Doritos and Kool-Aid.

"It's for a case I'm working on," I said. "Client confidentiality. You know."

Her flat eyes told me that, in fact she did not know. "I'm not calling him without a good reason."

"It's a good reason. I promise."

She shook her head. "If Skip is involved, it's a bad reason."

"Trust me. Please."

She sighed. "I don't like it."

"I know. It's important. It may keep me out of jail."

She shook her head again, but that time it was more in resignation than refusal. She would help me. Her cousin, Skip Balinor, worked as a programmer for one of the many financial-services software firms up in Lake Mary, just north of Orlando. But that was just his job. His passion was hacking.

As a college freshman he had been kicked out of a prestigious

East Coast liberal arts school for hacking into the administrative computer network and changing his all grades to A's. He ended up getting an associate's degree from Seminole Community College, where he had underperformed in class and spent his evenings trying to hack into government and corporate networks. He had twice been questioned by the Secret Service and once by the FBI. There were rumors within the family that he was on a permanent government watch list. However, the worst part, the real reason that Cam disliked him so much, was that he was a first-class prick.

I didn't really need Cam to call him. I could have called him myself. But the odds of him helping me were better if Cam called. More important, though, I needed Cam to take the flash drive to him. I was pretty sure that I was being intermittently followed by the cops and by then I might have Norman Fitchburg and his knife looking for me. I didn't want anyone following me to Skip's house or his office. That might not only jeopardize my possession of the hard drive, it could put Skip in danger. My plan was to drive over to see Jimmy at the same time as Cam went to visit Skip with the hard drive. The cops and/or the bad guys would, I hoped, follow me, leaving Cam alone.

I did consider inviting Skip over to Cam's place so that I wouldn't have to let go of the hard drive, but I abandoned that strategy when I saw the look on her face. She wouldn't permit him in her home. Plus, Skip probably needed to use his own equipment and software.

Cam made the call. She tried to keep the disgust out of her voice but she couldn't keep it off her face. She handed me the phone.

"Hey, Skip," I said.

"Hello, Officer. Long time no speak," he replied. He always called me Officer, his unsubtle attempt to draw a clear line between my law enforcement career and his lawbreaking career. What a renegade.

"You know I'm not a cop anymore."

"Yes . . ." he said slowly, his voice drawing the word out. "Yes,

I saw you on the TV news. You are a 'person of interest.' I've been a 'person of interest' before, too. But never for homicide. That's impressive."

"I'm glad you think so. Listen, I have a proposition for you."

"Oh?"

I explained the general situation. I had a password-protected thumb drive. It did not belong to me. I needed to find out what was on it.

"And why should I help you?" he asked.

"Are you afraid you won't be able to do it?"

"Nice try. You'll have to use more-complex psychology than that. I can do it. That's not even a question."

"Then prove it."

"Please, Officer. Stop trying to bait me. How much are you going to pay me?"

"How much do you want?"

"Five thousand dollars."

I laughed. "That's a good one. I'm glad to hear you haven't lost your sense of humor."

"Then why are we even talking? Good-bye, Officer."

"Whatever is on this hard drive is dangerous. If the cops knew I had it, they'd take it from me," I said.

Skip paused. "I'm listening."

"Whatever it is, it's what got that kid killed the other night. I want to know why. You could be the one to figure it out."

"So this is a shady proposition?"

"The shadiest."

"Why didn't you say so in the first place?"

Cam and I pulled out of the parking lot at the same time. She went one way and I went the other; she was bound for Skip's townhouse in Lake Mary and I was heading to the Fashion Square mall.

I found Jimmy in the food court, waiting in line for a corn-dog combo.

"Hey, dude," he said when I approached. He squinted at my bruised cheek. "You walk into a wall or something?"

"Yeah. Something like that." I filled Jimmy in on the basics of my encounter at Schumacher's place. We found a table and, with his mouth full of corn dog, Jimmy recapped his day at Victor's high school.

"He was a good kid," Jimmy said. "Like, totally popular with his own crowd. Not a jock so he wasn't, like, known all over the school, but, from what I can tell, he was just a generally cool guy."

"Were any of the friends surprised about the suicide?"

"Totally. They couldn't believe it. The girls are still crying about it. They all said he planned to go to college. One of 'em told me he was thinking about being a priest but then changed his mind. He wanted to study astrology. Or maybe astronomy. I don't blame him. I couldn't be a priest. . . ." He shook his head.

"The no sex thing?"

"Duuuude . . ."

"What about the drugs?" I asked, stealing a french fry. "Where did he get them?"

"The friends don't know. They swear. But I asked around to some other kids. Dude, I found at least two guys who could hook me up with whatever I wanted. Xanax. Ludes. Acid. X. Pot. The back of that school was like a freaking pharmacy."

"Yeah . . ." I nodded, not surprised. The modern high school was a complex minicity of good neighborhoods and bad ones, politics, commerce, alliances, and betrayals. "So, what do you think? Suicide?"

Jimmy shrugged. "It happens. I knew a guy in the army. He had been, like, trained and tested and everything. But one night, while the rest of us were on leave, he put a pistol in his mouth and said good-bye. It was a total shock. No note, no clues, nothing."

"Could Victor have been an accident? An OD?"

He shrugged again. "The friends swear he wouldn't kill himself. Anything's possible."

"Even murder?"

Jimmy raised an eyebrow. "Dude?"

"Just asking. We have to ask all the questions, even if we're just ruling them out. Did Victor have any enemies? Any fights or arguments recently?"

"Dude, the dude was, like, gonna be a *priest.*"

"I knew a lot of priests growing up. Believe me, some of them had long lists of enemies." I stole another fry but didn't eat it. "Some of the meanest bastards I've ever met were priests."

"I'll keep askin' around, if you want. See if I can learn anything."

I nodded. "Good idea." I put the french fry on a napkin and looked sincerely at Jimmy. "Nice work . . . I mean it." Jimmy smiled, satisfied with the compliment. Then, mouth full of the last bite of corn dog, he looked past my shoulder at something behind me. He squinted curiously. "What is it?" I asked.

He pointed his chin. "You know her? She's been lookin' at us."

I swiveled in my seat. Standing a few feet away, in front of a trash can with plastic trays piled on top, stood a woman in a loose T-shirt and black jeans. She watched me carefully, almost smiling— but not quite. Her scalp was visible through a thin crew-cut fuzz of hair.

Debbie.

I blinked at her for a beat, debating how to play it. Should I get up and approach her? She saved me the decision by walking over to us. She looked casual but still pretty, even with the buzz cut. She carried herself differently than she had the last time I'd seen her—more confident, less reserved. The set of her shoulders was squarer, her spine a bit straighter, and her gait had a little more swagger in it.

"Hello, Mike," she said.

"Hello." I.

"Mind if I join you?"

"Please do." I gestured at an open chair.

She sat. "Perhaps we can speak in private."

I considered Jimmy. "That's not necessary. Jimmy knows everything."

"Everything?" Debbie said, eyeing me meaningfully.

"Everything important."

Debbie sighed. "Okay. Whatever. Doesn't matter. Do you have the hard drive?"

"Not on me."

"Of course not. How quickly can you get it?"

"Whoa, babe. Slow down. Why would I give it to *you*? I'm thinkin' I should hand it over to the cops. It's my best chance of clearing my name."

"Not a good idea. A very bad idea." She leaned forward onto the table. "Look, it wasn't part of the plan to set you up as the doer. You stuck your nose in at the wrong time."

"Yeah . . . I'll say. So, what exactly *is* 'the plan'? What am I mixed up in here?"

She smiled coldly. "We just want the hard drive."

"Was sleeping with me part of 'the plan'?" I saw Jimmy's eyes widen.

Debbie offered a half shrug. "That wasn't so bad."

"Stop. You'll inflate my ego. So that was just . . . what? To soften me up? Distract me? That wasn't even necessary, you know. I would've helped you anyway."

Debbie nodded. "Probably. But I couldn't have you asking a lot of questions. I had to spoon-feed you just enough so you wouldn't ask too many questions and, as you said, *distract* you enough so you didn't ask more. And you did it, Mike. You did it. We had been looking for him for a couple of weeks. But you found that little fucker right away. You're good." She pulled out a pack of Camels from her purse. "You mind if I smoke?"

"You smoke?" I'd never seen her smoke or even smelled it on her.

"Every chance I get."

"You're not allowed in here," I said.

"Tough shit." She lit up a cigarette and sucked in a long, defiant drag.

I thought about the information she had given me: the kid's name; his last job; his city of residence. She had given me everything I needed, including a big fat lie about him being adopted. But, with everything else being accurate—his name, job, hometown—why would I doubt the adoption? She gave me just enough to prevent me from looking on my own and discovering the lies. I was a complete and total sucker.

"That was one hell of a performance," I said. "The tears. The big scene about wanting to meet your son before you died. I mean, it was Academy Award caliber."

"I'm glad you liked it."

"Oh yeah. Very entertaining." I leaned forward. "What about the cancer?"

"What about it?"

"All a lie?"

"All a lie."

I felt the anger inside me boiling up. "How could you do that? How could you lie about having cancer? Shave your head? Your eyebrows, for chrissakes . . . What kind of a person pretends to have cancer?"

She fixed me with her dark eyes. "A professional."

"A professional? A professional what? So, are you and your boyfriend—what—a couple of hired grifters? What's in it for you? Why do you want the hard drive? Who are you working for?"

She scratched the back of her fuzzy head. "You can't possibly think I'm going to answer you. You know better than that."

"Those people in the support group, they're out there, fighting for their lives, every day. Andrew just died. Did you know that? You made a mockery of them." I fixed her with a withering stare. "You may be the single worst person I've ever met."

She blew out a long plume of smoke. "I'll take that as a compliment."

"Go to hell."

"Look, Mike, as much as I'm enjoying this witty repartee, let's get down to business—"

Jimmy suddenly stood. "I think I *will* give you guys some privacy after all. I'll just take a walk." Before I could protest, Jimmy strode off into the food-court crowd.

"Business?" I asked, thrown somewhat off-balance by Jimmy's sudden departure.

"Sure. You got caught up in this more than you should have. That's an inconvenience. I understand. In exchange for the hard drive, I'm willing to make you a generous offer. To compensate for the trouble."

"Oh yeah? How generous?"

"Ten thousand dollars."

I nodded and made a "not bad" face. "I'm gonna have to think about that. So, what exactly is on that drive?"

"Couldn't get past the password?"

"No luck."

"Let's just say it's sensitive."

"And valuable."

"Ten large, Mike."

"What if I want fifty?"

She didn't even blink. "I'm sure we could come to some reasonable figure."

"Your money isn't gonna keep me out of jail."

She waved her hand dismissively. "Ah, the cops are just rattling their sabers. You didn't cut Jonathan. They'll figure that out. They probably already have."

"So who *did* cut Jonathan? Your boy toy Norman?"

She smiled. "*Norman.* I can't believe he picked that name. Really, do you think he looks like a Norman?"

"I guess not. What *does* he look like?"

"You can stick with Norman. That'll do."

"What about you? Is it Carol? I feel stupid calling you Debbie."

"Why? Don't I look like a Debbie?"

I considered her for a second. "No. Not anymore. Maybe not ever."

She shrugged. "Sorry. Debbie's all you get." She stubbed out her cigarette on Jimmy's corn-dog plate.

I looked at the cigarette butt. "Those'll give you cancer, y'know."

"Cute." She put her palms flat on the table. "Come on. Let's go get that hard drive."

I smiled at her. "You sure are a glass-half-full kinda person. I told you—I gotta think about it."

"Ten thousand dollars, Mike. More if you want it."

"Shove your ten grand. I want to stay outta jail."

Debbie sighed and gave me an exasperated look. "Okay. We tried this nice. You're going to give me that hard drive. Now get up and come with me or we're going to have to do this not-so-nice."

Behind her, I saw my buddy Norman Fitchburg step around a crowd of loitering mall teens. He was in a tight black T-shirt designed to reveal his steroid biceps. His left arm had a white bandage around it where I had shot him. His expression was devoid of humor.

"You remember *Norman,* don't you?" Debbie asked. "Norman's going to help you retrieve the hard drive. If Jonathan had just told us where he hid it, he would be alive and well right now. Instead, I'm sitting here asking *you* where it is."

Message received: If I didn't give it up, I would end up like Jonathan. Fitchburg moved quickly toward me. As he did so, I saw a black fanny pack around his waist. He reached into it as he approached.

"Hi, Norm," I said. "How's the arm?"

"How's your face?" he said, checking out my shiner.

"Touché. I see you've been working on your material."

"Get up," he said.

I blinked at him. "What's the magic word?"

"What?"

"What's the magic word? Manners . . . What do you say when you want someone to do something?"

"What the hell are you talking about? Get the fuck up."

"Sorry. That's not it. *Please*. Get up, *please*. It's simple manners."

I was stalling, trying to figure out my next move. I drew a blank.

"You actually had sex with this guy?" Fitchburg said to Debbie.

"Drop it, *Norman*," Debbie said.

"You can't blame her," I said. "With how steroids shrink everything, y'know, important, you can't expect her to be satisfied with, well, y'know . . . *you*."

Fitchburg's short fuse, whether innate or 'roid-induced, got the better of him. His right fist shot out and caught me in the temple, sending a bright flash through my vision and making me wonder if he'd popped my skull open where the doctors had sewn it back together after my tumor operation. I felt serious pain—more than a simple punch would have caused. I had, unfortunately, been punched a lot in my life. I was semiused to it. However, this was different. This was exacerbated by my recovering surgery. The blow was hard and snapped me sideways. Before I toppled out of the chair, Fitchburg grabbed the back of my collar and yanked me upright.

A few other food-court patrons looked over. However, it had happened so fast that not many people noticed. Fitchburg pulled me out from the table and, hand still gripping my collar, walked me to the escalator. I felt a hard jab in my ribs. Looking down, I saw Fitchburg's other hand holding a small .22 pistol to my side. He had pulled it from the fanny pack and kept it well hidden from sight as we walked. But I sure felt it. Add another bruise to my growing collection.

I knew that I was in trouble. Fitchburg was huge, mean, and armed. At that moment, I was none of those things. My feet barely touched the ground as Fitchburg propelled me to the escalator. Debbie walked in front of us, her face set in a stern, businesslike expression.

And then, in an instant, I felt Fitchburg's grip vanish from my collar. Turning, I saw the big man twist to the right. Someone had grabbed his arm and hauled him away. The .22 skittered across the tile. Debbie was already on the escalator, heading down. She turned to make sure we were still behind her and her eyes went wide.

I looked back and saw a fist pound Fitchburg's arm bandage, eliciting a guttural grunt. Then a leg swept Fitchburg's feet out from under him, sending him sprawling to the floor. That's when I finally saw who had intervened. And I couldn't believe my eyes.

CHAPTER 20

It was Jimmy. He stood poised over Fitchburg, knees bent, arms up, ready to fight.

As Fitchburg righted himself and started to rise, Jimmy struck with a powerful kick to his chest, sending the big man tumbling backward onto the descending escalator and directly into Debbie, who was desperately rushing back up. They both toppled down the moving stairs to the ground floor.

Jimmy grabbed me by the arm. "Come on," he ordered, pulling me through the food court and into the second floor of a JCPenney. "He might have another weapon." We moved fast, running full tilt through the racks of bras. We passed through stacks of towels, then bolted down the store's descending escalator. In another minute we were in the parking lot, jumping into Jimmy's green Jeep Wrangler and disappearing into traffic.

From the front passenger seat, I gave Jimmy a long, hard look. "What exactly did you do in the army?" I asked.

"You know," he said with a half shrug. "Different things."

"Like what?"

"I was in some different units." He paused, still looking through the windshield. "Special Forces mostly."

"Doing what?"

"What else? Triple R. Recon, raids, and revenge. I'm not allowed to talk about it. Operational-security stuff. Some of it was pretty hairy, though."

"And how long were you in Iraq?"

Jimmy shook his head. "Too long, dude. Too long."

There was obviously more to Jimmy than I had first thought. "Thanks for saving my ass back there."

"It's cool. I saw the big dude lurking around right after your gal sat down. I figured he might be trouble, so I circled around, just in case."

I nodded. "Good call. I owe you one."

I pulled out my cell phone and called Cam. I owed her one, too. She answered on the third ring.

"So, how's my buddy Skip?" I asked.

"Odious," she replied.

"Any problems?"

"None besides the usual. I gave him the hard drive. He was his typical smug self. He's gotten fatter and added some pimples. He thinks he's growing a beard."

"Did he figure out the password?"

"I have no idea. I didn't even go into his apartment. It was dark and smelled like Cheetos."

"Were you followed?"

"How should I know? I don't think so. I didn't notice anyone."

"Okay . . . Are you still in the car?"

"Yes. I'm almost home."

"Don't pull in yet. Circle the block a couple of times. If it looks like someone's behind you, call me back. If you can't reach me, drive to the police station and find Big Jim."

"Jeez, Michael. Is that really necessary?"

"Yes. Promise me."

She sighed heavily. "All right. I promise."

"Thanks, Cam. I love you."

"You better."

She disconnected. My next call was to Skip.

"Hello, Officer," he said.

"Skip," I said as a greeting. "So, what do you think?"

"The security is good. Above average. I'll need to work on it."

"Tell me you can do it."

"I said I'll need to work on it." Skip's tone was testy. "Whose drive was this?"

"The dead kid. The one the cops think I killed."

"What were his skills?"

"Skills? What do you mean?"

"*Skills*. What were his computer skills? How good was he?"

"Hell, I dunno. He was some kind of IT guy. Worked for the city."

"Hmmm." Skip's voice was barely audible. I pictured him pursing his lips and nodding to himself. Cam had said that he'd put on both new weight and pimples. Neither would help his social life. "IT . . . He probably knew what he was doing."

"So do you, Skip. You know what you're doing."

"Don't patronize me, Officer."

"Find out what's on that drive, Skip. It's important. Life-or-death important."

"I couldn't care less about life or death. But I refuse to be beaten by some pissant DB hack for the city."

"Right. Whatever that means. Just let me know as soon as you have something."

I disconnected and rubbed the bridge of my nose. I looked out the Jeep's passenger's window at the passing trees and buildings.

"Uh, dude?" Jimmy asked from behind the wheel. "Where am I driving?"

That was a good question. I considered for a moment. "To the office. It's time to crack open all that new kick-ass spy gear you have."

As I suspected, there was a cop driving around Schumacher's girlfriend's house. The cop was trying to be inconspicuous, waiting fifteen or twenty minutes between passes, but I immediately saw the pattern.

I knew I couldn't get anywhere near the place. If Schumacher spotted me walking up the drive, he'd immediately be on the phone to Joe Vincent. But Schumacher didn't know Jimmy. Jimmy had at least a chance of getting close enough to talk to him. Schumacher might, understandably, have a hair-trigger paranoia and call Joe Vincent anyway if Jimmy rang the bell, but it was worth a shot. I was tired of playing catch-up on the whole situation. I needed to get out in front and start acting rather than reacting. For that to happen, I needed information.

We were still in Jimmy's Jeep. My truck, which at that moment sat harmlessly in the mall parking lot, would have attracted too much attention. Too many people had seen it too many times. Its repeated presence at Schumacher's apartment before and after Jonathan's murder had made it a bright, glowing beacon. Cops were looking for it. Debbie and Norman Fitchburg were probably looking for it. Jimmy's Jeep, on the other hand, was just another car.

We parked down the block and watched the house, ducking below the dash as the cop made his slow patrol up the street. I trained my new binoculars on the kitchen window. I figured that if Schumacher was home, he'd eventually wander into the kitchen. We had no idea if he was, in fact, home. After he bolted from his apartment while Norman Fitchburg and I had our little spat, I had no idea where he went. Maybe he had called a friend to come pick him up. Maybe he was hiding somewhere. Maybe he'd called a cab. Maybe he'd just run.

I didn't think the cut on his arm was bad enough to send him to the urgent-care center or the emergency room, but I didn't know for sure. He might have been sitting in a waiting room somewhere, checking the group number on his insurance card. That was the only lead I had. I assumed that he would eventually return, if he planned to continue staying there. After getting an eyeful of his disproportionately hot girlfriend, he'd be crazy not to stay.

I adjusted the focus on the binoculars and saw movement through the kitchen blinds. There was a reflection on the glass, so it was hard to tell for sure, but I was pretty sure that what I saw was the figure of Steven Schumacher drinking from a can.

"Jackpot," I said.

That got Jimmy's attention. He adjusted the wires snaking under his shirt, pushing tape down onto skin and rolling his neck back and forth.

"Showtime?" Jimmy asked.

"Showtime."

We waited for the cop to complete one more pass up the street. Then Jimmy hopped out of the Jeep and hustled down the sidewalk to the house. I watched Jimmy for a few seconds, then flipped on a small, portable video monitor I held in my hand. The view on the monitor was from a tiny video camera disguised as one of Jimmy's shirt buttons. I saw Jimmy approach the house and heard his breathing as he moved.

"Check, dude," Jimmy whispered. "Check check. Are we online?"

I adjusted a thin headset with a microphone attached. "I can both hear and see you, Jimmy. Be careful."

"Always."

We had discussed taking the direct approach—having Jimmy simply knock on the door and ask to speak to Schumacher. But we figured that wouldn't work. After the week he'd had, Schumacher was probably more than a little jumpy. So we opted for the indirect approach.

On the monitor I saw and heard Jimmy pound on the front door.

"Carly!" he shouted. "Carly, open up! It's me." He pounded again. "Carly—come on baby, open up. Don't be mad."

I switched my gaze from the monitor to the binoculars and the kitchen window. I saw a blur of human-size shape move past it.

"Movement in the house," I said into the microphone. "Watch yourself."

Jimmy banged again on the door. "Caaarly!" he shouted like Brando screaming "*Stella*." "I'm sorry, baby. Open the door. Carly!"

"Who's there?" came a muffled male voice through my headphones. Schumacher was speaking through the unopened door.

"Hello?" Jimmy said. "Hey, dude—is Carly home?"

"Who wants to know?"

"Just tell her it's Jimmy. Tell her I'm sorry."

"Sorry for what?"

"She'll know. Just open up, dude."

"Carly's not home."

"Aw, man. Don't lie. Just open up. Please."

"Who the hell are you?" Schumacher said, the anger in his voice audible even through the door and the headphones.

"She'll know." Jimmy pulled a small box from his front pocket, making a big show of it because Schumacher was undoubtedly watching through the door peephole. "Okay, listen, dude. Just give her this. And tell her I'm sorry."

"Go away. She's not home."

"Right. Okay. I believe you. Just take this and give it to her."

Schumacher paused. He had to be wondering who the hell the guy was and why his girlfriend had been cheating on him. He had to be curious about what was in the box. The moment of truth was approaching. He'd either open the door or retreat into the house. "Just leave it on the mat."

"And have someone steal it? Hell no. I ain't leaving no diamond ring on the mat. Just take it for me."

Diamond ring? Jimmy and I hadn't discussed that particular detail. That was a nice touch.

I heard the latch click and saw the door open a crack. I got a fleeting glimpse of Schumacher's face before Jimmy slammed himself against the door, driving Schumacher back into the house. Jimmy leaped through the opening and kicked the door closed.

CHAPTER 21

"Okay, dude," Jimmy said in voice that held more authority than I would have thought possible using the word *dude*. "I'm not gonna hurt you. But you need to answer a few questions."

"Jesus," Schumacher whimpered, pulling himself up from the living-room floor. He was having a hell of a week. First, his friend had been slashed to death in his apartment. Then the morning's joy ride and souvenir arm slice from Norman Fitchburg. Then some stranger shows up asking for his girlfriend. Now a home invasion. I almost felt bad for the guy. Almost.

"Relax, dude," Jimmy said.

"This isn't about Carly, is it?"

"No. I never met her. Sorry about that."

Schumacher nodded. Then he bolted toward the kitchen. The monitor blurred as Jimmy pursued him over a couch. I heard a crash of furniture. When the images cleared, I saw Jimmy's hand gripping Schumacher's wrist, bending it backward so that Schumacher was forced to his knees. It looked painful and effective.

"Come *on*, dude," Jimmy almost whined. "I told you nobody would get hurt. But I can hurt you if you want. Is that what you want?"

"No—" Schumacher grunted.

"Okay, then . . . What's on the hard drive?"

"Hard drive?"

"Yeah. The hard drive from the coffee cup. The one you gave to the big bald dude this morning."

"How many times do I have to tell people—I don't know." Jimmy twisted the wrist. Schumacher reacted with a small squeal. "I don't know!"

"Why didn't you tell the cops about it?"

"I completely forgot about it until the big guy asked for it this morning. I swear. Jon hid it up there, but he never said what was on it."

"Come on, dude. Jonathan was hiding out. You knew that. You lied to Mike Garrity about him staying with you. Don't lie to me now."

"No—I swear. I mean, yeah, sure, I figured Jon was in some kind of trouble. But he was more excited than scared. It was like he won the lottery or something and didn't want anyone to steal his ticket. He never told me what it was. He just asked to crash at my place. Said not to tell anyone he was there. He was just a guy I knew from work. I was doing him a favor."

"You expect me to believe that you didn't know what was going on? Gimme a break." Jimmy turned Schumacher's wrist a little farther.

"Ow! God. Stop! You're gonna break it. I swear. I didn't know! I wish I never let him stay with me."

"Who's the bald dude?"

"I have no idea. I never saw him before this morning."

"Did you call the cops after you left your apartment this morning?"

"No. The big guy threatened me. In the car. He told me not to or I'd end up like Jon."

Jimmy paused, watching Schumacher squirm. "So what are you gonna do?"

"Do?"

"Yeah," Jimmy said. "You're mixed up in it now, dude. What are you gonna do about it?"

"I don't know, man. This is a goddamn nightmare. I just want it to go away." Schumacher's voice cracked. "Who *are* you, anyway?"

Jimmy ignored the question. "What's on the hard drive?"

"I don't know!"

"I don't like your answers, Steve. They're not helping me."

"It's the truth. I swear. Please let go. Please."

I heard Jimmy sigh. But he didn't let go. "So, Mike," he said. "What do you want me to do? Want me to break his arm?"

"No!" Schumacher yelped. "Who is that? Who are you talking to? Is that Mike Garrity? Tell him I'm sorry. Tell him it was a mistake."

I positioned the microphone in front of my mouth. "You think he's telling the truth?" I asked.

"I dunno. Probably. At this point, why would he lie? The drive is gone."

"Maybe. There might be more to the story . . . but, I agree. I think he's telling the truth. This looks like a dead end."

"So what do you want me to do? I can't leave him here. He might call the cops."

"I won't!" Schumacher shrieked. "I won't call anyone."

"Right," Jimmy said. "We could drive him somewhere and dump him. Make him walk back."

"Nah," I said. "I don't want to deal with him anymore."

"I could immobilize him," Jimmy said.

"Jeez, don't really hurt him."

"Not like that. I could tie him up. His girlfriend will let him out when she gets home. Unless she digs it, if you know what I mean."

"They'll definitely call the cops then," I said.

"Probably. But that'll give you time to relo somewhere else."

"Yeah," I said. "Okay. Immobilize him."

"Roger that."

"Uh, Jimmy?"

"Yo."

"Would you really have broken his arm?"

"Just say the word, dude."

Jimmy left Schumacher duct taped to a kitchen chair. Schumacher even got to take a supervised pee before being "immobilized." Jimmy put the small box for Carly in Schumacher's lap. It contained an eight-dollar rhinestone ring. The duct tape notwithstanding, I thought that the whole thing was rather civilized.

"So how'd the gear work?" Jimmy asked as we drove away in his Jeep.

"Bitchin'," I said.

Jimmy laughed. "Bitchin'? Cowabunga, dude." He pulled the wires out from under his shirt as I drove. "What's our next move?"

"I'm not sure. I was hoping Schumacher had some answers. But it looks like we're back to square one. We'll see how quickly Skip can crack the password on the hard drive. Once we know what this is all about, we can better plan a course of action. I *really* hate being in the dark."

"When Schumacher's girlfriend gets home, they'll probably call the cops. You should crash at my place. The cops will be on the prowl for you."

"You too, now."

"Maybe. But Schumacher doesn't know who I am."

I shook my head. "Joe Vincent's no fool. He's been to the A-Plus office. He's met you. As soon as Schumacher provides a physical description, he'll figure it out. I appreciate the offer, but I'll either stay at Cam's or grab a motel room. You should think about doing the same."

"Okay. What about your gal Debbie?"

That was a good question. I had no idea where Debbie or her boy Fitchburg was. I needed to stay sharp, though. If one thing was sure, it was that they would find me again. And they weren't going to be too pleased about our last encounter.

"There's no way I'm giving Debbie the hard drive," I said. "I'm taking her and her boyfriend down."

As we drove, Jimmy and I discussed his attendance at Jonathan's upcoming funeral. The cops would surely be present, so I couldn't show my face. We agreed that Jimmy should disguise himself so that he wouldn't be recognized by Schumacher, if he showed up. Jimmy would pass himself off as one of Jonathan's friends. I would monitor the whole thing remotely, using the gear we had just used. I could tell that Jimmy really liked the idea of donning a disguise and using his spy gear again. To him, this was what being a PI was all about. Despite my earlier skepticism, I was starting to agree with him.

We drove back to the mall, where I hopped out of the Jeep and got into my pickup. Jimmy and I agreed to check in with each other later. The Jeep drove off. Before I could put the key in my ignition, my cell phone rang. I looked at the caller ID: Cam.

I "Hi, Cam. What's up?"

"Michael? Where are you?" Her voice was shaky. She was scared.

My adrenaline immediately surged. "What is it? What's wrong?"

"I don't know. I think I—I think I need to go to the hospital."

"What happened? Where are you?"

"I'm home. Michael—it's the baby. Something's wrong. It hurts. And I'm bleeding."

I ran every red light and broke every speed limit in my dash from the mall to Cam's condo in Winter Park. She was waiting for me at the door. I swooped her into her Porsche and rocketed the three miles to Winter Park Hospital, weaving in and out of the casual suburban drivers, none of whom were in the middle of a medical crisis. Cam and I said almost nothing to each other on the way. She was too frightened and I was too focused on getting her to the emergency room as quickly as possible.

I skidded to a stop in front of the ambulance doors and helped her into the waiting room, which was filled, as usual, with various people in states of distress. A kid with a broken arm in the corner. A Latino landscaper with a gash on his forearm. A bearded guy with his head in his hand who simply looked miserable. The triage nurse wrote down Cam's information and, to my surprise and concern, immediately took her back to see a doctor, bypassing everyone in the waiting room.

A guard told me that I had to move the Porsche or it would be towed, so, while Cam was led through the examination-area doors, I dashed back to the car. I eventually found a parking spot and rushed back into the emergency room to find out where Cam had gone.

I was told that she was being examined by the doctor and that someone would come to get me when I could join her. I expressed a strongly worded opinion that this simply wasn't good enough. I wanted to join her right away. I was then told to wait in the reception area or be escorted out of the hospital by security.

So I found a seat not too far from the kid with the broken arm. He was probably ten or eleven years old. His mother sat with her hand on his uninjured arm. They smiled at me when I sat down. They regarded my black eye, probably assuming that's why I was sitting there. I wished that were the reason.

"What happened?" I asked.

"Apparently," said the mother, "jumping off the roof wasn't such a good idea after all."

I nodded. "Boys."

"Boys," she agreed.

I winked at the kid. Inside, however, I winced. I wondered if I was still a father-to-be. I wondered if Cam was still pregnant or if the bleeding meant that she had miscarried. I wondered if I would ever be sitting in an emergency room with a child who had jumped off the roof. The thought of what might be happening with Cam at that moment made my hands shake.

I turned my attention to the television blaring in the corner. It was a local news channel. It seemed that Hurricane Lorraine was still intent on visiting Central Florida. As she churned ever closer, the media frenzy had officially begun. People were swarming the Home Depots and other hardware stores all across Central Florida, buying up all the batteries, generators, and plywood on the shelves. The supermarkets were being stripped clean of bottled water and canned beans. After the last few hurricane seasons, in which a barrage of storms had pummeled the Sunshine State and residents had been forced to endure weeks without electricity, people weren't taking any chances. Three weeks without air-conditioning in Florida's humid summer was cruel and unusual.

The weather folks on television didn't help. With their Super Dopplers and on-the-scene reporters in rain slickers, they stirred up a community frenzy of barely controlled panic. That particular station already had a half-dozen reporters stationed at various East Coast beaches and the storm was still days away. Other reporters were at the hardware stores, grocery stores, county emergency-management centers, trailer parks, potential shelter locations, and any other places that might be impacted by Lorraine's landfall.

It was both informative and annoying. But, most of all, it was diverting. I needed to keep my mind off Cam's situation; otherwise, I might have charged directly into the examination area and started yanking back curtains. I let the hurricane hype wash over me. I welcomed it.

Then a nonhurricane story popped up, catching my attention. There was Nate Hungerford, with microphones shoved in his face. He was answering questions about the new downtown construction project, smiling his polished smile and gesturing with a gold-trimmed fountain pen. I leaned in closer to hear what he was saying.

"Mr. Garrity?"

It was a voice behind me. A male voice. I turned and saw an olive-skinned kid in a white lab coat. He looked like he had been up for three days straight.

"That's me," I said.

"I'm Dr. Patel," he said. I blinked at him. Doctor? He seemed so young. Weren't doctors supposed to be older? "You can come back now." He turned and started walking.

I stood and hurried after him. "How's Cam?"

"Perhaps you should ask her yourself."

CHAPTER 22

Dr. Patel pulled back the curtain. Cam was sitting up in the adjustable bed, wearing a dotted hospital gown. She looked relieved to see me. I stepped in and took her hand.

"How are you?" I asked.

"I'm okay."

"What about the bleeding—the baby?"

Cam looked up at the doctor.

"The baby's fine," Dr. Patel said. "We ran some tests, including another, more-detailed ultrasound. I thought it might be placenta previa, which is when the placenta covers the cervix—a potentially dangerous condition. Or a placental abruption, where the placenta partially separates from the uterine wall, which can be very serious. Fortunately, it wasn't either one of these conditions, which is good. It seems that the placenta, which should be higher up in the uterus"—he gestured across the top of Cam's abdomen—"is actually down here. That's lower than normal, but nothing to be too concerned about. The placenta usually corrects itself during the course of the pregnancy."

"That will cause bleeding?" I asked. "Being too low?"

"Not in and of itself," he said. "But when the baby decides to kick it for fun, it can cause bleeding."

"The baby is kicking it? Is that dangerous?"

"It's not ideal, but there really isn't too much we can do about it. As I said, the placenta should migrate higher up as the uterus expands to make room for the growing baby. When that happens, it should be out of kicking range." He looked at Cam. "Just have your OB monitor you closely. Make an appointment within the next week." Cam nodded.

"Thanks, Doc," I said. "That's good news. I can't tell you how worried I was."

Dr. Patel smiled. "You may have a future soccer star on your hands. He really gave that placenta a good whack."

I nodded. Then I looked up at him; then at Cam. "He?"

Cam beamed at me and nodded. "He."

"It's a boy?" I asked.

Dr. Patel nodded. "You're going to have a son. Congratulations."

That was legitimately momentous news. A son. It was a big enough deal to make me temporarily forget about my current legal predicament. However, predicaments have a way of inserting themselves back into our everyday lives.

When we returned to Cam's condo it was late—well after dark. We grabbed a quick bite and immediately started getting ready for bed. I was beat. Fortunately, I had some clothes stashed in a drawer in Cam's bedroom, so I could change.

I took a long, hot shower and tested the tenderness of my punched face. It was pretty sore and the bruise was at its purple peak. I consoled myself with the knowledge that it wasn't the worst I had looked.

I was dripping on the mat, attempting to towel off, when I heard the doorbell. My adrenaline immediately kicked in. I had a vision of Norman Fitchburg standing out there with his knife glinting in the moonlight.

"Don't open it!" I yelled while throwing the towel around my dripping waist and charging out of the bathroom. "Don't open the door!" I took a half step into the bedroom to grab my 9 mm.

But it was too late. Cam was already swinging the door wide open.

Much to my relief and terror, in walked Jim Dupree. He and Cam embraced. She all but disappeared in his huge arms.

"Jim," she said. "It's been too long." Cam closed the door and welcomed him into the condo.

"Too long, baby," he said. "Too long. How you been?" He saw me standing there dripping in the hallway but he didn't acknowledge me.

"I'm okay. We just got back from the hospital."

"Hospital?" Then he looked at me, his eyes narrowing, zooming in on my surgically repaired skull.

"No, nothing like that," Cam said. "Mike's fine. I just had a little scare. That's all. But I'm okay. Everything's fine."

"A little scare? What was it?"

Cam looked at me. "You didn't tell him? You didn't tell Jim?"

I cleared my throat. "We've, uh, kinda had other things going on. It didn't come up." Cam rolled her eyes.

"What didn't come up, Cam?" Jim asked. "Are you okay?"

"I'm pregnant," she said.

Jim blinked at her. Opened his mouth to say something, then closed it. He looked at me, then back at Cam.

"Well, that's wonderful," he said. "Congratulations. Really." He hugged her again and kissed her cheek. "You say everything's okay?"

"Everything's fine."

"Good. Good. If you need anything, let us know. Lydia's been through this a couple of times. She'd love to help."

"Thanks," Cam said. "I'll call her."

"We still might have some baby clothes in boxes. Lydia would know."

"Thanks. I'll take any of Nathan's old stuff."

Jim raised an eyebrow. "Nathan's stuff? You're having a boy?"

Cam smiled. "We just found out."

"Boys are great," Jim said. "They'll drive you nuts, but they're great." He sighed. "So, should I assume that this soaking-wet fool is the father?"

"I'm afraid so," she said.

Jim nodded. "You make him change diapers. You hear me? He needs his share."

"I hear you."

"Assuming I'm not on death row," I interjected. That stopped the conversation cold. Each looked at me for a moment.

"So," Cam said. "I assume this isn't a social call about the baby."

"Cam, honey," Jim said. "If I had known, I would have come a long time ago. But no. I need to talk to your boy here."

"What's he done?"

"You *don't* wanna know."

"Is it bad?" she asked.

"Bad ain't even the half of it. If it was just *bad,* that would be good. I *wish* it was just bad."

"Are you here to arrest me?" I asked.

"I'm tryin' to *help* you, you stupid son of a bitch."

Cam started toward her bedroom. "Well, I'll leave you boys alone to chat. Help yourself to anything to eat or drink, Jim."

"Thanks, baby. And congratulations again."

I chewed the inside of my cheek. "Okay," I said. "Let's *chat.*"

Jim made a disgusted face. "I ain't doin' nothin' until you put on some damn pants. Lord, man, didn't your momma teach you no shame?"

"So, how stupid are you?" Jim asked.

That was a great question. It's right up there with "How fat does this dress make me look?" Answering it just makes things worse.

"I dunno," I said. I held my hands about a foot apart, like someone describing the fish that got away. "About this much?"

"Being a smart-ass ain't gonna help you."

We were in Cam's living room, drinking diet sodas. I was, mercifully, dressed by then.

"So what *is* gonna help me?" I asked.

"Tellin' me the truth is a good place to start."

"What do you want to know?"

"Let's see . . . Where to start? How 'bout this . . . Did you really shoot somebody in front of Steven Schumacher's apartment?"

"Yeah."

Jim simply stared at me for a long beat. Then he slowly shook his head. "I don't even know what to say to you."

"Yeah." I sighed. "I take it Schumacher called the cops?"

"His girlfriend did. When she came home and found him tied to a chair."

"We didn't hurt him. We even let him pee before we taped him up."

"Uh-huh. You're a regular fuckin' Mother Teresa." Jim scratched the back of his neck. A bad sign. "Schumacher didn't even want to give a statement. Said he was sick of it all and just wanted out. But his girlfriend made him spill it."

I nodded. "Not to interrupt, but what's a girl like that doing with Schumacher?"

"No clue, bro." We both sighed, lost for a moment in the image of Schumacher's gorgeous girlfriend. Jim snapped out of his reverie first. "So, did you kill him?"

"Who? Schumacher?"

"No, dumb-ass. The big bald guy you shot."

"Oh. Him. No. He's alive and well and, at this moment, somewhere out on the mean streets of Central Florida, hunting me."

"He the one that punched up your face?"

"Yeah."

"What's his name?"

"Dunno. Goes by Norman Fitchburg. He's teamed up with the gal who set me up. She goes by Debbie Watson. I have no idea how to find them. I tried to tell Joey V about both of them but he wasn't interested."

"Where's the flash drive you took?"

"I don't have it."

"That don't answer my question. Where's the flash drive, G?"

"Elsewhere." When Jim gave me a look that portended a throw out the window, I elaborated. "I gave it to a computer expert I know. It was password protected. He's trying to crack it for me."

Jim shook his head. "C'mon, G. You know better than that. Give it to me. I'll get the nerd squad on it. They'll crack it open in no time."

"You don't understand. That flash drive is what got Jonathan Dennis killed. It can clear my name."

"That's why you need to put it in my hand. We need a chain of custody. You need to keep your damn fingers off it and stop contaminatin' its authenticity. You ain't no rookie. You know better than that."

I gritted my teeth. I loved Jim like a brother, but I was getting frustrated. "If I give it to you, you've gotta turn it over to Joey V. He's the primary. And he wants my blood. I don't trust him."

"I'll protect you, G. I got your back."

"No offense, Jim. But once it's in Joe's hands, you're outta the loop. He knows we're friends. He'll cut you out. He wants my head on a stick." I took a deep breath, trying to relax. I was getting agitated. "No. I gotta find out what's on that drive myself. I gotta know what the hell's going on before I give up control. I'm the one Joe wants to send to Starke." Starke, Florida, was the location of state penitentiary that housed death row.

Jim took a deep breath, but he didn't argue. "I hope you know what you're doin', G. I'll give you one, though. You're right about Joey V. After he heard about the little stunt at Schumacher's apartment and then at his girlfriend's house, he went on the warpath."

"That doesn't sound good."

"It *ain't* good. He talked to the district attorney and you just gave him enough for an official arrest warrant. He's probably at your apartment right now."

"Shit."

"It won't take long for him to come here knockin' on Cam's door or Becky's door. He's an asshole, but he's a good cop."

"So why aren't you arresting me?"

"I can't arrest you. I was never here." He stood and clapped his hands together once. "But I gotta go before Joey V shows up." He looked meaningfully at me. "So do you."

I got the message. "What about Jimmy Hungerford?"

"He's needs to go, too."

I walked Jim to the door. I shook his huge, granite hand before he left.

"Thanks, Jim," I said. "I really appreciate the visit. It means a lot."

"Yeah. What's one more favor between old partners?"

"Just put it on my tab."

"That's gettin' to be a big bill, bro." He gave me an extra squeeze of the hand, which all but popped my fingers from their sockets. "Congratulations on the baby. That's big. What do you Catholics say? Mazel tov?"

"Yeah. Mazel tov. Shalom, brother."

He exited the condo. Before I could close the door, he said over his shoulder, "Try not to shoot anyone else for a day or two, okay?"

"I'll do my best."

I closed the door and immediately dialed Jimmy Hungerford. He answered with a guttural grunt, as if he had been sleeping.

"Jimmy. Wake up. It's me, Mike."

"Dude." Jimmy sounded instantly awake.

"There are arrest warrants issued for both of us. The cops are probably on their way to your place now. Unless you wanna get pinched, you need to get out."

"I'm gone, dude."

"I'll call you later. Stay off the cell phone unless absolutely necessary. They can triangulate and find you."

"I know all about it, dude."

I'll bet he did. I had to keep reminding myself that Jimmy Hungerford had been a Special Forces commando.

"I'll be outta here in five minutes," I said. "I'll probably find a motel somewhere. You do the same. Stay outta sight."

"Dude, if I don't want anybody to see me, I can be the frickin' invisible man."

I didn't doubt him for a second.

CHAPTER 23

I wanted to talk to Jennifer. If I was going to be arrested, I needed to set things straight with her before it happened. The last thing I wanted was for her to learn about my incarceration on the evening news. But I didn't want to do it on the phone again. I'd be lucky if Becky even let me talk to her. Plus, I wanted to lie as low as possible for the time being. I didn't want my cell-phone usage to pop up on Joe Vincent's watch list.

I rolled out of the lumpy motel bed a little after nine in the morning, much later than I'd intended. A quick shower and change of clothes helped me feel more like a human being, although my bruised cheek was pretty horrid. I had grabbed all the clothes I had stashed at Cam's place, so I had a couple of changes. I was good for a few more days before having to buy more or find a coin laundry place.

When I checked in the night before, the desk clerk had told me that I was smart to grab a room then. I asked why and he explained that when Hurricane Lorraine finally arrived, every room in the place would be filled with coastal evacuees. That's me, I replied. Mr. Smart. I paid in cash to keep my credit-card records off the grid.

I helped myself to some complimentary burned coffee and a half-frozen cheese Danish from the motel's continental-breakfast spread. The food quality made me feel like I was back on the job. After a quick scan of the parking lot, I determined that the coast was relatively clear. I slipped into my truck and fired up the engine.

I made my way across town, sticking to neighborhood streets where possible, staying off the main roads. A few minutes later I was parked in the first spot I could find at Jennifer's public high school, an empty space at the back of the student lot. I had a momentary flashback to my youth at a Catholic high school. The kids back then dressed nothing like what I saw now on this campus. Although, to this day, a plaid skirt still gets my attention.

I had no idea where Jennifer was in that giant building filled with almost three thousand kids. Then it occurred to me: her cell phone. It was probably turned off—a school rule during class. But I thought I might get lucky with a text message. I knew from overhearing them that Jennifer and her friends often snuck text messages to one another throughout the day. Although sending a text message still exposed me to cellular-location tracking, I hoped that it would stay under Joey V's radar. I figured that it was worth the risk. I quickly texted Jennifer.

—*where r u now?*

I felt stupid abbreviating my words as Jennifer had taught me. But it really did cut down on the button pressing. There was a long pause and then my phone chirped.

—*school. duh.*

—*what room? i'm outside now.*

—*212. geometry. ugh.*

—*i'll b right up. stay there.*

—*???*

I made my way into the building and up the nearest stairs, deliberately not heeding the signs ALL VISITORS MUST CHECK IN AT THE OFFICE. I pushed through the stairwell door into the main second-floor corridor. It was deserted. Class was obviously still in session. A quick scan of the door numbers told me which way to head. I soon found room 212.

I peered through the long, narrow window in the door and saw a middle-aged woman writing on a white board. A few students were taking notes. Most were not.

A cacophonous bell erupted overhead and, like ants from a nest, kids swarmed into the hallway. Before I was swept away in the rush, I spotted Jennifer emerging from room 212, chatting with another girl.

"Jennifer!"

She turned and saw me. She gave me a quizzical look and stepped over.

"What are you doing here?" she asked.

"I need to talk to you. Can we go somewhere quiet?"

"I guess. It's the first lunch period." She looked across the hall. "Mr. DiNardo's room is empty."

"Great."

We fought our way through the crowd and slipped into the empty room. Jennifer flipped on the light. It looked to be a social studies or history room, based on the posters of famous landmarks lining the walls. I blinked at a small banner over the back wall. On it was printed, in large letters, the preamble of the Constitution. I suddenly remembered my vow to memorize it for Megan, the busty occupational therapist.

"We the people of the United States, in order to form a more perfect union, establish justice, insure domestic tranquility, provide for the common defense, promote the general welfare, and secure the blessings of liberty to ourselves and our posterity, do ordain and establish this Constitution for the United States of America."

It all came back to me as suddenly as Jennifer flipping on the lights, except that the recollection was accompanied by the *Schoolhouse Rock* soundtrack from the Saturday-morning cartoons of my youth. Maybe if I went next door to an English classroom, I'd suddenly start singing "Conjunction Junction, what's your function . . ."

I could go back and see Megan now. I'd show her some god-damn brain exercises. Hamburger hamburger hamburger. I still had it.

"Dad?"

Jennifer snapped me out of my trance. She was waiting for me to say something.

"Sorry," I said. "Listen, there's a chance that the police will arrest me after all. They think I'm involved in a serious crime, but they don't have all the information."

"Are you involved?"

"Well, I am now. But I didn't do what they think I did. I just have to convince *them* of that."

"When are you getting arrested?"

"I dunno. It could happen at any time. If it does happen, I may not be able to talk to you right away. I wanted to tell you not to worry. I wanted you know that I'm innocent. Just hang in there."

"You're scaring me."

"I'm sorry, Jen. I don't mean to scare you. Just don't worry, okay?"

"I'll try."

Great . . . *That* was effective. All that little chat did was inject a gigantic worry into Jennifer's otherwise worry-free day. At that moment, the classroom door opened and a rumpled guy with glasses and salt-and-pepper hair shuffled in.

"Oh," he said when he saw us. "Excuse me." Then: "Jennifer?"

"Hi, Mr. DiNardo," Jennifer said. "This is my dad."

A flicker of something crossed his face. He had probably seen me on the news as "a person of interest." I'm sure it was the talk of the school. I felt bad that I had affected Jennifer that way. The high school social scene was already fragile enough without having your dad accused of murder.

"Nice to meet you," DiNardo said, extending a hand.

"You too," I replied, shaking his hand. "I needed to talk to Jennifer for a minute and your room was open. We're done now."

"Sure. No problem. Anything for Jennifer." He smiled at her.

When I had turned to speak with him, I faced the white board at the front of the room for the first time since I had entered. There were some lecture notes still scribbled there, along with what I assumed was a drawing of the three branches of the federal government. However, up in the corner of the board, written in red ink in what looked like a girl's handwriting, were the words *Victor M. We love and miss you.*

"Did you have Victor Madrigas in your class?" I asked.

DiNardo blinked at me through his oversized glasses. The question was unexpected. "Yes, I did."

"Do you think you could spare a few minutes to talk about him?"

"I—I don't know. I suppose. Not now, though. I need to prep for this afternoon. Why do you want to talk about Victor?"

"His family has hired me to find out what I can. I'm a private investigator. They're just trying to understand. It's been very difficult on them."

"I can imagine. It's been difficult for all of us. Everyone liked Victor. It was just such a shock."

"Did you know him well?"

"I think so. I've been a faculty sponsor for some service projects he was working on—a car wash; a canned-food drive. I got to know him pretty well outside of class."

"Here," I said, grabbing a Post-it note from his desk. I wrote down my phone numbers. "Call me and we'll arrange a time to talk. I think it will really help his family."

He took the Post-it. "Okay."

We said good-bye and Jennifer and I exited the room. The hallway was almost deserted again. The late bell rang with an ear-splitting clang.

"Tell me about Mr. DiNardo," I asked as we walked.

"He's great. One of the good ones. I think he was really sad about Victor."

I nodded. "You're not late for lunch, are you?"

"Nah. I'll be okay."

When we were halfway to the door of the stairwell, it opened. An Orange County deputy in a green uniform pushed out. He was a little shorter than I, under six feet, but he was solid. His hair was dark brown and trimmed neatly. His torso bulged from the Kevlar vest under the uniform. The deputy eyed me closely as he approached, obviously trying to assess who I was and why my face was bruised. Then he looked at Jennifer.

"Hi, Jenny," he said. *Jenny?* Since when did people call her *that?*

"Hi, Officer Lou," she replied. Then I understood who he was: the school resource officer. He turned his gaze back to me.

"I'm sorry," he said. "Are you a teacher here?"

"No," I replied. "Just stopping by."

"Do you have a visitor pass?"

"No. Did I need one? Sorry. I'm on my way out now anyway."

"Really? I'll show you the way."

"No need. But thanks."

"It's no trouble. I insist."

Jennifer watched this exchange with growing anxiety. Officer Lou looked at her.

"Where should you be now, Jenny?" he said.

"Lunch," she replied.

"Then why don't you head down to the cafeteria. Okay?"

She looked at me for confirmation. "I'll see you later," I said as a message that it was okay for her to go.

"Okay," she said. "Bye."

Jennifer turned and headed down the stairs. Officer Lou considered me.

"How do you know Jennifer?" he asked.

"We're family," I said.

"Family . . . And you're related how?"

Officer Lou was no moron. He had put it together. I could lie and say that I was her uncle or something, but that would do little good. It was highly likely that Joe Vincent at the Orlando Police Department had notified the Orange County Sheriff's Department to be on the lookout for me. He may have even placed a special call to Officer Lou, as the resource officer at my daughter's school. This was not good.

"I'm her stepfather," I said.

Officer Lou made no reaction. "What's your name?"

"Wayne Graddo," I said. Becky's husband, the orthopedic surgeon and Jennifer's legitimate stepfather. "*Doctor* Wayne Graddo."

Officer Lou twitched an eyebrow. "Would you mind hanging out for just a minute, Dr. Graddo, before I walk you out?"

"Actually, Officer, I'm in a bit of a hurry. I can find my way out."

"I'm sorry, sir. Without a visitor pass, you have to be escorted. School rules. I just have to do one quick thing first. Please wait right here. I'll just be a minute."

He stepped across the hallway and pulled out a two-way radio. That was the point at which he would call in to his dispatcher and check the physical description on Joe Vincent's APB. He might have known Jennifer's stepfather's name and my dropping it might have put a seed of doubt in his mind. He'd need to check the bulletin's physical description to see if I matched. And, of course, I would. Wayne and I looked nothing alike.

As soon as the description was confirmed, he'd put the cuffs on me and I would soon be the newest resident in a very undesirable neighborhood: the county jail on Thirty-third Street. I couldn't prove my innocence from behind bars. I needed to get the hell out of there. But I couldn't simply bolt. Officer Lou was a lot younger than I and looked to be in far better shape. He'd catch me without even getting winded.

I made a big show of sighing in annoyance and sauntered over to lean against the wall while I waited. When I leaned, I found myself a few inches from a red fire-alarm pull station.

Pulling a fire alarm as a hoax is a crime. I knew that. But, at that point, I was already in too deep. I'd shot someone the day before. There was an active arrest warrant for me for homicide. A false-alarm prosecution was the least of my worries. So I did what anyone would do in my place.

I pulled the alarm.

CHAPTER 24

The noise was deafening, a high-pitched ringing that immediately filled the hallways with students, teachers, and staff. I threw myself into the current of bodies streaming to the stairs. Officer Lou turned toward me just as I was bolting down the stairwell. I knew he was right behind me. The stairwell was crammed with people which slowed us both down, but I had momentum and a head start on my side.

Kids were jostling and goofing on one another as we made our way down the stairs. I shoved past them, taking two and three steps at a time.

"Hey, no running during a fire drill!" some kid yelled at me, laughing with his friends.

I hit the bottom and emerged into the crowded first-floor hallway. I had to make a snap decision—charge out through the exit and risk Officer Lou overtaking me, or double back and hide in the bathroom or a broom closet or somewhere until Lou charged past and then I could slip out. I almost ducked into a nearby boys' room. That was the craftier way to play it. But time was not on my side. If I were Officer Lou and I lost the guy I was chasing, I'd immediately lock down the campus and call in the SWAT team. Schools don't mess around when it comes to security. In such a scenario, Officer Lou would probably seal the parking lots and, even if I did slip out of the bathroom, I'd never get my truck off the property. That would then make me a fugitive on foot, which has very low odds of escape. I'd be run down by younger, faster, stronger cops or spotted by the chopper that would immediately be mobilized.

No, I had only one chance. I had to get the hell out of there before that sequence of events was put in motion and take my chances out on the streets. I dashed out the school's doors to the parking lot, bumping into a group of teens taking their time exiting the building. I muscled past them and sprinted to my truck. I threw myself into the cab and jammed the key into the ignition. The engine rumbled to life and I slammed it into gear. Just as I was pulling onto the street, I spotted Officer Lou charging around the corner of the building. He had chosen another exit and was now going from the staff and visitor parking lot to the student lot. I was glad that sheer laziness had compelled me to park in the first spot I had seen, which happened to be in the student lot. It had bought me a precious few minutes.

With the enormous crowd milling around, I didn't know if Officer Lou had seen me drive off. He might have; he might not have. I was taking no chances. I needed to put as much distance between me and that high school as quickly as possible. I sped through some nearby residential neighborhoods as the sirens grew louder. Fire trucks probably. Cops, too, by now.

In my head I was mapping a route back to my roadside motel when my cell phone rang, startling me and causing me to steer wildly. I swerved back onto my side of the street and fumbled with the cell phone, pulling it up into view. I looked at the caller ID, expecting it to be Joey V. But it wasn't. It was much more intriguing. Despite my high-speed flight from justice, I decided to answer and risk the signal being traced to the nearest cell tower.

It was Skip Balinor, Cam's cousin.

"Talk to me, Skip," I said into the phone. "I need that hard drive."

"Hello, Officer," Skip said in a languid tone, drawing the words out. "Yes, you do. And so do some very interesting people."

"Tell me you got in."

"Was there ever any doubt?" he paused. "Do you have any idea what's on that drive?"

"No, Skip. No, goddammit. Why do you think I asked you?" He was just being a jerk, milking the moment for whatever glory and adulation he could get, however reluctantly offered. "What's on the drive?"

"As I said. Interesting. I'd rather not say over the phone."

"Then I'm coming to see you," I said, spinning the steering wheel hard to make a left from the right-hand lane. A Prius behind me honked.

"That's not necessary."

"Yeah. It is." I honked back at the Prius. "Don't move. Don't answer the door. Don't answer the phone. Don't do anything, Skip. You hear me? I'll be there in thirty minutes."

Thirty-three minutes later I skidded my pickup to a stop in the parking lot of Skip's apartment. I grabbed my 9 mm Glock from the glove compartment, vowing not to go anywhere without it again. I shoved it into the back of my jeans and untucked my shirt to cover the handle. I sprinted across the parking lot to Skip's ground-floor apartment. I pounded on the front door.

"Skip! Open up! It's me, Mike Garrity!" There was no response. "Skip! Open the door!"

After a seemingly interminable pause, I heard Skip's voice, a petulant, nasal whine. "You told me not to open the door." I heard him snickering.

"Open this door or I'll kick it in, I swear to Christ. Then I'll shoot you in the foot."

I finally heard a deadbolt slide and a door chain clink. The door opened a crack and I charged in, bouncing Skip back into his apartment.

"Hey!" he protested. "Ow! Watch it, ass-head. That hurt."

"Ass-head? That's new."

Cam was right. The place smelled like week-old Cheetos. It was dark, the blinds were drawn, and there were sci-fi movie posters tacked on the walls. The furniture consisted of two or three mismatched pieces picked up from garage sales and curbside discard piles. The only matching items in his decor were the consistent rips and tears in the fabric. The majority of the living room, however, was dominated by computer equipment, vast racks of hardware stacked from floor to ceiling. Monitors, printers, cables, boards, wires, plugs, peripherals, and great, unkempt stacks of CDs and DVDs. The place looked like Bill Gates's junk drawer.

Skip was indeed heavier and pimplier than the last time I had seen him. He was also desperately trying, with minimal success, to grow a scraggly black beard. His round gut stretched a black T-shirt to its shiny limit.

"Look at you," I said. "Why do you have to be such a nerd cliché?"

"Ass-head."

"Where's the hard drive?"

"Go screw yourself."

I sighed. "Look, Skip. Either you can give me the hard drive or I can take it. But, either way, I'm walkin' outta here with it."

Skip rubbed his shoulder where the door had struck him. "Don't you want to know what's on it?"

"Yes. Of course I wanna know what's on it. That's why I'm here." I waited a beat. "So?"

"How much would you charge for that information?"

"Aw, c'mon, Skip. We've been through this. I told you—I'm not paying you."

Skip shook his head. "You're not listening, Officer. Typical police. Never listen." He placed his palms together almost as if he were in prayer. "I didn't ask you how much you would *pay* for the information. I asked how much you would *charge* for it."

I shook my head slightly, trying to clear my thoughts. "What are you getting at?"

"We need to decide pretty soon."

"Why?"

"Because I'm going to have to give them a number."

"A number? What are you talking about? Who do you have to give a number to?"

Skip leaned against a counter in his kitchen. He affected a sly smile, which merely stretched his coarse, sparse beard into a disturbing rictus. "As I said, there is some interesting information on that hard drive." He reached behind himself and grabbed a CD from the kitchen counter. It was not in a case. "Here."

I took it from him. "What's this?"

"A backup. Everything on the flash drive."

"Thanks." I slipped the CD into the back pocket of my jeans. "Where's the flash drive?"

He patted his front pants pocket. "A safe place. I even reencrypted it so no one will know."

"Give it to me." I held out my hand.

"I don't think so."

"Who do you have to give a number to, Skip?"

He grinned the grotesque grimace again. "Once I cracked the security, I started reading what was stored. E-mails, mostly, but some documents, too. And I learned a lot. A lot. I can see why Jonathan Dennis saved it and encrypted it. He was good, too. But not good enough."

"Listen to me, you moron. Jonathan Dennis is *dead*. Whatever is on that hard drive got him killed. *Who do you have to give a number to?*"

"One of the most interesting things I learned while reading was the names. One name in particular. So I called him. For a small financial consideration, I would give him the drive back and forget all about it."

"Oh my God . . . You didn't . . ."

"Of course I did. You would, too. That's why you want it so badly."

"No. *No!* I want it because the cops think I cut Jonathan's throat for it. I want to know what the hell's going on so I can prove I had nothing to do with it. You dumb schmuck. Do you realize what you've just done?"

"Yes, I do. I just won the lottery. I'm thinking a million dollars. If you saw what I saw on there, you'd know that was a bargain."

"You dumb, stupid, idiot, moron . . ."

His phone rang suddenly. Skip crossed the dinette area to pick it up.

"Wait!" I said. "Just wait! Don't answer that. Let the machine get it."

Skip regarded me with bemused disgust and put his hand on the receiver. He lifted it.

"Hello?" he said cheerfully. "Hello?" Skip twisted his lips and placed the phone back in its cradle. "Must have been a wrong number."

In what seemed like slow motion, a tumbler clicked into place in my head. I blinked at Skip.

"Get down!" I barked, throwing myself on the floor. "Get down and behind the kitchen counter. Is there another way out of here?"

"Don't be ridiculous—"

"Is there another way out of here?" I repeated, with a little more urgency.

"The sliding door in the bedroom. It leads out to the pool area. Get up, Officer. You're embarrassing yoursel—"

Skip's front window exploded in a hailstorm of bullets.

CHAPTER 25

Glass rained down everywhere. Bullets tore through the apartment for what seemed like minutes, chewing up the drywall and sending plaster and wood splinters flying all over me. In reality, it might have lasted ten seconds, which is still a long damn time to be under automatic-weapon fire.

I lay on Skip's vinyl kitchen floor, my arms over my head, feeling the pieces of wood and drywall bounce all over me—my back, my legs, my arms. But, thankfully, I didn't feel the hot, piercing pain of a bullet impact. When the barrage finally stopped, I knew I had to act quickly. The shooter was probably on his way into the apartment at that very moment. I looked over and saw Skip next to me on the floor.

"Skip!" I whispered. "Skip—follow me. We gotta get out of here."

But Skip wasn't moving. Skip would never move again. A dark red puddle seeped out beneath him. His body was perforated with a half dozen or more bullet wounds.

"Aw, crap . . ." I muttered. "I'm sorry, man." I shoved my hand into the front pocket of his pants. My fingers found the pocket's contents and closed around them. I pulled out three Certs stacked in a frayed foil wrapper and the flash drive I had taken from Norman Fitchburg.

I pushed the flash drive into my pocket and bear-crawled as quickly as I could to the master bedroom. I found the sliding door

Skip had mentioned and unlocked it. I hauled it open, the door scraping noisily along the aluminum runner. Just as I leaped through the blinds, I heard the crack of Skip's front door being kicked in.

The Glock was in my hand—when had I grabbed that? I moved quickly to the pool area, where mostly young adults were scrambling for cover under towels and deck chairs. Did the shooter know I was in the apartment? I had no idea. The blinds were drawn, so he couldn't have seen me through the window. I might have arrived just early enough to slip into the apartment before the shooter made his call. But if he (they?) had been watching, I would have been spotted going in.

If they didn't know I was there, I could buy a few extra seconds while they tore the place up, looking for the flash drive. If they did know I was there, I could expect ruthless pursuit and a large-caliber shell to fill the empty place in my head where my tumor had been.

I needed to circle back around the building to reach my truck in the parking lot. I had to get the hell out of there. If the shooter—who I assumed was Norman Fitchburg—didn't ventilate me, then the numerous cops currently en route would have their chance. I had the CD in my back pocket and the flash drive in my front. All the answers to the deadly puzzle were in my pants, so to speak, but I was closer than ever to losing them all.

I slipped between Skip's apartment building and its adjoining neighbor and peeked around the corner. My truck was less than ten feet away. I saw nobody out front, but I did see what looked like Debbie's Camry double parked, with the grille pointing toward the exit. I took a deep breath and bolted, yanking open the driver's-side door to my truck and throwing myself inside.

I cranked the ignition, threw it in reverse, and squealed backward, executing a perfect J-turn, flipping the car around so that I would go forward. It was a maneuver I rarely executed while I had been a cop, but I'm glad that the training stuck with me. I floored the accelerator and caromed over the parking lot speed bumps. I knew I had only seconds. Fitchburg and Debbie had to know that their full-frontal assault would result in numerous 911 calls from all over the apartment complex. They would have to vacate the premises, too.

The shooter obviously wanted not only the flash drive, he wanted Skip dead—and dead with a message. Skip's blackmail attempt had backfired spectacularly. The assault was a message for anyone else thinking of doing the same. Plus, Skip had revealed what he knew. Whoever had ordered the hit didn't want anyone with that knowledge to remain alive.

The mirror on my driver's-side door exploded in a burst of metal and glass as a bullet vaporized it. I heard other shots ping the truck's tailgate. Before I drove out of the apartment parking lot, I glanced up at the rearview mirror and saw Norman Fitchburg's big bald head. He held a handgun and was shooting at me. I saw Debbie rush out of Skip's apartment carrying what looked like an Uzi submachine gun. The image shattered as one of Fitchburg's bullets came through the back window and destroyed the rearview mirror.

I instinctively ducked and pulled the steering wheel hard to the left, bouncing over the curb at the apartment entrance and charging out into traffic. A UPS truck swerved to miss me and the driver laid on his horn. I mashed my foot down on the pedal as hard as I could and sped off down the street.

I needed to get off the road and hide my truck. After the morning at Jennifer's school and then Skip's murder, my truck would be the hottest vehicle in the county. Cops from all jurisdictions would be looking for it. I saw a Burger King and pulled into the parking lot. There was an alcove between the drive-through lane and the restaurant itself, with a cinder-block wall meant to hide a Dumpster. But there was almost enough room for me to pull the truck completely into the alcove.

I eased into the space and stopped when my front bumper made contact with the Dumpster. The alcove was too narrow for me to open either of the doors, but, by rolling down the driver's-side window, I could slip out and hop into the truck bed.

I climbed down out of the truck bed and brushed the remaining shards of glass from my broken back window and rearview mirror off my pants. The alcove was meant to be blocked by a large chain-link-fence door that was covered in a green plastic screen. The fence was open when I pulled in. I grabbed the fence and swung it three-quarters closed. The tail end of my truck stuck out too far to close the gate completely, but it blocked the casual viewer from seeing it. Hanging overhead was a large oak tree, and its branches provided not only shade but, more important, cover from the helicopters that would soon be circling.

I wandered into the restaurant, ordered a Coke so that I wouldn't look suspicious, and glanced around for a pay phone. I had been on my cell phone way too much. Joe Vincent probably already had a printout of my day's movements, based on my cell-phone usage—texting Jennifer and talking to Skip. I hadn't exactly been lying low, as I had intended.

I wondered briefly if I should call 911 for Skip. Poor bastard. He was a jerk, but he was brilliant with computers and didn't deserve to die like that. And he was Cam's family. Her aunt and uncle were going to be devastated. What a waste. I quickly concluded that the cops had already been called to the scene by the other residents at the apartment building. You spend ten seconds shooting up a place and you should expect a call or two to the authorities. Plus, unfortunately, I had seen enough homicides in my career to know that Skip was already gone. Rushing an ambulance to the scene wasn't going to make a difference.

I found a pay phone outside the restaurant, not far from the Dumpster alcove where my truck sat. I looked in my wallet and found Jimmy Hungerford's business card. On the back was Jimmy's cell number. I dialed it and let it ring. I said a silent prayer that Jimmy would ignore my warning about not using his cell phone. Jimmy answered on the fourth ring.

"Hello?"

"Jimmy—it's Mike. Are you alone?"

"Hey, dude. Yeah. I'm alone."

"I'm in trouble. I need some help."

"Okay. Don't move. I've got your number on caller ID. I'll call you right back." He hung up. I did the same. A moment later the pay phone rang. I answered it.

"I'm on a safer line now," Jimmy said. "Tell me what you need." His whole demeanor had changed; not significantly, but enough for me to notice a sense of seriousness and professionalism poking through, even on the phone.

"I've had a couple of incidents today. I'll explain later. But I can't drive my truck and I have to stay off my cell phone. I need a ride and a safe place to hide out for a while. And a computer, if we can get one."

"Where are you now?"

"I'm at a Burger King in Lake Mary." I gave him the location.

"Okay. I'll be right there."

"Be extra careful, Jimmy. There will be cops everywhere. And somewhere out there are Debbie and Norman Fitchburg, packing at least one Uzi. Maybe more."

"Incidents, huh? Okay, go in the bathroom and lock yourself in the handicap stall. You have a weapon?"

"Yeah."

"Anybody tries to force his way into the stall, you shoot 'em. Get low and watch the feet under the door. If you don't like the shoes, shoot 'em. If they bend down to see if you're in there, shoot 'em."

"There won't be anybody left by the time you get here."

"Just you, dude. And that's the plan."

Jimmy arrived more quickly than I had expected, given traffic and being cautious to avoid attention. I saw him enter the bathroom. More accurately, I saw his shoes enter the bathroom.

"Dude. You in there?"

I unlocked the door to the handicap stall and stepped out. "Am I glad to see you."

"Anybody try to get in?"

"Just a lactose-intolerant guy who should have avoided the vanilla shake and a young dad who needed the changing table for a poopy diaper."

"Did you let 'em in?"

"No. I felt bad, but hey, I got my own problems."

"Did you shoot 'em?" Jimmy asked with a grin.

"No, but the lactose-intolerant guy all but begged me to shoot him."

Jimmy led me out of the bathroom and into the parking lot, where a silver Mercedes SL550 sat with the top down.

"Nice ride," I said, slipping into the passenger's seat of the roadster.

"My dad's car," Jimmy said as he slid behind the wheel. "One of my dad's cars." He reached behind the seat. "Here." He handed me a plastic grocery bag. Inside were a blond wig, a baseball cap, and a pair of drugstore sunglasses.

"Are you kidding?" I asked.

"Put 'em on. There are freakin' cops *everywhere*."

I plopped the wig on my head and topped it off with the baseball cap. Then I slipped on the sunglasses and slid back in my seat. Jimmy put a Sea World beach hat on his head, grinned at me, and pulled out into the street.

We scrupulously obeyed the speed limit as we drove away from the Burger King. A Lake Mary police cruiser came flying by with its lights flashing, followed quickly by two Seminole County Sherriff's cars. They were all heading to Skip's apartment complex. Jimmy put on his turn signal and we pulled safely up onto the I-4 on-ramp. We were soon heading west, away from blood and glass and shell casings. I pictured my old buddy Death zooming in from the opposite direction, maybe driving a black Corvette, on his way to pick up Skip.

Jimmy turned to me. "You ever wonder why they call this an interstate? I mean, dude, it goes from Daytona to Tampa. What other state does it go through?"

"Disney World," I offered.

"Right." He passed a blue minivan in the left lane. "So, you gonna tell me about your *incidents?*"

"Yeah." I told him about Jennifer's school and Mr. DiNardo. Then Officer Lou and the fire alarm. And my short but eventful visit to Skip's place.

"An Uzi, huh?" Skip asked.

"Yeah. Tore up everything. Including Skip."

"Sounds like Fallujah," Jimmy said.

We stayed on I-4 until we reached Sand Lake Road on the southwest side of Orange County, near the attractions. Jimmy drove west for several miles, past shopping centers, restaurants, and townhomes. We wound our way through some residential neighborhoods until we reached the gated entrance to Fieldstone West, an exclusive golf community. Jimmy drove through the "residents" gate and zoomed off. We passed perfectly manicured greens and fairways, with a few gray-headed golfers scattered around.

Jimmy turned into a cobblestone driveway that led up to a gigantic house with a red tile roof. Huge palms lined the drive. We pulled the Mercedes past the four-car garage and parked under a covered portico. I could see the golf course extending beyond the backyard, but there was plenty of lush vegetation to provide privacy.

"Uh, nice place," I muttered.

"Yeah, it'll do," Jimmy said. "So get this. One day I'm sitting in a tent, eating cold beans in a can mixed with sand. Frickin' sand got in everything. There are, like, no trees. People are shooting at me all the time, trying to seriously kill me. Bullets, RPGs, even rocks.

Every day. They hated my ass. It's like a hundred and fifty degrees. Imagine the worst place you've ever been. Then multiply it times a thousand. It's the worst goddamn place on earth. The worst. So, I finally get shot and get shipped to the hospital. It's not too bad. My leg. But I can't go back to my unit. My tour's almost up, so they send me home and within a couple of weeks I'm here, in this house, with satellite TV and an Xbox, all the food I want, a swimming pool, pizza delivery. It took me, like, two months to deal with it. It was too much. Like sensory overload or something. I had forgotten what normal was, you know? Not that this frickin' mansion is normal for most people, but you know what I mean. Not having to put on body armor to take a piss. Not worried that someone's hiding behind every garbage can with a grenade launcher. Not waiting to drive over an IED on my way to the office . . . I don't know . . . Going straight from the tent to this mansion was, like, mental whiplash." Jimmy shook his head, struggling to find the words to express what he really wanted to say. "Anyway, getting shot was the best thing that ever happened to me. Saved my life. After I left, an RPG hit one of our tents. Took out two of my buddies."

"I'm sorry."

"Yeah. I'm sorry about your cousin today."

"My ex-wife's cousin."

"Right." We got out of the car and I followed Jimmy around the back of the house. We walked across the pool deck to a small bungalow about thirty yards from the main house. Jimmy unlocked the bungalow's door.

"I stay back here sometimes," he said. "In the guesthouse. This is where I came when you told me to bug out of my apartment." We went in. I was surprised at how . . . *nice* it was. The decor was understated and stylish. I had expected Coors cans and Hawaiian Tropic posters. Instead, I got a leather couch and a teak coffee table. "You can stay as long as you need to, dude. My mom used to come back here sometimes, but, since the divorce, she isn't around much. I think she's in Europe or someplace now. Nobody comes back here now, except maybe Richie. But I can make sure he doesn't know you're here. He's the only reason I still stay here. I mean, my dad's not the easiest guy to live with—I couldn't stay in the same house. But Richie needs someone to watch out for him. I can do that from here. It's not a bad little place."

"I think it's great," I said. "I really appreciate this, Jimmy. You have no idea."

"That's cool. There's only one bedroom but you can have it."

"The couch is fine for me."

"Are you sure? I don't mind. After the army, I could sleep on a pile of rocks. I actually *have* slept on a pile of rocks."

"I'm sure. Thanks anyway."

"Okay. Oh—I almost forgot." Jimmy opened a kitchen drawer and pulled out two phones. "These are prepaid cells. I picked them up earlier today. You can't use your phone anymore. They're gonna nail you."

"I know. Good thinking." I looked around the living room and spotted the flat-screen television. "You mind if I turn on the news? I'd like to see what's going on."

"Help yourself." Jimmy handed me the remote.

I turned on the local all-news channel. One story was dominating the coverage, but it wasn't the shooting in Lake Mary. It was the sudden acceleration of Hurricane Lorraine, churning out in the Atlantic. Its projected landfall had been moved up and the Central Florida media was in full panic mode. They had begun mandatory evacuations for the coasts and were sending everyone in the trailer parks to shelters.

After maybe ten minutes of breaking storm coverage, the anchor finally turned to another story. There it was. Skip's front window, what was left of it. Yellow police tape circled the area in front of the apartment building. It looked far too much like Schumacher's apartment after Jonathan's murder.

And then there I was. My picture in a big box on the screen. My name in white letters underneath. They were saying that

I was wanted for questioning as a person of interest and that anyone with knowledge of my whereabouts should contact the authorities.

I actually did plan to call the police. But I had a couple of other calls to make first.

CHAPTER 26

"Hey, Jimmy," I said. "Can I borrow a computer?"

"You wanna look at the CD?"

"Damn right."

Jimmy sighed. "Here's the thing. I don't have one anymore. I only had a laptop, right? I carried it back and forth to work. But the cops took it when they raided the office. Now I got nothing."

"What about your dad? He has to have one somewhere in that big house."

"Yeah. Probably. We're not real, y'know, close. I'm gonna have to go over and look around. It might be in his office, which he locks when he's not home. Dude, he even locks it when he's working in there. And I know he pays the maid extra to tell him when I go in the house and what I do over there. He's got, like, trust issues. I'm gonna have to wait until I can sneak in."

"This is pretty important, Jimmy. This is worth the risk."

"Believe me, dude. If he figures out you're here, it's gonna be bad all around. He'll probably call the cops."

I rubbed a hand over my chin, where a day's growth of stubble sprouted. My cheek still hurt like hell from Fitchburg's punch. I didn't like waiting. I had all the answers sitting there on this CD, but I had no way to access them. I considered marching across the pool deck and straight into the house, going room to room until I found the computer that had to be there. But, if Jimmy was right, and I had no reason to doubt him, that would be risky. Even though Nate Hungerford probably wasn't home, if there really was a maid acting as a spy, then I'd be toast. And, if she had seen the news, she might even call 911 herself.

I considered calling Cam and asking her to bring me a computer. No. Absolutely not. If she wasn't already being watched by the cops, then Debbie and Fitchburg would be tailing her. I'd be putting her in danger and leading them straight to me. I couldn't call Jennifer, for the very same reason. What about Becky?

Yeah, right.

I'd think of something, but, for the moment, I'd wait for Jimmy to come through. Right then, however, I needed to talk to Cam and tell her about Skip. It really didn't matter if I called her on Jimmy's home line or on the prepaid cell. If Joe Vincent had been able to persuade a judge to give him a warrant to monitor Cam's calls, then they'd find me no matter what—either through directory listings for Jimmy's number or the closest cell tower for the prepaid.

But I doubted that Joey V had been able to move that fast. When I'd last left Cam, the cops hadn't revealed that they'd connected her to me—although Big Jim had said that it was only a matter of time. Joey V would need some sort of justifiable rationale for monitoring Cam's calls, and that would be tough to get.

There was, however, a record of my bringing her to the hospital. That would probably be enough to prove a current relationship and recent contact, and might convince a friendly judge to issue a surveillance warrant. Would Joe have dug that up yet? He wouldn't get it from Big Jim, but my pretty face had been all over the TV news. Me and Hurricane Lorraine, what a cute couple. Someone from the hospital might have made the call. A lot of people had seen me. Maybe a nurse. The Indian doctor. The mom with the kid who jumped off the roof.

It was too risky. I couldn't call Cam. I couldn't call anyone who would help. But then I had an idea. There was only one person I *could* call. I opened the prepaid cell phone.

"Mike? Is that really you?"

"Yeah," I said. "How you doin'?"

I heard my lawyer, Mark Lindemann, sigh. "You want the truth? Or should I lie?"

"I dunno. You're a lawyer now. Which comes more natural?"

"Hey, I think I lied more when I was with the FBI."

"The truth, then," I said.

"Shitty. Before we say anything else, let me advise you that, for the record . . ." he cleared his throat and said in a stiff, rote manner, obviously fulfilling a requirement that he wasn't especially happy with, "there is an arrest warrant issued for you and you need to turn yourself in as soon as possible to the nearest law-enforcement officer. If you want to come down to my office, I will accompany you to the police station. If you reveal your current location to me, I may be compelled to provide that information to law-enforcement authorities." He cleared his throat again and returned to his normal voice. "Anyway, you ask how I am? Not good, my friend. What the hell do you think you're doing?"

"Yeah. I know how this probably looks."

"You're going to have to pay me extra."

"Before I give you the whole story, I need a couple of favors."

"Oh, really?"

"Yeah," I said. "I don't suppose there's any way I could borrow a computer."

"Not without me learning, even indirectly, where you are. Are you prepared to turn yourself in yet?"

"Hell no."

"Then let that decide if you should ask to borrow a computer. What do you want a computer for?"

"I'll get to that in a minute. First, I need you to call my ex-wife

Cam and patch me through in a conference call. That way, the number calling her place will be yours, not mine."

Mark had been with the Bureau, so he knew what I wanted to do. By having Mark call Cam and patch me through on a conference bridge, the number that would show up on Cam's record would be Mark's. I doubted that they were listening in, but I wouldn't have been surprised if they were checking all her incoming calls. Going through Mark's office line wouldn't help the cops find me.

"Okay," he said. "Give me the number."

Since I wasn't sure if she'd be home, I gave him her cell-phone number. It rang a few times before she picked up.

"Hi, this is Cam." That was her business greeting, the one with the smile in her voice, the one she used with receptionists and nurses as she made her rounds, trying to get sixty seconds with a doctor so that she could share the wonders of the pharmaceutical products she sold.

Mark introduced himself and explained the situation. He also explained that he would be staying on the line.

"So, Michael's on the line right now?" Cam asked. The smile had disappeared from her voice.

"Hey, babe," I said.

"Where are you?" she said.

"Yeah, uh, I can't really say. Sorry. Listen—have you seen the news today?"

"The news? No. I'm in my car. I just had an appointment." She paused. "What happened." It wasn't even really a question, more an expectant statement, filled with dread.

"I'm sorry, honey. Skip's dead."

"What? Oh my God . . ."

"Yeah."

"How do you know?"

"I was there. I was talking to him when it happened. He got into the flash drive and figured out what was going on. He thought he could blackmail them, and they shot up the apartment. I'm really sorry."

"You were there? Are you okay?"

"Yeah. I'm okay. It was a close call, but, y'know . . . I just wish I could have done something else."

Cam sighed loudly. She sounded sick. "This is awful. Aunt Gwen is going to be devastated."

"I know. I'm sorry."

"You have to go to the police," she said. "This has gone too far."

"I can't yet. I haven't exactly been minding my own business. There's a warrant for my arrest. That's why I had to leave so suddenly. I need to find out what's on that drive first."

"Skip didn't tell you?"

"No. He didn't get the chance. I have the drive, which is locked, and a CD backup. But I don't have access to a computer at the moment and I can't really go someplace conspicuous to use one."

"That's why you want to borrow my computer," Mark interjected.

"Yeah. I'm sitting here holding all the answers in my hand, but I can't get at them."

"Michael," Cam said. "I'll come get you. Tell me where you are."

"No," I said. "You need to stay as far away from me as possible. In fact, I suggest that you not stay in your condo for a few days. If they connect Skip to you, they may come after you to get to me."

"You can't be serious," Cam said.

"I'm very serious. Two people are dead. I've got a murder-one charge hanging over me. This is as serious as it gets. Just do as I say, Cam. Please."

I heard another sigh. "Okay. I can call my sister, I guess. The news about Skip is probably already being spread to the rest of the family. They might want us all to be together anyway."

"Good," I said. My relief was palpable, like taking off a heavy wool coat. Cam had to stay safe. "Good. Am I still allowed to tell you I love you?"

"Allowed? If you had said it a little more often when we were married, we might actually still be married."

"I'll call you when I can."

"Be careful, Michael."

"You, too, babe."

Mark disconnected the call. "So how much danger are you really in?" he said.

"It's hard to quantify," I said. "Somewhere between a lot and a whole lot."

"All right. Tell me everything."

So I did. I filled him in on everything I had done since he and I had last spoken. He wasn't exactly happy with my actions, but it was too late to berate me now.

"So you can see . . ." I said, "why I need to find a computer. Once I know what's going on, I'll at least have a chance to clear myself."

"I could drive a laptop out to you now," Mark said. "But you'll have to tell me where you are."

"And a judge might compel you to reveal that."

"Maybe. But I'm a good lawyer. I can delay and stall with the best of them. I'll pile up a fortress of motions and briefs."

"I'm tempted. I am. But the more I think about it, the more paranoid I get. There's a decent chance that I can get my hands on a computer before tomorrow. If I don't, then I'll call you and we'll figure something out."

"Okay. Jeez. Be careful." He exhaled loudly. "Is there anything I can do for you now?"

"Yeah. Let's make one more call."

"Who do you want to call?"

"Joe Vincent."

CHAPTER 27

"Well, I suppose you can save me the trouble of telling him we talked," Mark said. "But, as your lawyer, I must advise against speaking directly to him. Let me do the talking."

"I appreciate the advice, Mark," I said. "But Joey V and I go way back. I know what to say and what not to say."

"Trust me, Mike. It's a bad idea."

"Well then, it's right up my alley. I've been making bad decisions all week."

Mark didn't laugh. "I need to save you from yourself."

"Just make the call, Mark."

He sighed in resignation. "I'll cut you off if I don't like what I'm hearing."

"Fair enough."

Mark dialed a number. I heard it ring. The line clicked as someone picked up.

"Detective Vincent."

"Hi, Detective," Mark said. "This is Mark Lindemann, Mike Garrity's attorney."

"Oh yeah?" Joe said. "Your client is in a lot of trouble, pal. You don't happen to know where he is, do you?"

"As a matter of fact, I do not. However, Mike would like to talk to you."

"I'll bet. When and where?"

"How 'bout now?" I said.

"Garrity? You on the line, too? Well, ain't this a goddamn party."

"Save it, Joe," I said. "Listen, you need to back off. I'm not the guy you want."

"Back off? What are you, a comedian? Not the guy I want . . ." Joe chuckled to himself. "Let me tell you about the guy I want and then you tell me if he sounds familiar, okay? This is a guy who is on record searching for Jonathan Dennis and was seen in the vicinity of his apartment more than once. A guy who happened to be found at Jonathan's murder scene, in the victim's room."

"Joe—" I said.

"No, wait. I ain't done. A guy who, after being questioned about the murder and released, had an argument with someone at the same crime scene, stole a computer USB drive at gunpoint, shot someone in the front yard, and somehow ended up cutting the arm of the primary witness."

"I didn't cut him. Fitchburg did."

"Shut up, Garrity. A guy who then threatened the primary witness and used duct tape to tie him to a chair in his girlfriend's house. A guy who pulled the fire alarm at a local high school so he could escape a sheriff's deputy and then drove to the apartment of someone named Skip Ballinor. Was present in Ballinor's apartment when a massive gunfight ensued, resulting in Ballinor's death. Any of this sound familiar?"

"Some of it might ring a bell."

"These are not the actions of an innocent man. You're a cop, Garrity. You're smart enough to avoid situations like that. Unless, of course, you're involved and can't avoid them."

"There's more to the story."

"It's over, Garrity. It's time to turn yourself in. Hell, I'll even come get you myself. That's the kind of guy I am."

"Yeah, you're a peach, Joe."

"Tell me where you are, Garrity."

"I can't do that. I can't do that because I don't think you're interested in the truth. You've already made up your mind that I'm involved and want to lock me up as quickly and neatly as possible. You're not interested in my explanation or, really, anything I have to say."

"The truth? The *truth*? And what exactly is the *truth*?"

"I'd love the chance to really explain it to you."

"In person. I'll come get you."

I sighed. Joey V was a lost cause. "Let me take a guess. Everybody in the department is freaking out because of the hurricane. They're all preparing for the storm and you don't have anyone to help. You just want me locked up so you can check it off your list."

"I'll spare someone for you, buddy."

"Gee, thanks."

"So, why the call, Garrity? Huh? If you aren't turning yourself in, what are we doin' here?"

"I just wanted to remind you how to work a case. Don't prejudge. Gather all the evidence. Listen to all the statements. *Then* draw a conclusion. You don't have all the evidence yet. Do yourself a favor: find Norman Fitchburg and Debbie Watson."

"Thanks for the advice, Dad. So what's on the USB drive?"

"I'll let you know as soon as I find out."

"I'm gonna find you, Garrity. And then I'm going to put you away. You can tell your story to the jury."

"I'll see you soon, Joe."

"You bet your ass you will."

I spent the night on Jimmy's couch. Considering the day I'd had, I was surprised by how soundly I slept. I rolled off the cushions, rubbed the accumulated crust from my eyes, and looked around. I felt groggy and disoriented. My muscles ached. My bruised cheek throbbed. I needed a shave and some mouthwash. I tried in vain to mash down a cowlick jutting out from the side of my head. A typical Mike Garrity morning.

Jimmy was nowhere around, so I shuffled into the adjoining

kitchen and stuck my head in the fridge. I found some orange juice and poured myself a glass. The clock read 7:22.

As I sipped, I gazed out the guesthouse window at the sparkling pool. It was bigger than your average suburban tract-home swimming hole. And it was not screened, a rarity in mosquito-filled Florida. The ice-blue water rippled in the morning sun, casting shimmering reflections on the undersides of the big palm fronds that surrounded the brick paver deck. With the big house in the background, the place looked like a luxury resort, not a private residence. It was amazing to look out at the sunshine, the gentle breeze, the cloudless sky, and know that a giant tempest was bearing down on us within the next forty-eight hours.

I thought about nothing and everything as I stood in the kitchen drinking OJ. Despite all the troubles of the last few days, I was still very aware of how lucky I was. To be standing upright, breathing and blinking, was a gift. More than a few people had thought I would be dead by then, myself included. Bob had been quite persuasive.

But there I stood, defying all the odds—so far. Even if I did get arrested, there were worse things. I was still as lucky as hell. Luckier than Jonathan Dennis. Or Skip Balinor. Or poor Victor Madrigas.

I was alive. Jennifer was safe. Cam was safe. The unborn baby was okay. Anything else I could endure. I hoped.

I thought about the different styles of the two cops in my case orbits, Boyd Bryson and Joe Vincent. Bryson was haunted by the missing 1 percent of information on the Madrigas case, that last loose end he wanted to tie up. Joey V, on the other hand, wanted me in shackles. It would take a hell of a lot more than 1 percent to keep Joe Vincent up at night.

The bungalow door opened and Jimmy burst in, a desktop computer in his arms.

"Dude," he said. "I found one. It was in one of the guest rooms. I couldn't get in my dad's office, but I found this one. It's kinda old, but it should work."

I stepped forward, took it from Jimmy's arms, and set it on the coffee table. Jimmy stepped back out through the door and quickly reappeared with a keyboard, a mouse, speakers, and various wires looped over his arms.

"Dude," he said. "Can you help with the monitor?"

I stepped outside and saw a full CRT computer-monitor sitting in a plastic Playskool wagon. I scooped it up and brought it into the bungalow.

"Nice wagon," I said.

"It's Richie's. But thanks." Jimmy closed the front door. "Do you think you can set this up by yourself?"

"Sure. You need to get changed anyway."

"Right." Jimmy checked his watch. "I don't have much time."

Jimmy disappeared into his bedroom and I began untangling computer cables. He came back into the living room a few minutes later, just as I was plugging the mouse into the back of the computer.

"How do I look?" Jimmy asked.

"Not bad," I said. And it was true. He didn't look bad. He was wearing a dark, three-button suit with a black silk tie. His hair was combed, his shoes were shined, his face was shaven—all good army habits ingrained into his psyche. But none of those features was why I said he didn't look bad. I was referring to his disguise. "Your mustache is peeling up. No, the other side."

"Thanks," he said, tapping the fake mustache back down. It's amazing what a few little touches can do to alter your appearance. A pair of glasses. Some fake teeth. An adhesive mole. A stick-on mustache and goatee. Any one addition on its own might not be enough. But, taken in the aggregate, the small changes added up to an entirely new look. "Think anyone will recognize me?"

"I doubt it. They'd have to be looking hard. Let's test the gear."

"Check."

Jimmy reached into his jacket pocket and I heard a soft click. I picked up the handheld surveillance monitor from the couch beside me and saw myself on the screen. The view was a little distorted from the fish-eye lens, but there I was, captured from the lapel pin of Jimmy's suit jacket. I waved at myself.

"I feel like Alan Funt," I said.

"Who?"

"*Candid Camera*? Never mind. Before your time." I held a headphone up to one ear. "We have picture and sound. All systems go."

"Okay," Jimmy said, picking a speck of lint from his sleeve. "You see what you can find out from the CD and I'll see what I can find out at Jonathan's funeral."

CHAPTER 28

The cops were everywhere. I saw them in the monitor, moving past Jimmy as he walked into the church. I felt like I was watching some kind of bizarre shark documentary, the image on the monitor screen grainy and slightly distorted, Jimmy acting as the underwater camera, the cops gliding by like great whites looking for blood. I felt a small pang of guilt for having sent Jimmy directly into those infested waters without a cage.

But he did have a cage, of sorts: his disguise. It was a good idea to send Jimmy to the funeral in one of his superspy disguises . . . and to keep me the hell out of there. I would have been spotted and arrested within thirty seconds of arriving in the church parking lot. Jimmy did his best to avoid the sharks, both uniform and plainclothes, but he couldn't help crossing their paths.

Fortunately, Jimmy was the right age to look like one of Jonathan's friends, so he didn't stand out from that group. And the disguise kept the cops from recognizing him. As much as I had mocked Jimmy's espionage gear, it was coming in handy now.

With one eye on the funeral, I took a deep breath and popped the CD into the computer. The disk spun up and I clicked it open. Several folders displayed and I scanned through them quickly, not opening anything yet. There were more than two hundred files stored in about a dozen folders. The folders were named by month, the earliest being just over a year ago: "August." Might as well start from the beginning, I thought, and clicked it.

I wasn't wearing the headphones, so the music from Jonathan's funeral filled the small bungalow, tinny and flat through the external speaker. The August folder contained nine documents with .doc, .txt, and .htm file extensions. I started with the earliest one.

It was an e-mail message sent from someone named Ken Billings. I recognized the name. He was an Orlando city commissioner. The message was short and I didn't really understand what it said. Something about ensuring that some paperwork was submitted. I couldn't tell what paperwork was being submitted or why. But one fact did jump out at me. I had to read it twice to make sure I wasn't seeing things. It was the name of the recipient. I blew out a sigh and sat back.

The recipient was Nate Hungerford.

Jimmy's father. The owner of the bungalow I was sitting in and the computer I was using.

The minister presiding over Jonathan's funeral started speaking: "Why? That's the natural question to ask ourselves on a day such as this. Why has Jonathan been taken from us at such a tender age, in the bloom of his youth?"

I was pondering the same question and wondering what Nate Hungerford had to do with it. I opened the next file and worked my way through the remaining August files. Then the September files. As I read, a picture started to emerge. It was a disorienting way to learn. Each e-mail message—and that's what most of the files were—offered a tiny piece of the overall puzzle. I could glean a general sense of the bigger picture only by looking at enough individual pieces and letting them connect in my mind.

I felt like one of the blind men feeling the elephant. Each new e-mail revealed an unknown feature of the animal. But, after working my way through more than half the files, the creature was starting to take shape. And an ugly beast it was.

"Jonathan was not only a friend," the minister said. "He was a son. The only son of his parents, Nancy and Carl. As the prophet

Zechariah said, 'They shall mourn for him as one mourns for an only son, and they shall grieve over him as one grieves over a first-born.' And it's a loss that God understands only too well, having watched his own son die on a cross more than two thousand years ago. But, like the Prodigal Son, God has brought Jonathan back to his home, with a loving embrace, and a welcoming feast." Someone sitting next to Jimmy sniffled and blew her nose.

I jotted down some notes, trying to organize my thoughts so that I could figure out what I understood and recognize what I still needed to learn. The paperwork mentioned in the first e-mail was a set of forms that officially registered Nate Hungerford and the Hungerford, Reilly and Osman law firm as a lobbyist in Orange County. A later e-mail even attached the forms.

The story, as best as I could figure it . . . Nate Hungerford had registered as an official lobbyist, representing the Lawrence Company in their efforts to win the construction bid for the downtown redevelopment project. Hungerford and Lawrence had a kickback arrangement with Commissioner Ken Billings and none other than the mayor of Orlando himself, Glen Jenkins. Hungerford had cut a deal with Billings and Jenkins to ensure that the Lawrence Company won the bid. Which they just had, to the tune of $110 million.

Jonathan Dennis, an IT administrator working for the city, had happened upon the scheme as revealed through e-mails sent by city accounts. Or maybe he'd gone snooping and found it; I couldn't tell. But Jonathan began saving and archiving everything related to the correspondence. Some of the messages between the parties even specifically referenced the fact that they were being deleted by the parties involved after being sent or received. But Jonathan had scooped them up as they passed through the server and put them in his electronic pocket.

Jonathan hadn't been saving e-mails in the service of the public good, however. He'd had no intention of telling the police. Jonathan had eventually revealed himself to those involved and attempted to extort them. This, as we now knew, had been a bad decision. It was the same decision that Skip had made, with the same tragic results.

Although I couldn't tell from the e-mails whom Jonathan or Skip had contacted, I had a pretty good idea. And I was pretty sure that each had contacted the same person.

The mourners at the funeral were singing by then and I heard Jimmy's out-of-tune voice joining in. "How great Thou art . . ." I turned to the monitor and watched for a moment, listening to the collection of voices. The view on the screen was the back of an overweight man's suit.

The person whom Jonathan and Skip had called would have to be someone with the resources to pay a blackmail demand. While neither Jenkins nor Billings could have been considered poor, or even middle class, their incomes were far from grotesque. I was pretty sure that they didn't have, say, a poolside bungalow next to an opulent mansion.

In other words, they weren't Nate Hungerford, Esquire.

All the e-mail correspondence radiated into and out from Nate Hungerford like a web. He was the one common player in all the conversations with Lawrence and Billings and Jenkins. Neither Lawrence nor anyone from his company had any direct contact with any elected official. Nate's fingerprints, on the other hand, were all over almost every document on the disk. That made him the most visible target for a blackmail scheme. Plus, he could afford to pay.

If Jonathan and Skip had called Nate with their blackmail demands—and, based on the e-mails, Nate was the person I'd have called . . . A gruesome conclusion occurred to me. That would mean that Nate Hungerford had ordered the hits on both Jonathan and Skip.

"Hey, Mike." It was Jimmy's whispered voice through the speaker.

I jumped, startled out of my thoughts.

"Mike—you there?" Jimmy whispered.

I grabbed the headset. "What's up?"

"Anything you want me to do? The service is about over. There won't be a burial. I think his parents are having him cremated."

"Do you see anybody you recognize?"

"I saw one of your cop friends. One of the detectives who raided the office."

"Joey V? Stay clear."

"Not him. The other dude. The tall, skinny guy."

"Gary. Stay clear of him, too. Neither one of them is stupid. They might recognize you."

"Okay. So, what do you want me to do?"

"Make one more circuit and see if you can spot Debbie or Fitchburg. If so, let me know. They're probably nowhere near the place, but you never know. If you don't see them, head back home." I took a deep breath and closed my eyes. "We need to talk."

I put the down headset and turned back to the computer screen. Boy, did we need to talk.

I sat Jimmy down on the couch and took a seat next to him in a chair. My stomach was tense and my palms were sweaty. I hated delivering bad news. I hated every moment of informing the next of kin about the death of their loved one. I especially hated delivering bad news to people I knew—something I had been practicing a lot that year.

Hi, guess what? I have a terminal brain tumor. . . .

I leaned forward and looked at Jimmy's unsure, expectant face. Sitting there, in that position, I flashed back to when Jennifer was little and Becky and I sat her down exactly like that and told her that we were getting divorced. That news had not been received very well, with both Jennifer and Becky collapsing into sobs.

"So, dude," Jimmy said. "What's with the face?" He imitated my creased brow and pursed lips.

I sighed. "I think I figured out the gist of what's going on. But

I'm afraid you won't like it." Jimmy cocked his head and I launched into it. I explained what had I found on the CD. The e-mails and the trail of evidence pointing to his father. The city commissioner and the mayor. The Lawrence Company and the $110 million downtown-reconstruction award. The very high likelihood that both Jonathan and Skip had contacted Jimmy's father to extort him. The suspicion that Nate was probably the one who had ordered the hits on both of them. Jimmy listened to all this with no expression. He looked at his knees the entire time I spoke. I paused. Tilted my head down to try to see his eyes.

"Jimmy?" I asked. "Are you okay?"

He said nothing for a moment. Finally, he looked up and said, "You don't know anything for a fact."

I nodded slowly. "That's true. I don't know anything for sure. But there's more." I took a deep breath. "How many other guys did you interview for this job besides me?"

"What? What are you talking about?"

"Just answer the question. How many other people did you interview for my job?"

Jimmy blinked at me. "None . . ." he said slowly, trying to get his head around the reason I was asking.

"None. That's kinda strange, don't you think?"

"I dunno. Maybe, maybe not."

"There are a lot of qualified PIs in town. People with a lot more experience in private investigation than me. Why didn't you talk to any of them?"

"We found you first. Dude, you have a ton of experience. We called around. Checked you out. You were the one that everyone recommended."

"Who's 'we,' Jimmy?"

"What do you mean?"

"You said *we* found you first. *We* called around. When you say *we*, you really mean your father." Jimmy opened and closed his mouth, trying to find some grounds on which to object, but he said nothing. He knew that I had spoken the truth. I continued. "Your father called my buddies at OPD. Your father found out I had cancer. Your father arranged for me to interview with you. He coached you to stress the health insurance. He told you to hire me. He set the whole thing up."

Jimmy didn't like hearing that. His face grew red. "Why would he do that? You brought the Jonathan Dennis case with you when you were hired. It doesn't make any sense."

Jimmy had a point. I wasn't sure that I had that part figured out yet. But I gave him my theory anyway: "He knew I was gonna take the job. He set it up perfectly for me. He handpicked me so he could keep tabs on the case. He didn't plan on me being so uncooperative about sharing information, but he could still keep an eye on me."

"But you brought the case with you." Jimmy sounded almost like he was pleading.

"Don't you get it? He must have sent Debbie into that cancer support group. It was a setup from the very beginning. She showed up at the group just after Jonathan disappeared. She targeted me and invited me out for coffee. Hell, she even told me I should take this job. She played me like a piano, and your dad was writing the music." Jimmy wrung his hands together in an agitated kneading motion. "It all makes sense, Jimmy. Everything leads back to your father. He wanted me to find Jonathan so Debbie and Norman could kill him and take the flash drive. They're working for your father."

"I don't know, dude." Jimmy shook his head, looking down at the floor. "I don't know."

"A hundred and ten million is a lot of money. The kind of money people kill for."

"You're talkin' about my dad, dude."

"I know. I'm sorry. I really am."

Jimmy shook his head again, "I don't know. I just don't know about this . . ." He blew out a sudden exhale and stood. "I'm gonna call him."

"No!" I grabbed his sleeve. "No—you can't. Not yet. We'll talk to him. I promise. But you can't tell him any of this. Not now. If I'm right, then he can't know that we know. It's too dangerous."

"What? You think he'd kill *me*? My own dad?"

"I don't know Jimmy. Two people are already dead. If Skip really called him like he claimed, then your dad knows that the scheme could get out. He's gonna be jumpy. He's gonna want to ensure containment."

"So what are we supposed to do? I can't just sit here on my ass and do nothing—not after what you just told me."

"I know. I'm working on an idea. I've got a few details to work out first, though."

Jimmy sat back down and looked at me, his eyes full of hurt. I didn't have the heart to tell him that I really had no idea what to do next.

CHAPTER 29

The first squall line from Hurricane Lorraine was passing over when I got into the Mercedes. Luckily, the top was up. The sudden blast of wind bent the palm trees and flapped their fronds like silk hankies. The rain pummeled the windshield. It didn't last long, five or six minutes, but it was a small teaser for the coming main attraction.

I needed to make some calls on the prepaid phone Jimmy had bought. But I didn't want to call from Jimmy's place; just in case I got traced, I didn't want to be tracked back there. My plan was to make the calls from another cell tower's zone and then speed back to Jimmy's place before the cops showed up. The storm was actually on my side. I wasn't kidding when I told Joey V of my suspicion. All law-enforcement and emergency-management personnel would be on duty, preparing for the storm and its aftermath. If you ever wanted to rob a liquor store, that would have been the time.

I drove a few miles to what I hoped would be a different cell zone and parked in a 7-Eleven lot. I suspected that my first call would be a waste of dialing, but I knew that I had to go through the motions. I called Debbie's cell phone—that was the only number she had ever given me.

As I'd expected, there was no answer. In fact, there wasn't even a number anymore. I heard the triple tones from the phone company, followed by a mechanical female-voice recording informing me that the number I had dialed was not in service. Please check the number I was calling and try again. No need, ma'am. Thanks anyway.

My second call was to another cell phone. But I knew that one was in service.

"This's Dupree." He picked up after the first ring.

"Big Jim," I said. "How ya' doing?"

"God damn you, G. Where the hell are you?"

"I can't really say. And I'd be grateful if you didn't try to find me. At least not right away."

"You realize how deep you're in it? What's the matter with you? Runnin' all over town acting like an idiot. Pullin' fire alarms. Shootouts up in Lake Mary. What happened to your brains, fool? Didn't you listen to a word I said?"

"Believe it or not, I can explain all that."

"Yeah. I bet. I stuck my neck out comin' to you the other day. I still have a career here, y'know. And this is the thanks I get? This is how you stay outta trouble?"

"Yeah. I'm sorry. But, like I said, I've got my reasons."

"So why you callin' me now? On my personal cell?"

"I need a favor."

"You gotta be kiddin' me."

"No," I said. "I really need a favor."

"Your favor is that I'll wait five minutes before giving your number to Joey V."

"Give him the number. It's a prepaid cell. He'll have to track it down. I'll be gone by the time he finds it and traces it back to the cell tower. Plus, with the hurricane coming, he won't have anyone to send out to get me anyway."

"Well. Listen to you. You got it all figured out, huh? Like some kinda criminal mastermind."

"Jim, seriously. I know what was on the hard drive. All of it. It's all gonna come out and you'll see why I've done what I've done. Assuming I don't get killed first. I just need a favor."

"What's on the drive?"

"I don't have time to go into it all now. But it's big. It's a major scandal. You have to trust me. This is me talking. I need you to trust me, Jim." I heard him breathing heavily and scratching the back of his neck. He said nothing. I took his silence as a reluctant willingness to consider my request. "The guy who was shot in Lake Mary. That was Cam's cousin. He was my computer expert. I need you to check the last three outgoing and incoming calls to his house."

"Why?"

"I can't tell you yet. Come on, man. I'm sure Joey V's already got the report from the Lake Mary cops. Just read me the numbers."

Jim again said nothing for long moment. "Okay. I'll call you back. But if you keep doin' stupid, dumb-ass things, I'm gonna kill you myself."

Jim called back a few minutes later and read me the numbers. I had my answer.

Among the last of Skip's outgoing calls was one placed to the main switchboard of the Hungerford, Reilly and Osman law firm. Two of the last received calls were from a cell phone registered to the same law firm—I presumed they were from Nate Hungerford, calling him back—and one listed only as "wireless caller." The wireless caller was Debbie or Norman Fitchburg calling from a prepaid cell phone, the call being the wrong number with no answer that Skip had picked up just before the bullets started flying. That call had been to verify that Skip was home before they opened fire.

I drove back to the pool guesthouse through another squall. I used the security-gate remote in the car to get back into the neighborhood. The rain was getting harder and the wind more intense. Lorraine was on her way.

I pulled into the driveway and parked behind a Lexus that

hadn't been there when I'd left. I dashed through the rain back to the pool house, where Jimmy sat on his couch in the dim light, holding but not drinking a can of Sprite.

"Dude," he said without looking at me.

"I talked to my friend. Skip called your father's law firm. A cell phone registered to the firm called him back. Within two hours he was dead."

Jimmy nodded. "He's home."

"Your father?"

Jimmy nodded again.

"Well," I said. "Let's go talk to him. You wanna come or should I do this alone?"

Jimmy downed his soda. "I'll come."

"You realize that if you come with me, everything will change for you. A-Plus won't ever be the same."

"I know."

"No more fancy office. No more spoon-fed cases from up-stairs."

"I said I know."

"Are you okay with that?"

He considered me for a beat. "Do you plan to stick around when this is all over?"

"I will if you'll have me."

"Then let's go, dude."

The rain had let up, so I didn't get much wetter than I already was as we walked around the pool deck and through a set of french doors that led into the gourmet kitchen. I pulled out my Glock, chambered a round, and stuck it into the back of my pants. Jimmy eyed me warily.

"Is that necessary?" he asked.

"I dunno. Hope not. Does your father keep a gun in the house?"

He shrugged. "Never seen one. But there seems to be more to my dad than I ever knew. . . ."

"I'm not taking any chances. You don't know who else could be here."

The house was quiet. Jimmy led me through the living room and into the master bedroom. The place was straight out of *Architectural Digest*. Thick carpet. Marble columns. Rich people really did live differently than the rest of us. We worked our way through the remainder of the first floor. There was no one else around. We crept back into the living room and stepped as silently as we could up the hardwood stairs to the second floor.

As I reached the top step, I heard a faint clacking noise. It was coming from a room down the hall. I put my fingers to my lips and pointed. Jimmy nodded.

"Richie's room," Jimmy whispered.

I put my hand on the Glock and brought it out. We padded slowly down the hall. Jimmy and I each took a different side of Richie's door, which was slightly ajar. Jimmy and I moved into position silently, without conferring, my cop training and his Special Forces experience clicking into sync. We each knew what to do. It was an oddly reassuring feeling.

We listened for a moment, but heard no voices, just the quiet clicking noise. The sound was random, with no discernible pattern. I gave Jimmy a questioning look and he shook his head. He didn't know what the sound was.

I put an open palm on the door and gently pushed. It creaked open. Jimmy and I peered in.

Jimmy's brother, Richie, sat in the middle of the floor, surrounded by a pile of multicolored LEGOs. As he swept his hand through them, searching for pieces, they made a soft clacking sound. Richie was working on a large yellow tower and picked out a yellow piece from the pile.

Sitting on the floor next to him was Nate Hungerford. Nate's tie was undone, his collar loose. His hair was wet and uncombed. His soaked suit jacket was heaped on the floor next to the LEGOs. A highball glass filled with an amber liquid and a couple of ice cubes sat on the floor in front of him. Nate was applying a piece to his own LEGO construction when the door opened. He didn't look up. He just kept building his project with an intense concentration.

"Hi, Jimmy," Richie said. "Hi, Mike."

"Hey, Richie," Jimmy said. He cut his eyes at me and looked back. "What're you guys doin'?"

"Building," Richie said. "I'm making a tower. Dad's making a truck."

"Is that right, Dad?" Jimmy took a half step into the room. "You building a truck?"

Nate was silent. He pressed a block into place.

"Dad?"

"That's right," Nate said, still not looking up. "A truck."

"Since when do you play with LEGOs?" Jimmy asked.

"Since now," Nate said. His speech was slightly thickened. He took a sip from his highball glass. He held up his "truck," a solid block of red bricks. "Do you like it?"

"What are you doin' home, Dad? You're never home this early. It's not even dark yet."

Nate put down the LEGOs and finally looked up. His eyes went back and forth between Jimmy and me, not quite focusing. "Hurricane. Hurricane Lorraine. They sent everyone home." He smirked and picked up his project, muttering to himself, "Hurricane Lorraine . . . took a plane from Spain . . . to bring me pain . . . in the rain . . ."

I slipped my 9 mm back into my waistband and stepped slowly into the room. "Nate. We need to talk."

"You think so?" he said, applying a red brick to the top of his "truck." He held it up and considered it for a moment. Then he pulled back his hand and flung the piece at the wall with all his might, leaving a large dent in the drywall. The object shattered and pieces bounced in all directions. Nate picked up his glass.

Richie looked up, startled and afraid. After glancing at his father, Richie immediately turned to Jimmy.

"It's okay, pal," Jimmy said. "Why don't you take a break? Go downstairs and watch TV."

"I want to keep doing LEGOs."

"I know. You can keep 'em out and come back to it in a little while. Just take a break and go downstairs. You can watch TV."

"Can I have a cookie?"

"Sure. You can have two."

"Chocolate chip?"

"Whatever you want."

Richie's face lit up and he pulled himself to his feet. He trundled out of the room and we heard his footsteps descending the stairs.

Nate snorted and downed his drink. "Can I have a cookie, too?"

"Do you know why we're here?" I asked.

"You like LEGOs?"

"This isn't funny, Dad," Jimmy said.

"No . . ." Nate said. "No, it isn't. So, how much do you know?"

"Everything that was on the flash drive," I said. "The e-mails. The documents."

"Ah. And what do you intend to do with this knowledge?"

"I'll do what I have to."

"I see . . . More blackmail. Well, get in goddamned line."

"I'm not interested in blackmail," I said.

"No? Are you sure? Blackmailing me is becoming quite popular."

"How could you, Dad?"

"How could I what? Exactly which of the many horrible things that I've done in my life are we talking about here?"

"The bribery," I said. "The e-mails. The hit on Jonathan Dennis."

Nate blinked at us for a moment and then snorted. He doubled over and made a hoarse, wheezing sound. It took me a second to realize that he was laughing. Jimmy and I weren't.

"On the long list of my sins," Nate said, coming up for air, "you actually pick the three things that I didn't even do. That's perfect."

"It's over, Nate. I have the flash drive. I read the e-mails. I know everything."

"You don't know anything!" Nate snapped, suddenly appearing sober. "It's a setup. I didn't send any of those e-mails. They're fakes."

"C'mon, Nate," I said. "Don't. It's too late for that."

"And you're supposed to be the hotshot detective. . . ."

Jimmy and I exchanged a look. I decided to play along.

"Okay," I said. "Why would someone blackmail you with fake e-mails?"

"You're standing in it. Look at this house. I'm rich. I'm the one who can afford to pay."

"Yeah, I get that. But why would you? If they're fakes, why not go to the cops?"

Nate sighed. Rubbed his face. "It's complicated."

"Simplify it for us."

"Right." Nate sighed again and looked up at the ceiling. He ran a hand along the side of his head in an unsuccessful attempt to straighten his mussed gray hair. "It's like this . . . I didn't send those e-mails. But I have a pretty good idea who did."

"Yeah? Who?"

"Carl Lawrence."

"Who?" Then it hit me. The short, balding guy who had been with Nate at his law office. "The Lawrence Company."

"My client," he said, lifting his glass in a mock salute. His voice was heavy with sarcasm. "I brokered the big development contract he just won. In the e-mail messages my extorters shared with me—messages that I did not write—I saw little expressions that he liked to use. 'Good to go' and 'outrageous opportunity.' Stuff like that."

"So you're saying Lawrence pretended to be you? Why would he do that?"

"Maybe to protect his company. In case the messages ever got out. I don't know. I haven't asked him."

"But if he hired you to represent him, why would he go behind your back and bribe city officials?"

"That's a pretty dumb question, Mike. There are a hundred and ten million reasons why he might do that. With money like that on the line, people will do all kinds of things to get an edge."

"Even murder?" Jimmy asked.

"*Especially* murder."

"Wait a minute," I said. "I don't get it. Why would this guy blackmail you if you were working for him—*and* you won the contract? Besides being a shitty thing to do, it doesn't make any sense. He wouldn't have anything to gain and everything to lose by revealing what he did. If it got out, they'd lose the contract. Why would he threaten to reveal it to squeeze money out of you?"

"You really don't get it. Lawrence isn't the one blackmailing me. Someone else got hold of those e-mails, saw my name on them, and figured I was an easy target."

"Who?"

"Well, that's the big question, isn't it? I have no idea. At first I thought it was those two psychos, since they're the only ones I've talked to. But now I think they're working for someone else."

"Two psychos—Debbie and Norman?"

"Debbie and who? No, their names were Vicky and Aaron."

"Big guy with a bald head, goatee?" I waved my hand over my head. "Woman with a bald head, too? No goatee."

"That's them," he said. "Vicky and Aaron."

"Call 'em off, Nate," I said. "It's over."

"Call them off?" He held up one hand in a half-pleading, half-aggressive gesture. His hand shook involuntarily. "I just *told* you. They don't work for me. They're the ones threatening me."

I popped the knuckles in my hands. The whole conversation had me off-balance. It wasn't at all what I'd expected. Could Nate have been telling the truth? He was a good lawyer. He could have concocted a story like that.

"If you didn't write the e-mails," I said, "why let yourself be extorted? Just go to the cops. If you're innocent, you have nothing to worry about."

"Maybe . . . Maybe I could convince them the e-mails were fakes. But then I'd have to give up Lawrence. And then the whole deal would go down the toilet."

And there it was. "So you were willing to pay a ransom on a bunch of e-mails you didn't even write, just to keep the deal."

"It's a big deal, Mike."

"So you're innocent?" Jimmy asked.

"Define innocent . . ." Nate replied.

"Did you order the hit on Jonathan Dennis?" Jimmy said.

"No. I had nothing to do with that. He was blackmailer number two. Somehow he got his hands on the same e-mails and saved them to the now-infamous flash drive. Then he disappeared. And Vicky suggested that we interview you, Detective Garrity, for the open investigator job."

"Suggested?" I asked.

"Strongly suggested. I was supposed to keep an eye on you. And then you found the kid. And then *they* found him. And eliminated the competition. I don't think the dumb bastard even knew someone else was already blackmailing me."

"What about Skip?"

"Who?" The pitch of his voice went up, as if he couldn't bear any more surprises.

"Skip Balinor," I said. "The guy who was killed in Lake Mary."

"Ah. Him. A real charmer. Blackmailer number three. Called me on the phone. Serenaded me with the fake e-mails. Eliminated for the same reason, I presume."

"So you have no idea who Debbie—I mean, Vicky and Aaron are working for?"

"None." Nate sighed. "It was supposed to be simple. I was going to pay an exorbitant sum in exchange for silence about Lawrence's bribes. But then Jonathan Dennis showed up with the flash drive and complicated things. I was forced into the scheme to recover it. The original blackmailer, whoever he is, didn't want anyone else with his leverage."

I stood over Nate, considering him. He looked older, diminished, in his wet, wrinkled suit and open collar. His power tie hung askew, signifying nothing but sadness. His hair was drying in an unruly mess and, sitting there on the floor amid the scattered LEGOs, he looked more like a dejected child than an influential lawyer. It was then that I knew his story was true. All of it. Everything came down to greed. Nate was willing to go along with the fake e-mails and the extortion if it meant that he could keep his deal. Now he knew that it was all over. There would be no payday. So he sat in a pile of plastic toys staring into a drink glass that might as well have been a sippy cup just emptied of apple juice.

"How do you contact Vicky and Aaron?" I asked.

"I have a pager number. When I want to talk, I page 'em. When they want to talk to me, they call my cell."

"Did you ever track the pager?"

"Yeah. I had another PI do it. The first one was registered to some fake name in Evansville, Indiana. I can't keep up with all the fake names." He jiggled the ice in his glass, brought it to his lips, and tilted it back, pouring out the last drop of watered-down liquor. "They keep changing phone numbers and pager numbers. I think the phones are prepaid cells."

"Page 'em now," I said.

"No use," Nate replied, putting down the glass and picking up two LEGOs. "I've tried three times in the last two hours. They haven't called back."

"When did you last talk to them?"

Nate shrugged. "Late last night? Early this morning? I don't really remember. After they killed the guy in Lake Mary."

"He was my wife's cousin."

Nate sighed. "I'm sorry."

"You know the cops already have Skip's phone records. They have him calling your office and then one of the firm's cell phones calling him back. If it weren't for the hurricane, they'd probably already be here to question you."

"Probably."

"You realize that your deal is gone."

"I realize."

"I'm going to call the cops now," I said. "It's over."

Nate was silent for a moment, staring down at the strewn LEGOs. "You know what?" he finally said. "I really do want a cookie."

At that moment Nate's cell phone rang. He made no move to answer it. After three rings, I dug into his wet suit jacket and found it. The caller ID read WIRELESS CALLER. I handed it to him.

"Answer it," I ordered.

He took it and flipped it open. "Hello? Yeah . . . A few drinks. Uh-huh . . ." He looked significantly at me. I didn't like his expression. As he spoke, he became more and more anxious. "Yeah, I think I can get in touch with him . . . Right . . . Who? No . . . Don't do that . . . No . . . Please . . . You don't need to—please . . . What? . . . Oh God . . . Yeah . . . I'll tell him . . . I said I'll tell him . . . Is this your number now? Okay. Don't do anything . . . Yeah, the money's no problem. I've got it . . . Yes. I'll tell him."

Nate sat for another thirty seconds, holding the cell phone to his ear, saying nothing. I thought he was listening, but, when I leaned down, I heard no other voice through the receiver. I pried the phone from his fingers and lifted it to my own ear. Silence. Whoever it was had disconnected.

"Was that who I think it was?" I asked.

Nate nodded. "That was Vicky. Or Debbie. Whoever . . ." He closed his eyes. "They know that it's a matter of time before it all gets out. Their leverage is gone. But they still want their money. They want the hard drive and eight hundred thousand dollars. They want *you* to bring them both to them. But they don't trust you. So they got some new leverage. They say they took your ex-wife. If you don't show, they'll kill her."

CHAPTER 30

My knees locked. I couldn't move. My throat went dry.

"Say that again . . ." I said, my voice a hoarse whisper.

"They have your ex-wife," Nate said. "They want me to get in touch with you and have you deliver the flash drive and eight hundred grand in cash. You need to do it."

"Do you have the money?"

"I do."

"When and where?"

"Tonight. I don't know where yet. They're going to call back and I'm supposed to convey to you the exact time and place."

I closed my eyes, trying to force my mind to slow down. They had traced Cam from Skip. That was exactly what I had feared. I had a horrible sense of déjà vu. I felt the same helplessness and rage that had overwhelmed me last summer when Jennifer had been kidnapped and held by a group of mob-connected thugs. I'd thought that lightning never struck the same place twice.

"If they touch her," I said, my eyes still closed. I couldn't finish the sentence out loud.

"I got your back, dude," Jimmy said.

"No cops," said Nate. "They said no cops or she's dead. I believe them. They've already killed at least two people over this."

I breathed deeply. Swallowed the lump in my throat. *Think, Garrity . . . No cops? Should I call Big Jim anyway? He'd help.* But the hurricane was blowing in. OPD couldn't arrange the proper setup or the security. There was also the chance that the minute I popped my head up, Joe Vincent would lock me up, taking me out of commission to make the exchange. Did I trust Joey V and his hurricane-depleted team to handle that and prevent Cam from being killed?

The answer was obvious. I did not.

So what other options did I have? I decided that I couldn't call Jim, even if I asked him to keep quiet and help me on a personal basis. Too risky. As he'd said, he still had a career at OPD. If I called him with something that big, he would have to tell others, probably Joey V. And I couldn't risk what Joe might do.

I would take the call when it came. I would follow instructions. I would pray that Cam would be okay. I prayed that she was okay right now. There was no telling what Debbie and Fitchburg might do.

I hated being forced to react. I felt like all I had been doing since I met Debbie was reacting. Hell, I had been reacting since my brain tumor, Bob, showed up. My life was one big reaction to adverse circumstances.

Stop feeling sorry for yourself. That won't help Cam. I needed to move from reactive to proactive. I needed to go on the offensive. But how? What did I have?

"Dude?" Jimmy asked, eyeing me. "You okay?"

I blinked at him. Jimmy. I had Jimmy. He was definitely an operational asset.

"Jimmy," I said. "Are you willing to help me?"

"Of course, dude. I got your back."

"What if it gets . . . messy?"

"I'm okay with messy. In the army, messy was my specialty."

I nodded, as much to myself as to Jimmy. "Yeah. Thanks." An idea was forming in my head. I didn't have the details yet, but at least it was something. "How much of your gear do you have here?"

"Most of it. Some surveillance stuff. Some tactical stuff. Some weapons."

"Go get it."

Jimmy nodded. Then looked at Nate, who was still sitting on the floor. Nate was idly sticking LEGOs together, listening to us.

"What about my dad?" Jimmy asked.

"Nate," I said. He didn't look up. "Nate," I repeated more loudly. He finally looked at me. "There's a strong hurricane blowing in. Richie needs you to take care of him. Don't do anything stupid, you hear me?"

"Don't worry about me," he said. "I'm just drunk. I'm not suicidal."

"When the call comes, Jimmy and I are leaving. You need to watch Richie."

"I'll take care of my son."

I looked at Jimmy to see how he felt about his father's sincerity. Not too well, judging by his anxious expression. He returned my look.

"What are you gonna do?" Jimmy asked me.

"I've got an idea. But first I have to make a couple of calls."

The first call was to my lawyer, Mark Lindemann. I pulled out the prepaid cell and found an empty bedroom—there were several—where I could speak undisturbed.

"So," Mark said, once we'd exchanged greetings. "Did you find a computer?"

"I did." I proceeded to tell him everything I had found on the flash drive as well as my conclusions. I told him about Nate and about the upcoming exchange. I told him about Debbie and Fitchburg taking Cam.

"You have to go to the cops," Mark said. "This needs a professional response."

"I agree. But I can't. The department is in lockdown by now. Nobody out on the streets, nobody allowed to leave HQ until the storm passes. You know the rules. They won't respond to a 911 call now. They're not gonna do anything about this. Even if he could, I know Joey V. He'd lock me up and try to handle this himself.

With the hurricane, he doesn't have the manpower. And, most of all, I don't trust Debbie and Fitchburg. They have Cam. They said no cops. I don't want to give them a reason to do anything we'll all regret."

"For God's sake, Mike, you can't go. If you don't get killed driving around in the storm, you could be walking right into a setup."

"I know. I need to stack the deck in my favor. I'm working on a plan."

I swallowed, took a deep breath, and told him the whole scheme.

It took a few minutes to find the number for my next call. Unfortunately, Cam's sister Wendy wasn't home. I was trying to find out anything I could about the circumstances surrounding Cam's kidnaping. When had Wendy last seen Cam? Had she seen Debbie or Fitchburg? I wanted any detail I could get, to arm myself with information so that I could formulate the best plan possible.

Then I remembered Skip's death. The family would probably be gathered together, perhaps riding out the storm in one place. They might be at Cam's aunt's house, but Cam's mother had a bigger place and that would be the more natural spot for the family to retreat to.

The phone rang a few times. Someone answered. I didn't recognize the male voice. Maybe the husband or boyfriend of one of Cam's cousins.

"Can I speak to Bev, please," I said, hoping that I could keep the panic out of my voice, in case Bev didn't yet know what had happened to her daughter.

"Just a sec," the guy said. A minute or so later, Cam's mother came on the line.

"Hello?" she said.

"Bev? This is Michael."

"Michael? My goodness. I haven't talked to you in so long.

I suppose you're calling about Skip. The whole family's here. You should come over, if the winds aren't too bad yet. Such a tragedy . . ."

"I know," I said. I had just learned two things: (1) she didn't know about my role in Skip's death and (2) she didn't yet know about Cam. "Bev, I have to ask you a few questions and I need you to give me the best answers you can. It's important."

"Of course, dear."

"When was the last time you saw Cam?"

She didn't answer for a moment. "Cam? I thought you wanted to ask about what happened to Skip. . . ."

"No, not now. I need to know exactly when you last saw Cam and where."

"I don't understand. Why do you want to know that?"

"I'm sorry, Bev. I don't have time to explain. Think about it. Please. When and where did you last see Cam?"

She hesitated again. "Well, If you want, Michael, I'll just put her on the phone. She's in the next room."

I said nothing for a few seconds. It was so different from what I'd expected that I couldn't process it.

"Michael?" Bev asked. "Are you still there?"

"Yeah . . . Did you say Cam was there with you? Right now?"

"Hold on." I heard her muffled voice call for Cam. A moment later I heard Cam's voice.

"Michael? What's the matter?"

"Cam . . ."

"What's wrong?"

"Are you okay?" I asked.

"I'm fine. Is that why you called?"

"Have you been at your mom's house for a while?"

"Most of the day. Before that I was at my sister's."

"Has anyone bothered you or . . . or approached you?"

"What, today?"

"Yeah."

"No. I just told you—I've been with my family all day. What's going on? Why are you asking me this?"

I concentrated on my breathing. I was completely off-balance.

"Just stay there," I said. "Don't leave the house."

"In case you haven't noticed, there's a category-three hurricane out there. I'm not going anywhere. Something's wrong, isn't it?"

"Yeah . . . I'm just not sure what."

"Don't do anything stupid, Michael."

"Why does everyone tell me that?"

"Because they know you. You should come over here. Before the storm gets bad. Come here and be with us."

"No . . ." I rubbed my face. "No. I gotta go. Just stay there. I love you."

I disconnected before she could really start grilling me. Why would Debbie and Fitchburg have bluffed me? It didn't make any sense. Surely they had known that I would check it out. If they didn't have Cam, then I had absolutely no incentive to show up with the flash drive and the eight hundred large. They hadn't struck me as the bluffing type.

And then it hit me. It hit me like a sucker punch to the back of the head while I was looking the other way.

It wasn't Cam they had taken. It was Becky.

CHAPTER 31

I called Becky's house. The phone rang only once.

Becky's husband answered it.

"Wayne. It's Mike."

"Mike . . ." He sounded surprised, like I was the last person he expected to be calling him.

"How are you guys doing?" I asked.

"I don't know. Have you heard from Becky?"

I closed my eyes. It was true. "No," I said.

"I'm getting worried here. She went out earlier to get some last-minute stuff for the storm. Extra batteries. A couple of DVDs to watch until we lose power. Some M&M's for the movies. But she's been gone a long time. She isn't answering her cell. I even drove up to Blockbuster but it was closed and there was no sign of her car."

"Wayne—"

"So I called the cops, but they told me there was nothing they could do until the storm passed, and besides, they couldn't look for someone who's only been missing for a few hours." I heard the anxiety in his voice. "Is that true?"

"Yeah. Listen, Wayne—"

"I'm starting to freak out here, Mike. I don't know where she is. There's a hurricane out there."

"What about Jennifer?"

"She's here. She's as worried as I am."

"I haven't seen her, Wayne." I couldn't tell him the truth. He was already freaking out, and there was no telling how he would react to the news that Becky had been kidnapped by a couple of homicidal blackmailers. If I had any hope of getting her back safely—assuming that was even possible—I needed Wayne and Jennifer to stay where they were. "I'll make a few calls to some friends in the department. I'll see what I can do."

"Thanks, Mike. Call me back, okay?"

"Yeah. As soon as I know something."

"As soon as you can."

"Right."

I cringed as I disconnected. I sensed Wayne's growing panic. He knew that something was very wrong. And, truth be told, I was not at all secure in my ability to pull off this hastily arranged rescue operation. I was worried that the whole thing would turn out badly.

Despite our antagonistic relationship, I did still love Becky. We had shared a lot of years together. We still shared Jennifer, the single best thing I've ever done in my life. I still felt a chauvinistic, spousal obligation to protect her. She was in that mess because of her relationship with me, and I needed to do everything in my power to get her out of it. If it all went bad, I couldn't even imagine having to explain it to Jennifer.

I closed the phone and left the spare bedroom. I passed Richie's room on my way downstairs and saw that no one was in there. I found him and Nate at the kitchen table, eating cookies and drinking milk. Through the kitchen window that overlooked the pool, I saw the trees bending in the wind, the rain slicing down in fat drops at a forty-five-degree angle. The pool looked like an apocalyptic naval battle in miniature, the surface erupting in watery explosions as the wind kicked up genuine waves. Hurricane Lorraine was introducing herself.

"Where's Jimmy?" I asked.

"Garage," Nate said, dunking a sugar cookie in his milk. Richie was beaming at him. It occurred to me that this might be the first time that Nate had ever interacted with Richie like that. I wondered if they had ever sat in the kitchen during a rainstorm before, dunking cookies.

I moved past them and pushed out into the garage. The light was on and I saw three vehicles parked in the four available spaces: a Lexus sedan, an Acura NSX, and a Hummer H1. The Mercedes sat under the porte cochere, which was inadequate protection from the storm. They needed to get that machine inside.

"Jimmy, you here?" I called.

"Dude." I heard him before I saw him. He popped up from behind the Hummer, where he had been securing gear. I blinked at him. He was dressed in dark, almost completely black, urban camouflage. His face was entirely obscured by black greasepaint. A black knit commando cap was on his head. He had secured various pieces of equipment to himself: a sidearm, knives, a flashlight, a radio, ammo packs, and I don't know what else. I'll tell you this, he didn't look like he was dressed up for Halloween. He was decked out for serious business and I was taken aback by the transformation. He lifted a Remington 700 sniper rifle with a long-range night-vision scope and slung it over his shoulder.

"You have what you need?" I asked him.

"Not sure. Depends on the terrain and the situation. But I'll be ready."

I nodded. "Thanks, Jimmy. I appreciate you coming along. I feel a lot better with you on my side."

"Dude." With that one word, Jimmy somehow communicated an entire range of feelings that not only acknowledged my gratitude but told me that he was totally committed. He adjusted a strap on his upper arm. "How many will there be?"

"At least two, plus the hostage, I hope. My guess is that the real blackmailer won't be there, but I don't know that for sure.

The main priority is getting the hostage out alive. That's all I care about."

"Understood."

I felt butterflies in my stomach. I always got nervous before a tactical operation, busting down a door or getting ready for a planned takedown. But what I felt then was more than nervous anticipation. It was a level of fear I wasn't used to. Jimmy saw it on my face.

"Y'know," he said. "I've done this before. Three times. The insurgents kidnap people all the time. Once we went in for a U.S. contractor and twice we went in for Iraqis who were on our payroll and important assets. These weren't Jessica Lynch deals, although I knew some of those guys. These are the kind of operations you don't see on TV."

"So how did they turn out?"

"Two successful recoveries. One unsuccessful. We lost one of the Iraqis. Fourteen dead between the three strikes. No Americans lost, although we did have three guys get wounded."

I nodded. I had no idea what to say to that. What response would be appropriate? I wasn't sure if it made me feel better or not.

"So, dude," Jimmy said. "When do you think they'll call?"

And, of course, that was the moment I heard Nate's cell phone ringing in the kitchen behind me.

The meeting was to be in an hour. The place was a public parking garage on Central Avenue downtown.

I checked the cartridges in the magazine of my Glock, chambered a round, and slipped it into the back of my jeans. I put the flash drive in my pocket. Jimmy suited me up and strapped a small .22-caliber pistol to my ankle.

"Are you ready?" I asked.

"Rock and roll, dude," he said.

We bade good-bye to Richie and Nate, who finished their

cookies and relocated to the living room, where a SpongeBob cartoon was just starting. I slipped into the driver's seat of the Hummer and Jimmy got in the back. He lay down on the seat so that no one who might be watching could see him. I put the gym bag with the eight hundred grand on the passenger seat. I had never been so close to so much money in my life.

The garage door rumbled up and we pulled out onto the driveway, where the torrential rain and howling wind assaulted us. I felt the big car lean as a gust hit us.

"Damn . . ." I muttered, saying a silent prayer that we would actually make it through the roads in one piece. Every year, some joker over on the coast refuses to evacuate during a hurricane, claiming that he'll be safe in his home. And every year those same jokers swear that they would never do it again, that it was the single most terrifying experience of their lives. And there we were, voluntarily going out into hundred-mile-an-hour winds.

Lorraine had come ashore a short time before, south of Cocoa Beach as a category-three storm, with sustained winds of 125 miles per hour. By the time it made its way across the Beachline Expressway to Orlando, the winds had dropped slightly to a category two. The readings at Orlando International Airport clocked Lorraine at 100 miles per hour. Propelled by the wind, the rain screamed out of the sky in a continual barrage.

Even in the Hummer, I didn't feel at all safe. As I pulled out of the driveway and onto the street, a ten-foot-long branch from a big magnolia tree cartwheeled past. It brushed along the side of the car with a sickening scraping noise.

"Dude," Jimmy said from the backseat. He was lying down and couldn't see the armageddon we were driving into. "What was that?"

"That was part of the tree from the neighbor's yard. Hold on. We're in for a bumpy ride."

Somehow, I made it out of the development. All the security

gates were up, the guardhouse abandoned. There were no other cars on the road. I could barely see—the wipers, even on full speed, couldn't hope to keep up with the deluge.

I remembered watching the news during a hurricane a few years earlier. The station had shown one of the cameras outside the parking lot of Universal Studios. At the height of the storm, with the camera image shaking violently from the wind buffeting the pole it was mounted to, I had seen a lone car speeding down the road. It wasn't a police vehicle or an ambulance. It was just a car. I recalled thinking, What sort of idiot goes out driving in the middle of a hurricane? Apparently the type of idiot named Mike Garrity.

I pulled slowly up onto I-4, ignoring the traffic lights, and eased into the center lane. Twin sheets of water sprayed along the sides of the Hummer as I drove. The water was coming down so fast that the roads were covered several inches deep. It couldn't drain quickly enough to prevent what had become an interstate river. I suddenly remembered my pickup truck, sitting at the Burger King in Lake Mary, the back window shot out and the driver's window rolled down from when I'd had to climb out. The cab was probably flooded.

I drove as quickly as I safely could, which was still slow. I think my top speed was maybe twenty-five miles per hour. As a bit of irony, when I approached the Thirty-third Street exit, a tremendous gust of wind kicked up and blew the Hummer over one lane, toward the exit and the looming prison beyond. I slammed on the brakes and the truck hydroplaned. I skidded across the far lane and onto the shoulder, the truck buzzing over the ridged safety bumps.

I'm not ready for prison yet, I thought, and regained control of the truck. I steered back out onto the interstate and continued heading northeast, toward downtown. As I drove, I tried to process the story that Nate had told. If his whole story was true, that meant the original blackmailer was still out there somewhere. But who was it? An ambitious staffer of the commissioner, perhaps, or some low-level assistant at the Lawrence Company.

I finally made it to the Anderson Street exit, which led me down off the highway. The old oak trees shook like twigs and the rain swirled in howling curtains between the tall downtown buildings. I saw the glass windows of one building buckling in and out with the wind and low pressure. It was a terrifying sight, made even more disturbing by the familiarity of the setting. I had driven those streets thousands of times. I knew every sidewalk crack and manhole cover. Yet I had never seen anything like that. It was like seeing a trusted old friend suddenly erupt into a fit of uncontrolled rage: the familiar cast in a grotesque and frightening role.

I saw a tree leaning and knew that it was going to topple. It was a live oak, one of many downtown, and had to be at least a hundred years old. Its thick, gnarled trunk tilted at an unnatural angle, the roots on one side popping up through the unstable mud. When Hurricane Charley had torn through Orlando a few years earlier, it was shocking to see the devastating loss of trees. Southwestern Florida had rightly received the majority of the attention in Charley's aftermath, since the destruction in Lee County and its neighbors was devastating. But Charley had cut a swath of destruction right up the center of the state, pummeling sections of Orlando with winds in excess of 100 miles per hour, hopping onto I-4 and cruising right up the road to Daytona Beach, where it retained its hurricane status and exited as a category-one storm. The tree I now saw leaning over Magnolia Avenue had survived that storm, as well as Frances and Jeanne. It seemed unfair to knock it over now, after all that struggle.

But, if there's one thing you learn as a cop—and a cancer patient—it's that Death is a tricky guy to predict. Sometimes he just sneaks up on you and punches you in the mouth with no good reason and with no warning. I stood on the Hummer's brakes, fishtailing the big machine to a skidding stop in the center of the road.

"Dude?!" Jimmy called from his prone position in the backseat.

Then, with an earsplitting crack, the oak tree ripped from its moorings and crashed down onto the road, sending a swirling maelstrom of leaves and snapped branches into the raging sky. Mud splashed across the Hummer's windshield and then was immediately obliterated by the driving rain.

"Jimmy," I said, looking at the spot where we would have been flattened had I not slammed on the brakes. "Are you sure you want to get out early?"

"We don't want them to see me slip out in the garage. They'll probably be watching. And we don't want to take a chance that they'll search your vehicle. I can't stay hiding here. Just let me know when we're two or three blocks away."

"We're almost there now."

I spun the wheel and bounced up onto the sidewalk, cutting across a corner near a closed coffee shop to avoid the downed tree. I pulled up next to an alley, hoping that it would not only provide Jimmy some cover but keep him from being blown to Miami.

Jimmy looked at me with a startling intensity, grabbed the sleeve of my shirt, and said, "Give 'em what they want. Keep 'em talking. The hostage is the objective. Nothing else matters. Don't stay a second longer than necessary. Don't be stupid. Don't be a hero."

Now I even had Jimmy telling me not to be stupid. I nodded. "Jesus, be careful. It's really bad out there."

Jimmy gave me a small grin, a mischievous smirk that, combined with his wild eyes and blackened face, gave me the distinct impression that he was in his natural element. He gripped the Remington, popped the lock on the back door, kicked it open, and leaped out into the alley. I soon saw him disappear into the swirling rain.

I turned back to the road, navigated the Hummer two more blocks, and arrived at the entrance to the parking garage that Debbie had specified. All the gate arms were up and, naturally, the attendant's booth was deserted. I pulled into the garage and headed up. I circled my ascent for three floors, as directed, and stopped. Then I saw them.

They were standing there waiting for me.

CHAPTER 32

I shut off the engine, left the key in the ignition, grabbed the gym bag, and got out of the Hummer. Debbie and Fitchburg stood like sentinels in front of Fitchburg's Impala, the wind whipping through the garage, blowing rain and mist across the empty parking spaces. They had to adjust their stances as the wind rocked them sideways. They were both wearing jeans and dark sweatshirts.

Somewhat reassured by the pressure of the Glock against my back, I strode over to within maybe ten feet of them.

"Nice weather we're having," Debbie called, shouting over the howling gale.

"We *are* the sunshine state," I called back. "Where's Becky?"

"Show me your gun."

"What makes you think I have a gun?"

She deadpanned a look at me. "Slide it over."

I reached behind me and grabbed the Glock. So much for the reassuring pressure. I put it down and kicked it across the wet cement. Fitchburg then kicked it off to the side, where it came to rest against one of the half walls that ran the perimeter of each floor of the garage.

"Is that my money?" She nodded at the gym bag.

"All eight hundred."

Debbie gave Fitchburg a look. He stepped over and snatched the bag. He took it back, unzipped it, and pawed through the neat bundles of cash.

"No paint bomb," Fitchburg said. "Just a lot of cash." He pulled a brown plastic trash bag from his pocket and dumped the contents of the gym bag into it. Then he flung the gym bag aside. "That should take care of the GPS."

"No GPS," I said. "I just want my wife. You have your money. Where is she?"

"One more thing," Debbie said. "The computer drive."

"It doesn't matter anymore, y'know," I said. "Skip cracked the security. He made a backup. The contents are out. Nate Hungerford is through. You won't be able to extort any more money from it."

"Is that why you think we want it?" Debbie said. She and Fitchburg exchanged amused looks. "What did I tell you at the mall? I'm a professional. I was hired to obtain that flash drive and I *will* have it in my hands. I don't give a shit what's on it or why. Could be pictures of the governor wearing panty hose in bed with a goat. I don't care. Nothing on that drive has anything to do with us. But we're being paid for a job and we will complete that job. We have a reputation to maintain."

"You didn't need to shoot Skip."

She offered a half shrug. "Judgment call. We were getting frustrated. Plus, we hadn't shot up someone's place in a long while. That was fun."

Fitchburg walked over and held out a hand. I wanted to kick him in the balls, but I restrained myself. Instead, I reached into my front pocket and pulled out the flash drive. I handed it to him.

"It still has the password," I said.

Fitchburg held it out for Debbie, staying where he was. He couldn't toss it to her—the wind was just too fierce. So she stepped over, took it from his outstretched fingers, and brought it close.

"This looks like the real thing, Mike," she said.

"It is the real thing. I want to know where Becky is."

"You didn't switch it for a decoy? Try to pull a fast one?"

"No. Like I said, the info's out. It doesn't matter anymore. Just hand over my wife and I'll forget I ever saw you."

"Forget me?" Debbie placed the flash drive on the floor and crushed it with her boot heel. "After all we shared? I don't believe that."

Fitchburg was watching her. As soon as the flash drive had been pulverized, he turned to me with a malevolent grin.

"I've been waiting a long time to do this," he said. I saw a metallic glint in his hand. Uh-oh. I took a half step backward. But it wasn't far enough. Fitchburg lunged at me savagely, driving his knife blade directly into my stomach.

I went down, the air completely gone from my lungs. I couldn't speak. I couldn't move.

"What the hell?" Fitchburg said. He flexed his wrist, looking at his knife. The blade was clean. The blow hadn't felt right. He'd likely had a lot of experience stabbing people and knew that something was wrong. "You're wearing a vest. You son of a bitch. A vest." He raised the knife. "You don't have a vest on your neck, though."

Fitchburg brought the knife down toward my throat. His forehead suddenly burst open in a spray of flesh, blood, and bone. He toppled backward, the knife flopping out onto the wet concrete.

Jimmy.

I had recovered enough to immediately roll out of the line of fire. Then I fumbled for the .22 pistol strapped to my ankle. I didn't see Debbie. As soon as Fitchburg went down, she must have sprinted for the Impala, the stairwell, or up the garage incline to the next floor. I held the pistol out in front of me, looking for her.

The Kevlar vest had saved my life. Without it, Fitchburg's blow would have punched a hole through my gut and out the other side. Thank God for Jimmy and all his kick-ass new gear.

"Debbie!" I called. The garbage bag containing the money was gone. The Impala was still there. "Debbie!" There was no response. I crawled along the low concrete wall, taking care not to pop my head up. A four-foot piece of sheet metal careened into the garage through the open sides, rumbling like thunder, and eventually lodged itself against an interior wall.

Through the wind and rain I head footsteps running, getting louder. I raised the .22 and whirled around, ready to squeeze the trigger.

It was Jimmy. He looked like he had fallen into a swimming pool. The Remington was in his hands, presumably the weapon that had just scrambled Norman Fitchburg's brain.

"She's getting away," Jimmy shouted. "She went down the exit stairs. I saw another car on the first level. I thought it was just left there, but it was probably hers."

"What kind of car?"

"Toyota. Camry, I think."

It was probably Debbie's. Her insurance policy in case things went bad.

"What about Becky?" I asked.

Jimmy shook his head. "No sign. I looked in the car. Even pounded on the trunk and bounced the shocks. There was nobody in there. I looked in the stairwells on the first two floors and didn't find anyone. I didn't have time to do more. I had to get into position. Good thing, too . . ."

We both instinctively looked over at Fitchburg's prone form. The blood from his perforated head mixed with the rain into a dark, shiny puddle under his body.

"Check the Impala," I said. "Don't touch the body. Bag the knife. I'm going after her."

As Jimmy moved to the Impala, I put the .22. back in its holster and raced to the Hummer. I revved the big engine and slammed it into gear. I saw Jimmy shake his head over the Impala's opened trunk. Becky wasn't in there.

I spun the SUV's tires and nearly skidded into a concrete barrier as I careened down the floors of the empty parking garage. The Hummer thudded over the speed bump at the open gate and shot out into the raging maelstrom.

There was a flash of green to my left and I caught a glimpse of Debbie's Camry speeding down the street in the rain. I stomped on the brakes and jerked the wheel hard to the left. The big Hummer's back end switched places with the front end and I mashed my foot on the accelerator.

Keeping my eyes on the blur of green racing away from me in the torrent, I couldn't help but notice the flashing blue light in my rearview mirror.

CHAPTER 33

The light behind me was mounted on the roof of a black Suburban and was closing the gap between us. I heard the piercing whine of the police siren through the steady thrum of rain assaulting the Hummer. The idea of pulling over in the middle of a hurricane to show my license and registration was ludicrous. So, instead, I pressed harder on the gas.

The Hummer surged forward. I was traveling dangerously fast in my attempt to catch Debbie. I was going too fast for downtown driving under normal conditions. Going that fast in a screaming hurricane was suicidal. I knew that I had very little actual control of the three-ton machine I was driving. My breathing was rapid, my knuckles were white on the wheel, and my senses were infused with adrenaline.

The Camry made a hard right and I followed, sending a spray of water higher than the Hummer's roof cascading onto the sidewalk. We were all over the road. Yellow lines, speed-limit signs, and traffic signals were all meaningless. I chanced a half-second glance into the mirror and saw the Suburban keeping pace.

But I was gaining on Debbie. I saw the Camry more clearly through the driving rain. The Toyota couldn't handle the almost 100-mile-per-hour winds and deep water like the bigger vehicles. Debbie swerved again, fishtailing around another corner. I cut a sharper angle, bumping up over the curb and across an empty sidewalk. The move bought me some more distance. I was maybe a car length or so behind her.

A powerful gust swept through two decent-size buildings, creating a maniacal swirl of wind and water that caught the Camry and buffeted it sideways several feet. I felt the wind smack the Hummer but was able to maintain control of the truck. I fixed my grip on the wheel and plowed into the Camry's rear bumper.

The smaller car danced wildly across the road, water spraying up in twin jets from the wheels. It spun more than 180 degrees, so that it was facing sideways across the road, not far from an on-ramp to I-4.

I stomped on the brakes and skidded the Hummer to stop a few feet away. As I reached for the .22 pistol strapped to my ankle, I felt my body jolt violently sideways. I pulled myself up from the floor of the passenger seat and saw that the Suburban had been unable to stop in time and had clipped the back corner of the Hummer.

I looked out the windshield. Through the rain I saw the Camry's brake lights go dark. Debbie must have taken her foot off the brake. The siren whooped once loudly to get my attention.

"Everybody out and keep your hands where I can see 'em!" came an amplified male voice from the Suburban.

Debbie was going to run. I slid back into the driver's seat to chase her if she did. There was a loud tapping on the driver's window next to my head. I turned my head and had a close-up view of the barrel of a semiautomatic pistol.

"Out of the car!" shouted the man holding the weapon.

"She's gonna run!" I shouted back over the howling wind.

"You got three seconds!" the man said. "One—two—"

"Goddammit!" I yelled and shoved open the door. The man grabbed me by the collar and shoved me face-first to the flooded asphalt. As I went down I saw the Camry's tires spin and the car lurch forward. "She's getting away!"

Then a second man was standing over me. I couldn't get a good look at either of them.

"Are you Garrity?" the second man said. He had a very slight Spanish accent.

"Yeah. You have to go after her. She has all the money."

"Hungerford's money?"

"Yeah. Eight hundred grand."

"He's wearing a piece," the first guy said, and I felt his hands on my ankle.

"Let me keep it. I'm gonna—" And then it hit me. I suddenly knew where Becky was and who was behind the original blackmail scheme. Lying there between the two SUVs, my face pressed into the flooded road, being soaked by a category-three hurricane, it all fell into place. I guess I had just needed the right conditions.

The two guys hoisted me to my feet and I finally got a decent look at them. They were both in their midthirties. One was Caucasian with blond hair and the other looked Hispanic. Each held a semiautomatic pistol in his hands. Both were wearing tactical clothes, including dark blue Kevlar vests with FBI emblazoned on them. We were all being drenched and pummeled by the rain and wind.

"Listen," I said. "One of you has to go after her. The other one needs to come with me. I know where they're holding my ex-wife. I'll take you."

"Are you nuts?" the blond guy said. "This is insane. We need to get inside."

"She's getting away!" I shouted.

"Okay," the Hispanic guy said. "I'll go with him. You chase the car."

"Come on, Ruiz—" the blond guy protested.

"Go. Now!"

"There's also a buddy of mine babysitting a dead body on the third floor of the parking garage," I said. "You may wanna call that in."

I jumped back into the Hummer, my sodden clothes squelching as I settled into the seat.

"So," the Hispanic guy said. "How do you know Mark Linde-mann?"

"Name's Ruiz," the agent said, sitting in the passenger's seat. I drove crazily down the center of a downtown street as the mael-strom raged all around us. The top half of a palm tree sailed across our path. "Dead body, eh? You okay?"

"Thanks for coming out, but you were a few minutes late," I said.

"We had a little rain on the way over."

Rain pounded us like BBs and the wind rocked the huge truck. The tall downtown buildings channeled the gusts like canyons and created intense, raging currents of wind and water that swirled up streets and around corners. With so much water pouring out of the sky, you could literally see the wind.

"Sweet Jesus," Ruiz said. "This is insane."

"You get the warrant?"

"It's in the Suburban." Ruiz braced himself on the Hummer's dash as we thumped over a curb. "The judge thought we were crazy, too."

Before leaving Nate's house, I had called Mark Lindemann and told him the whole story. I knew I couldn't call the Orlando Police Department—both because of my own sticky situation and be-cause they would be locked down for the hurricane. But I hadn't wanted to go into the meeting with Debbie and Fitchburg without some backup. And I wanted them brought to justice. Not only would it clear me, but they both deserved a long time in a small cell. Of course, Jimmy had given Fitchburg what he really de-served.

Mark still had a lot of friends in the Bureau. He called a couple who he felt might get a kick out of the situation, with the raging storm just adding to the appeal. The possible political-corruption angle and unavailability of the local cops was just rationale enough for the feds to step in. The agents were able to get in touch with a friendly judge with a home fax machine to sign a warrant for the electronic recording, so that it could be used in court later. Mark had also arranged for Jimmy and me to be listed as volunteer associates cooperating with the FBI.

"You get anything good?" Ruiz asked.

"I think so." I reached behind me and pulled out the digital recorder clipped to my belt, unhooking it from the wires that snaked up my shirt and under the Kevlar vest. Before leaving Nate's house, Jimmy had outfitted me in protective gear and wired me up to record both audio and video. I handed the recorder to Ruiz.

"Where we going?" he asked.

"Not far." I navigated the Hummer through the streets, avoiding a significant number of downed trees, the wind pushing and shaking the big truck like a Tonka toy.

Becky . . . I hoped I was right about where she was being held. Debbie and Fitchburg obviously had someplace safe to stay. At first I thought it might be a hotel room. But they probably wanted to avoid being seen, and every room in Orlando was by then filled with coastal evacuees. Debbie and Fitchburg had probably lost whatever room they had been renting. No, the answer was a lot simpler.

I skidded the Hummer to a stop.

"This it?" Ruiz asked.

"Yeah."

I cranked the wheel and pulled into the empty driveway of the rental house that Debbie had shared with Norman Fitchburg.

CHAPTER 34

We sprinted through the stinging rain to the front door. It was locked, but between the two of us we were able to kick it open.

We moved carefully into the house, Ruiz going first, his weapon drawn. Fortunately, Ruiz and his partner had let me keep the .22. I now held the weapon in my hand. Ruiz signaled for me to move along the right side of the home and he would go left. We were conducting a textbook sweep, being cautious in case Debbie or any other "associates" were in residence.

All my old cop instincts kicked in. Heightened senses. Hyper-awareness. Weapon raised. After seventeen years on the job, being armed becomes part of your professional identity. It felt natural, an extension of my body, like a doctor with his stethoscope.

I prayed silently that Becky was okay. She had to be. It wouldn't have made any sense to kill her. Debbie couldn't have known what would happen in the parking garage. Killing Becky early would have eliminated their leverage. But I also needed to add into the equation the fact that they were unpredictable murderers. As soon as he had gotten what he wanted from me, Fitchburg had immediately tried to filet me like a red snapper. There was no telling what they would do. Becky's safety depended on the professionalism that Debbie wore as a badge of honor. There was no business case for killing Becky. Unless, like shooting up Skip's place, it would simply be "fun."

While Ruiz worked his way into the kitchen side of the house,

I peeked into the second bedroom. It was empty, as sparse as it had been the last time I had been there. The wind howled angrily outside. The shady oaks rocked back and forth like feather dusters, shaking leaves and branches loose into the gale.

I moved into the tiny hallway, the hardwood floor creaking beneath my feet. I turned the knob of the master bedroom and pushed the door open. My heart stopped.

It was Becky. Her hands and feet were tied together with multiple wraps of silver duct tape. She was on the floor, strapped to the foot of a heavy mahogany bed frame. Pieces of tape covered her eyes and her mouth. The bed was slightly askew where she had tried to drag it in what had probably been a failed escape attempt. And she wasn't moving.

"Becky—" I said. And her head turned toward me. She grunted something. I rushed to her. "Don't move. It's me, Mike. This might hurt a little." I got a grip on a corner of the tape covering her mouth and pulled. It was really stuck. I did the best I could to remove it gently, but I know it must have hurt like hell.

"Mike—" she said, starting to cry.

I smelled urine. She must have been left like that for hours, forced to relieve herself where she sat, fully clothed, strapped to the leg of a bedpost. It made me furious, and I was all the more satisfied with Fitchburg's fate. But Debbie was still out there.

"Shhh," I said. "Listen to me, Becky. Is there anyone else in the house?"

"Yes—"

There was a noise behind me. I whipped around, gun raised, finger tightening on the trigger.

"It's me," Ruiz said. He stood in the doorway and lowered his gun.

"There's someone else in the house," I said. And I knew who it was. It all clicked into place. Someone who had the same access to the city's e-mail servers as Jonathan Dennis had. Someone, in fact, who had better access. Someone who knew everything there was to know about the mayor's IT security. "He's about my height. Has a little soul patch on his chin. His name's Ed O'Malley, but he prefers Edward."

"Is he armed?" Ruiz asked.

We both looked at Becky. But, before she could respond, there were two loud, unmistakable cracks. Ruiz jerked sideways and hit the floor. I threw myself in front of Becky and raised the .22.

"More than one?" I asked.

"No," Becky said, her voice breathy and terrified. "I've only seen one."

I waited for a moment, weapon held in front of me, shielding Becky with my body. But no one appeared in the open bedroom doorway, so I inched forward and reached for Ruiz. He wasn't moving. I found his neck and felt around for a pulse. Blood was seeping out under him. There—I found the pulse. He was still alive. I couldn't tell where he had been hit. The vest would have protected his vital organs, but his head was exposed. I didn't know where the blood was coming from.

"It's over, O'Malley!" I called. "Put the gun down!"

I crawled to the doorway, trying not to step on Ruiz's legs. I peeked out for a half second but couldn't see anything. Then, with a loud pop, all the power in the house went out. Everyone expected to lose power at some point during the hurricane, but the timing couldn't have been much worse for me. The entire structure was drenched in shadow.

"Is that you, Garrity?" O'Malley's voice carried through the darkened home.

"Yeah. Your hired muscle has abandoned you. Debbie took off with Hungerford's eight hundred grand."

"She'll take her cut and deliver the rest."

"Right. She's gone, brother. And Fitchburg's dead. You just shot an FBI agent. Put down the gun before this gets any worse."

"In case you haven't noticed, there's a hurricane out there. Now that I know the money's been delivered, all I have to do is cap you and your wife, douse the place in gasoline, and light it up. My car is hidden out back. It'll be hours, maybe days, before the cops can get here."

I figured that my best strategy was to keep him talking. If he was talking, he wasn't shooting, and that would buy me some time to think of something.

"So, let me guess," I said. "An ambitious guy like you, sitting at your desk in City Hall, you see the e-mails coming in about the redevelopment and figured your ship has come in." There was no answer. "O'Malley? You still out there?"

"Where else would I be?"

The tone of his voice was a little different: the resonance had changed. He had probably moved position out there in the darkened house.

"So why not go after Jonathan yourself?" I called. "If he was moving in on your action, you had access to a lot more information about him that I did."

"I was his boss. I couldn't go chasing him down. I needed some distance."

"So why not send Debbie and Norman?"

"They're not hunters, like you. They're grifters. They're professional scammers. I mean, she not only shaved her head, she shaved her *eyebrows*. Damn."

"You're not so bad yourself, you know. I really thought you didn't want to help me when I came to see you."

"I couldn't have you suspect me. But I made sure you had the information you needed."

I inched forward some more, staying low to the floor, peeking around the doorjamb into the hallway. It was too dark to see anything but large, black shapes that were probably pieces of living-room furniture. I saw no movement. I adjusted my grip on the .22.

Crack! The wood of the doorjamb just over my head splintered and I jerked back into the room. He had seen some movement when I peeked out but it was too dark to get a proper bead on me. I still had no idea where he was

I slithered over and pulled a Beretta 9 mm from Ruiz's motionless hand. A much more powerful weapon than the .22. I would need all the help I could get. Blood was pooled on the hardwood floor under Ruiz. He needed medical attention soon or he was a dead man.

I checked the Beretta and made sure that a round was chambered. I heard a floorboard creak in the hallway. I pushed myself against the wall next to the open doorway. If he poked his head in, I'd have a clean shot.

There was suddenly another loud crack and a chunk of the plaster wall about six inches from my head exploded. The bastard had pressed his weapon against the other side of the wall and indiscriminately fired. He'd almost gotten lucky. The bullet lodged in the opposite wall not far from Becky. Her nostrils were flared in terror, her eyes still obscured by duct tape.

I hit the floor and began crawling back toward the doorway. Another piece of plaster burst from the wall, lower and closer to my new position. The bullet thunked into the night table, even closer to Becky. It was a large-caliber shell, judging from the damage to the wall. He was going to hit one of us if he kept it up.

I pressed the Beretta against the wall at about waist height, where I though he might be if he was still moving toward the doorway. I pulled the trigger. The gunshot was deafening and the gun kicked back in my hand. I heard a scuffling in the hallway as O'Malley reacted to the bullet.

That was my chance. I threw myself out into the hallway, gun raised, and squeezed off four or five shots before I slammed into the opposite wall. I just aimed into the inky-black shadow, hoping to get lucky or drive him out into a pool of dull gray light.

I hit the floor and saw a muzzle flash erupt from the shadow and felt a bullet impact the wall less than an inch from my ear. I pumped three more shots at the spot of the flash and heard a body thump against the wall. It was a sound I had heard before in my career. I leaped up and covered the six or eight feet of hallway, weapon raised and ready to fire.

I finally saw him, partially illuminated by a battery-powered blue night-light in the living room, around the corner. He was on the floor, slumped against the wall. I had hit him twice, once in the leg and once in the neck. The neck wound would be fatal. Blood pumped out of his severed artery and soaked his clothes.

I kicked the pistol from his hand and knelt down. His eyes were open. He looked at me and opened his mouth. His lips moved but no sound came from them. Blood, tinted black in the colored night-light, bubbled from his mouth and down the corner of his chin, soaking his ridiculous soul patch. He blinked once, looking at me with expressionless eyes. Then he gagged, wheezed a weak inhale, and exhaled a long, gurgling breath. His eyes dilated and his head lolled to the side.

There were no last words, no pithy comments, no more revelations. This wasn't the movies. His was a messy, awful death. A death at my hands.

I pressed a finger on his neck to make sure that he was dead and then dashed back to the master bedroom. I rolled Ruiz over and saw two wounds. One bullet had hit his shoulder above the vest. The other had grazed the side of his head, carving a groove through his scalp and hair over his right ear. It was bleeding like crazy, but it didn't seem to have penetrated the skull. It looked like the shots that had struck him had snapped his head into the doorjamb, knocking him unconscious and probably giving him a concussion. He needed to get to a hospital as soon as possible.

"Mike?" It was Becky. "Mike, is that you?" She was terrified. With her eyes still covered by tape, she wondered if she was about to be executed.

"It's me," I said.

I removed the tape from her eyes as gently as I could. Then I used a kitchen knife to cut her out of her bonds. The emotional weight of everything she had just been through finally crashed down on her. I held her for a minute while she sobbed on my chest.

"Becky," I said. "Honey—we need to get him to a hospital. He's going to bleed to death. Can you stand?"

"I—I think so."

I helped her to her feet. I grabbed a washcloth from the master bathroom and had Becky apply pressure to Ruiz's shoulder wound while I pulled the Hummer up into the yard as close to the front door as possible.

Although she was weak, Becky was able to help me maneuver the unconscious Ruiz into the truck. She couldn't help but see O'Malley's blood-soaked body as she stepped over him. I caught a glimpse of two gasoline cans on the kitchen floor and knew they hadn't been intended to fuel a generator.

We loaded Ruiz into the backseat and I drove—again—through the swirling maelstrom to Florida Hospital near Loch Haven Park. I knew that calling 911 would have been useless until the storm had passed. And Ruiz didn't have that much time.

We got Ruiz into the emergency room and they admitted him right away. The fact that he was still wearing his FBI Kevlar vest got some folks' attention and they moved quickly to treat him. As they pulled the vest off him, I saw the telltale indentation of a deflected bullet strike in the center of his back. If he lived through the night, it would be due largely to that vest.

The hospital examined Becky and gave her fresh clothes to change into. She was able to reach Wayne and Jennifer on a landline phone and let them know that she was okay. All cellular service was out.

I reached Mark Lindemann and we filled each other in. Debbie had gotten away. She had too much of a head start. She had pulled up onto I-4 when the FBI grabbed me and could have slipped off onto any side street before Ruiz's partner had started his pursuit. When he realized that she was gone, vanished into the storm,

Ruiz's partner had returned to the parking garage and found Jimmy sitting vigil over Fitchburg's corpse. Jimmy was fine and currently giving a statement. My recording would back up his version of events.

I found Becky reclining in an ER bed, looking out a window at the storm. It was still torrential outside, but the severity had lessened somewhat. We still had several hours of it before Lorraine would end her visit to Central Florida.

"So," Becky said, turning from the window. "Are you going to tell me what this was all about?"

I sighed and sat next to her. "Yeah . . ."

With a sinking feeling in my gut, I realized that this little episode would do nothing to improve our already complicated, dysfunctional relationship.

CHAPTER 35

Hurricane Lorraine was a decidedly unpleasant storm. When the proverbial dust settled, she had caused nearly $10 billion in damage and smashed her way across the center of the state from Cocoa Beach, through Orlando, and then back out into the Gulf north of Homosassa. Six deaths had been attributed to the storm: three of them had occurred when one of numerous spawned tornadoes targeted a downtown duplex, one when a giant tree had crashed into the bedroom of a sleeping retiree, and one from the combination of a downed electrical wire and a very large puddle. Fitchburg and O'Malley didn't count because they were not storm related.

Ruiz made it through the night and the doctors predicted a full recovery. Becky received some outpatient counseling. She was measurably better when she was finally reunited with Wayne and Jennifer, although she wasn't quite sure how to reconcile her complicated feelings about me. While I had figured out where she was and been the one to rescue her, I was the reason why she had been abducted in the first place. Let's just say that, combined with her already conflicted feelings about me as a result of our marriage and divorce, this only added to her internal tension.

Depending on where you lived, the power was out anywhere from a day to two weeks. The power at my place was back in three days. That was fine with me because I really wasn't home for much of that time anyway.

I spent the bulk of those three days sitting in a conference room at the Orlando Police Department, explaining everything, providing evidence, and then explaining everything again. I spoke with Joe Vincent, Gary Richards, Jim Dupree, some guys from internal affairs, the county prosecutor, a state prosecutor, my own attorney, the FBI, and a host of other folks who paraded into the conference room at various times. Then I explained it all again. And again. The cops by then had the crushed flash drive and the CD backup. They had Fitchburg's knife, which had indeed been Jonathan Dennis's murder weapon. They had one of the weapons used at Skip's place, found in the trunk of the Impala and matched by ballistics tests. They had my hidden recordings of the encounter at the garage. They had my testimony, Becky's testimony, Cam's testimony, Jimmy's testimony, and, most important, Nate Hungerford's testimony. Nate spilled the whole story, including the real author of the e-mails, Carl Lawrence.

Joe Vincent hated that he had been wrong, but he was no fool. He was by then the lead cop on a major investigation. Four deaths (including Fitchburg's and O'Malley's) and a big-time scandal. That was the kind of case that could make a career. Mark Lindemann negotiated for the cops to drop all charges against me, including the fire alarm at Jennifer's school, in exchange for my testimony against the Lawrence Company, Commissioner Ken Billings, and Mayor Glen Jenkins. Nate Hungerford cut his own immunity deal in exchange for his testimony. He would lose the redevelopment payday, but he would stay out of jail and retain his law license.

I felt bad for Sally. She really liked the mayor and I was about to help put him away. But Sally would survive. She always did. She'd probably still be sitting at the same desk as the new mayor's office manager when Jenkins finally got out of jail in a few years. I'd buy her a sandwich and a Diet Dr Pepper to make it up to her.

My truck was a total loss. Yes, the open driver's window and shot-up back window had let a considerable amount of rain into the cab, which had caused significant damage. But not nearly as much as the giant tree that had crashed down on its roof. It seemed that the very same tree in the Burger King parking lot that had obscured my truck from prying helicopters in Lake Mary had crashed down on my F-150, flattening it like a beer can. In addition to my truck, the tree took out a corner of the restaurant, scattering once-frozen patties and empty deep-fryers into the parking lot. I would have to rent a car for a few weeks until I could go buy another nice, "preowned" F-150. I was a creature of habit and I liked my truck. But I did plan on one accommodation. Because of my impending new fatherhood, I intended to buy an extended cab. This would, after all, be a family car soon.

Norman Fitchburg's fingerprints identified him as one Edward Tavis, most recently of Dallas, Texas. He was unmarried and there was no indication in his records of anyone who might have been Debbie Watson. Or Vicky. Or Carol. Or whatever her name really was. The cops never found Debbie or her Camry. Or Nate Hungerford's eight hundred grand. Ouch.

I knew that both the local cops and the FBI would keep looking for Debbie. But I also knew that they wouldn't find her. Like she had said, she was a professional. She knew what she was doing. None of us would ever likely see Debbie again. And that suited me just fine.

About a week after power had been restored, most of the streets had been cleared, with huge piles of chainsawed limbs stacked along most roads. I was in my apartment, eating cereal, when my phone rang.

"Hello?" I said, chewing my Cheerios.

"Mr. Garrity?"

"Yeah?"

"This is Richard DiNardo. Jennifer's teacher. We met at her school right before the hurricane."

"Yeah. Mr. DiNardo. The day of the fire alarm."

"Right. Right. Um, I'm sorry to call you at home like this, but, when we met, you mentioned that you wanted to talk to me about Victor Madrigas."

"Yeah. I do."

"Well . . . I wonder if you could meet me somewhere. So we can talk."

"Sure. When and where?"

"How about now? There's a coffee shop down the street from my house. We could meet there."

"Now?" I put down my spoon. "Okay . . . What do you want to tell me?"

"I'd rather not say on the phone. I'm sorry." He gave me directions to the coffee shop and hung up.

I had a funny feeling about it. Why would DiNardo need to see me all of a sudden? Guilty conscience, perhaps? I didn't like it.

In less than an hour I walked into the Starbucks and ordered a strong "coffee of the day." I found DiNardo sitting at a small round table in the back corner. I joined him and we exchanged greetings.

He looked a little older than when I had seen him in the classroom. He was wearing a blue golf shirt and a pair of khaki shorts. Teacher-casual. His hands fidgeted nervously and he didn't touch the small coffee cup sitting in front of him.

"So, what's up?" I asked.

"School's out for a few days, as you probably know. Because of the hurricane. I got power back yesterday and thought I would use the free time to catch up on some personal e-mails. It's hard to keep up during the school year. Anyway, I have my settings set to Exclusive, to keep out the spam and junk. So, I was going through my junk folder, making sure there wasn't something in there that I wanted to keep. And . . ." He paused. Took a deep breath. He grimaced.

"You found something," I offered.

He nodded. He looked sick. "You said you were working for Victor's father, right?"

"That's right. He hired me to investigate Victor's death. To see if it could have been something other than suicide."

"Then I think you better see this." DiNardo pulled a folded piece of paper from his back pocket and handed it to me. "I got to know Victor a little better than most of my students. I was the faculty sponsor for some of his service projects. We just seemed to get along, you know? I assume that's why he sent this to me."

"Okay," I said and unfolded the piece of paper.

"That was in the junk folder. He obviously sent it before . . . It's been sitting in there this whole time. When I saw his name on the message, it kind of spooked me. Then, when I read it, I didn't know what to do. I remembered what you said, so I called you."

I read the page. It was a printout of an e-mail message sent from Victor Madrigas to Richard DiNardo. It wasn't very long and took only a minute or so to scan. When I was done, I locked my eyes on DiNardo. His brow was furrowed into worried creases. I read the message again, just to make sure I hadn't misread anything. I hadn't.

"Who else has seen this?" I asked.

"No one. I called you as soon as I read it."

I sighed heavily. The message was a suicide note.

It seemed authentic to me. In the message, Victor claimed that he could no longer deal with the pressure his father was putting on him. Victor wanted to go to college and study astronomy, but his father insisted that he enroll in a seminary and become a priest. Victor didn't want to be a priest, knew that wasn't his calling, knew he would never be happy in that life. But his father had made it clear that he would pay only for the seminary. Any other choice by Victor would be the greatest of disappointments. In fact, Ben Madrigas was so sure that Victor had been meant for the priesthood that, if Victor refused to follow that path, it would be a sin against God. A refusal of divine intention. Victor loved his father and couldn't bear the disappointment and shame. Yet, he couldn't face a life of unhappiness. He saw his way out: it was directly through a bottle of anti anxiety meds.

Oh, brother. I closed my eyes and visualized handing the message to Ben Madrigas. If his pain was bad now, wait until he learned that not only had Victor indeed killed himself, Ben himself was the reason.

I hadn't been to see my father in two years.

His grave was in a nice sunny spot, right next to my mother's. WILLIAM MICHAEL GARRITY, BELOVED HUSBAND AND FATHER. Husband and father . . . the two roles that defined his life. Unlike Victor Madrigas, who couldn't choose between the priesthood and secular life, my father had chosen both. But the secular life was the one that had ultimately fulfilled him. And I was the result.

The prodigal son had finally returned.

There I stood, waiting for my fattened calf. I was never one for speaking aloud to the dead. My father could no more hear me standing there above his bones than he could have in the linen closet of my apartment. But a lifetime in the Catholic Church had trained me to carry on a one-sided internal dialogue with those in the afterlife. Prayers to Jesus, to Mary, the saints, and deceased grandparents were a way of life. They still were. Something lost or stolen? Ask St. Anthony to help. Have a sick pet? St. Francis. My personal favorite was the patron saint of lost causes: St. Jude. Now my parents had been added to the list of people I talked to in my head.

Before the cancer had eaten him up, my father gave me a medallion. St. Michael, the patron saint of police officers. It had been his way of making peace with me, of finally, on his literal deathbed, accepting me for who I was, not who he had wanted me to be.

I almost never wore the medal, but I kept it in a velvet box in a dresser drawer. Every so often, I pulled it out and held it. I don't know how much stock I put in the power of St. Michael, but I knew what that small piece of metal meant to me. It was a sterling silver disk of paternal love and I cherished it.

I pulled the medallion out of my pocket and held it up, as if my father could see it through a secret spy cam in his headstone. A ridiculous gesture, I know, but I did it anyway. I rubbed my thumb over the raised image of St. Michael and sighed, my throat suddenly tight, my nose runny. I put the medal back in my pocket and blinked my eyes.

I glanced at the open plot next to my parents'. That was where I expected to be buried. When diagnosed with my brain tumor earlier that year, one of the doctors had suggested that it might be wise to "get my affairs in order." Great bedside manner. That was where I was presumed to be planted, next to my parents. Bob and I might be lying there right now, had I not elected to surgically evict Bob and gotten lucky, at least for the time being, with the results. But there were no guarantees. I knew that the odds were against me. The doctors had tried to get every last cell with their scalpels, but it was unlikely that they were 100 percent successful. Even with the postoperative chemo and radiation, I was pretty sure that there were still a few single-celled spawn of Bob floating around in my bloodstream. Like an undersea coral polyp, one of them would find purchase on my cerebellum and start to grow again. And, next time, it would probably become a much nastier tumor. But I'd keep fighting. The doctors would take it out again. What else can you do? If it grows back, you take it out, and you keep taking it out until you can't anymore. At some point—I hoped it would be more than a few years, but possibly not—I would be lying there with my own stone marker. The permanent return of the prodigal son.

It was a nice spot. My parents would have liked having me nearby. As they always used to tell me, I never spent enough time with them. Perhaps the perpetual complaint of the parents of only children. Perhaps the complaint of all parents.

For the first time in a while, I felt the cold presence of my old friend Death hovering nearby. But he wasn't interested in any of the cemetery residents—they had lost their appeal the instant that they gasped their last breaths. It was the living he was fixated on. His never-ending product pipeline. Although my thoughts of Bob probably had conjured him, he wasn't particularly menacing. He was in no hurry to snatch me. At least not that day. It was like Death was just hanging out, having a smoke, because he liked my company. I pictured him sitting on a nearby headstone, his long legs stretched out in front, just shooting the breeze.

Think the Dolphins finally have a quarterback this year?

Nah . . . Their playoff hopes are dead. . . .

I turned away from my eternal resting place and laid a small bouquet of grocery-store flowers on my mother's grave. Then I bowed my head and gave them both a gift: a Hail Mary and an Our Father for each of them. I prayed silently, in my head, like they had taught me as a child. They would have liked that.

I had no flowers for my father. He wouldn't have wanted them anyway. Instead, I pulled a bottle of Jameson Irish whiskey from a paper bag. I poured a belt into a plastic cup, saluted the old man, and tossed it back. It burned gloriously down my throat, smooth, woody, and spicy. Then I poured another belt, a double, offered another salute, and tipped it over onto the grass above his coffin. He would have liked that, too.

I stood for another moment, enjoying the warm October sunshine. Except for the trees and debris piled everywhere, you wouldn't ever have guessed that a major hurricane had recently blown through there. I took another swig from the Jameson. Then I pulled out my cell phone and dialed. A few warbly rings later, he answered.

"Hello?" said Ben Madrigas.

"Hi, Mr. Madrigas. It's Mike Garrity. I need to talk to you about Victor."

CHAPTER 36

I met Ben Madrigas at his office. He ushered me into the same seat as before. He again sat in the second guest chair, both of us on the same side of his desk. He expressed his relief that I had been cleared of all charges related to Jonathan Dennis's murder. I thanked him and expressed my appreciation for his support through the whole ordeal. After a few minutes, the conversation's inertia died and he looked at me expectantly.

"Have you found out anything about Victor?" he asked.

"Yeah. You could say. That's why I'm here."

"Please. Tell me." He was anxious and hopeful at the same time.

I cleared my throat. Took a fortifying breath. "Do you have any idea how easy it is to buy drugs at a suburban high school? No? Anyone can do it. Even kids that have never done it before. Within ten minutes you can have a bag of whatever you want." I looked Madrigas in the eye. "We talked to a lot of folks. Friends, teachers, other kids at his school. The stories were all the same. We're sure that Victor had never done drugs before. This was the first time."

Ben Madrigas nodded. "Yes. Yes. I knew it."

"Here's the thing. When someone has never done drugs before, they're sort of like an amateur. A lot of kids, especially good kids, like Victor, cut loose right before going away to college. They see it as a chance to try one crazy thing before leaving high school. Some kids drink. Some kids drag race down the neighborhood street. Some kids engage in unwise sexual activity. And some kids get high. It's a last blowing off of childhood steam. But some of those kids drag racing wrap their cars around a tree. And some of those kids having sex get pregnant or herpes. Or AIDS. And some of those kids who get high overdose. If you've never done it before, you don't know the limits. It's dangerous. . . . Do you understand what I'm trying to say?"

"Are you telling me that Victor's overdose was an accident?"

"Look, Mr. Madrigas. I'll level with you. We'll never know for sure. But, based on my investigation, that's my professional conclusion. He wanted to try something he had never done before and he didn't know the limits."

Emotion was welling up in Madrigas. I saw tears in his eyes. "An accident. He made a terrible mistake."

"Right. A terrible mistake. I don't have enough to overturn the official police report, but you deserve to know."

"Yes." He nodded his head. "Yes. I understand. An accident. An unintentional accident." He gripped my forearm. "Thank you, Mr. Garrity."

I nodded back at him. "Yeah. You're welcome."

I just couldn't see how the truth about Victor Madrigas would have helped anyone. It would have destroyed Ben, probably for the rest of his life. Perhaps the truth could have spared one of Victor's siblings from the same pressure that Victor had felt, but I doubted that it was a concern. I had the admittedly subjective sense that Victor's death had given Ben Madrigas an appreciation for the fragility of parenthood. I hoped that he would go lighter on his other children, grateful that they remained among the living.

I, too, had a new appreciation for the fragility of parenthood. Experiencing Jennifer's kidnapping during the summer, the scare with Cam's pregnancy, and Becky's abduction, I had a very tangible sense that everything that truly mattered could be taken away at any time. If my experience with cancer had taught me anything, it was that life hangs on a delicate, silken thread: some longer than others, filled with beautiful colors, and capable of snapping at any time.

Before I had left the Starbucks, I persuaded DiNardo to delete the e-mail from Victor. He was happy to abdicate the decisions to me. I tore up the printout of the message. Detective Boyd Bryson would never see it. He would have to live with his unresolved one percent. That was too bad.

Cam had an appointment in Winter Park, so I drove over to meet her for an early dinner. We found a table at P. F. Chang's. Cam had a craving for something spicy, so that's what we ordered. We talked about possible names for the baby. There were a few decent candidates. James was good. Or Brian.

"What about Michael Junior?" Cam asked, smiling through a mouthful of noodles.

"I don't think so. Why burden the kid with my baggage from birth?"

"I think it's nice. A type of immortality."

The subtext was obvious. When the brain cancer finally did me in, at least mini-me would still be around. That wouldn't be fair to the kid. He needed to be himself, not a shrunken version of me, God help him.

"Actually," I said, "I had something else in mind."

"Oh?"

"I was thinking of William." I looked down at the table. "William Michael."

Cam gave me a sad smile. "After your father." I nodded. Cam grabbed my hand. "I think it's perfect. William Michael Garrity. Our son."

We went back to her apartment to watch a movie. While I had reconciled myself to the fact that we would never remarry, if this was the reality of our divorce, I could do worse. I popped in the DVD while Cam sorted through her mail.

"What's this?" she asked. She held up a greeting-card-size envelope. It had my name on it with her address.

I shrugged. "Dunno. Open it."

Cam slit it open and took out the contents. She held up an enclosed gift card to Babies "R" Us. "It's a two-hundred-dollar gift card." Then she read the greeting card. "Who's Debbie?"

I stepped over to the kitchen table and took the card. The front depicted a powder-blue baby rattle. Inside, the printed message read, "Enjoy your new bundle of joy." Scrawled in cursive handwriting were the words: *Congrats on your son. ~Debbie.*

It was from her, of course. I'd have to show it to the cops and the FBI. But it wouldn't help them find her. The postmark read Tulsa, Oklahoma. She was probably in Seattle by then. Or San Francisco. Or Tokyo. Or Copenhagen. If I was lucky, the cops would still let me spend the two hundred bucks.

I don't think it was threat. More a case of Debbie thumbing her nose at all of us than anything else. Still, I might spring for an upgraded security system for Cam's condo. Just in case.

We nuked a bag of microwave popcorn and settled down on the couch. I put my hand on Cam's expanding belly.

"Did you feel that?" Cam asked.

"I think so."

"I think the baby just kicked." She grinned. "Our little soccer player."

Debbie, despite her ulterior motives, had once given me a very useful piece of advice. She had told me, as part of her manipulation, that I needed to commit to my future. She couldn't have been more right. Despite my cancer—hell, *because* of it—I had committed everything—my mind, my body, and my heart—to the future. This child, William Michael Garrity, was going to change my entire life.

And I couldn't wait.